PRAISE FOR RK JACK

"THE DEVOURER FROM BEYOND"

Book One of the OST Series

"RK Jack's *The Devourer From Beyond* turns the knob up to eleven then breaks it off. Nonstop action, chills, and a terrific storyline that sets a pace faster than *Raiders of the Lost Ark* and continues to deliver."

—Mark Everett Stone, author of *Things to Do in Denver When You're Un-Dead*

"In *The Devourer From Beyond*, RK Jack combines various genres to create a gripping page-turner. The author adeptly conveys the law enforcement representatives' way of thinking and their perception of hazardous circumstances, increasing the psychological and emotional depth of the narration. An enthralling twist promises more breathtaking discoveries, and the conclusion does not disappoint."

—*Readers' Favorite* 5-Star Review by Nino Lobiladze

RK JACK

CONTENTS

THE MIST FROM BEYOND

Published by Horizon View Press LLC

Denver, CO

Copyright © 2025 by Russell Jack (RK Jack).

All rights reserved, including the right to reproduce any of this book, in part or whole, in any form, without the author's express written permission. For information on permissions or to contact the author, email directly to rkjackauthor.com

This book is a work of fiction. All names, characters, and events that occur are fictitious. Thus, any relationship to any person, living or dead, or actual events is coincidental.

No part of this book may be reproduced in any form or by any mechanical means, including information storage and retrieval systems, without permission in writing from the publisher/author, except by a reviewer who may quote passages in a review.

All images, logos, quotes, and trademarks included in this book are subject to use according to trademark and copywriting laws of the United States of America.

ISBN: 979-8-9900568-2-4

FIC015000 **FICTION** / Horror

Cover design by Shira Atakpu, copyright owned by Russell Jack (RK Jack).

All rights reserved by Russell Jack (RK jack) and Horizon View Press LLC.

CHAPTER 1
THE MIST

Start of the School Year—Late August
Tonto National Forest—Tempe, Arizona
Dorothy

WE WERE *SO* WRONG.

As the first rays of dawn woke me, I could see the other women were also waking. I remembered with a start what had happened—

Oh my God, oh my God!

I frantically looked around and saw eight other women who looked as terrified as I felt. All of us were naked, as the ritual had called for, and I desperately wanted it to be just a dream, but I could see the blood all over us: human blood—and lots of it. None of us spoke as we put on our clothes. We didn't need a headcount, as we knew Amanda was the only one missing.

Or whatever Amanda was now.

I'm Dorothy Scranton, the president of Beta Zeta Sigma, our sorority at Arizona State University (ASU). I decided that the ten of us would perform a Wiccan-style "Summoning of the Damned" as outlined in an ancient tome—one that my faithful assistant Peter had found in an obscure occult bookshop in Sacramento. Late Saturday night, just last night, we performed the ritual right at midnight. We all believed it would be just a harmless initiation for Amanda Collins, our newest sorority sister.

Unfortunately, however, it looked like the summoning had worked. I vividly remembered what had just happened …

———

Hiking up the hill in Tonto National Forest is fun, and it's a cool night for Tempe, especially being late summer. We are all excited to see how Amanda reacts to our *evil summoning,* and I have to laugh at the thought of any of this crap being real.

I looked again at the crazy title of the tome, written in Italian. Luckily, I learned Italian while in high school, so thankfully, I can read this creepy book—oh, sorry—"The Tome."

"The Desolate Damned of the Planes." What a strange title! Since it's written in Italian, though, it looks fabulous. I mean, "La Desolazione Maledetta degli Aerei" does sound *way* cooler! The strange bindings and ancient pages only add to its authenticity; Peter must have paid a fortune for it!

Our short hike is over, and we are finally at the giant boulder high on the hill. I would call it a mountain, but really, it's just a big hill. While placing "La Desolazione" on the rock, I watch the other women already placing and lighting candles.

As the candles flickered in the light wind, everyone stripped and moved into their places to surround the "altar" (the big rock with the book on top). Amanda is next to it, sitting on another rock, as the sacrifice for the demon.

OMG, this is such BS. It is fun, though!

I can see the full moon's light shining brightly on our naked bodies. I want to follow every instruction to the letter, so I'm reading the summoning in fluent Italian while the others chant.

I must act serious (hee hee).

This will scare the hell out of Amanda.

As I deliver the final words, Laura plays an eerie recording of a wailing lost soul. I'm trying hard not to laugh. I can see Amanda jump as the haunting moaning begins, and she is clearly frightened.

Yes! It's working!—

Wait, what the hell is this?

A strange greyish mist is coming up all around us from the ground … I can't move; my feet are rooted in place. None of us can move!

Oh my God! What is happening?

The mist is transforming into something that can't possibly exist; the entity swirling in the fog is horrifying and indescribable. It is moving to Amanda first.

The mist thing swirls onto Amanda like a tornado of destruction. She is screaming as the mist forces its way into her eyes, nose, mouth, ears, and God knows where else. Blood is shooting out, and we can see the mist is turning red now as it feeds on her blood, going in and out of her.

Amanda is *still* screaming, and we can all hear a terrible slurping and gulping noise coming from *inside* her. Her blood is everywhere. Finally, she fell and lay still.

Is it satiated?

I watch helplessly as the last of the red mist enters her lifeless body. We all watch, transfixed, and unable to move our feet, as Amanda stands and smiles.

OMG, her smile!

Her inhuman smile revealed hundreds of long, razor-sharp teeth. Her body is covered in her blood—too much to have survived.

And she is coming over to me first—

No, no!

"Hello, Dorothy," Amanda says sweetly, with that impossible toothy grin.

"I … I … No, please …" I am begging her, crying uncontrollably, I don't want to die!

She is laughing as she comes near my face, and I can smell her fetid breath. I close my eyes as her horrible maw moves down near my neck …

CHOMP!

The pain is intense at first, but now it's starting to feel good! I want her to keep going—it feels sexual, even orgasmically satisfying. I never realized I was so into Amanda until now.

Sighing contentedly, I can feel my blood spurting and running all over our naked bodies.

CHAPTER 2
CRIME SCENE NEWS

Three Years Ago
Crime Scene News (CSN)—Denver, Colorado
Samantha

THE REPORT CAME in over the police band: "Shots fired at Perry's truck stop (in Colorado Springs)."

Harold Bigsby, my cameraman, was sitting next to me in our office. We were a well-oiled news team, so we looked at each other and then jumped up—no discussion needed. Lately, it seemed that all we covered were police brutality claims and tame crime scenes.

We had been covering the crime beat assignment together for over a decade, becoming quite adept at ferreting out the news. Although we both previously worked for KUSA 9News, we found some of their limitations stifling. No disrespect to them, as they are an excellent news team, but Crime Scene News offered us *full* leeway to investigate and report entire stories without the "help" of an editor. Nowadays, the editing process focuses less on accuracy and more on corporate self-censorship. While CSN was just a fledgling news agency, it had substantial resources from a trust fund. Someone wealthy wanted to see complete stories—factual, evidence-supported, and inclusive of *all* details, regardless of hurting anyone's feelings.

So that is what Harold and I gave them—and this one sounded interesting, for sure. Officers down, and SWAT is on the scene ...

Juicy.

We jumped into the news van and raced to get there. I knew Harold was speeding, but we figured most of the cops were busy heading there as well. By the time we arrived in Colorado Springs, the police tape was already up.

"Samantha Cox, CSN reporter," I told the officer, holding up my press pass. Harold was right behind me, already filming.

"Ma'am, this is an active crime scene; you cannot come past the tape. However, I'll send over our Public Information Officer (PIO), and he'll give you a full report."

With that, he walked away.

Humph.

Another cover-up, I bet.

The PIO person came a few minutes later. He gave me a BS story about a man with a gun who was killing people. The suspect had been "neutralized" (funny, how they never want to say "shot and killed") by the SWAT team.

While he was talking, I looked at Harold. He looked back at me, and I nodded.

We have mastered *the nod.*

It basically says, "This person is giving me a line of BS; go film the crime scene instead—they are hiding something."

Over the years, I have made many cops furious with me. However, most appreciated that I, at least, tried to tell the whole story (which isn't as common as you might think). Some cops even thanked me for running my stories. They found it refreshing that I called out the real story instead of just running only the parts that sensationalized it.

When a cop shot an unarmed man in the back, I covered everything they *both* did wrong. But I was the only news reporter who also told what the cop did right and that the suspect would be alive today—if he hadn't resisted arrest in the first place.

This did not put me on the "good liberal" side.

F—em.

I tell the truth—good, bad, or both (usually both). I tell the damn story of what really happened! This would never fly at most big news networks, so I'll never leave CSN.

News agencies get paid for the size of their viewership and subscriptions; they do not get paid for getting everything right. I was mad that journalistic integrity was a dying code…

As the PIO windbag fed me a line of crap, Harold was filming the bodies and the officers coming out. After Harold was done, he came back over, and I met him at the news van.

"Good job, Harold. That PIO was laying the lies on thick today."

He laughed. "Yeah, they're covering something up. Watch this video—"

After he connected his camera, we watched the monitor. The video started with my talking to the patrol officer and the lying PIO guy. But when Harold began to film the truck stop, things got interesting.

Two police officers and eight civilians were taken out in body bags, and we could clearly see where a rifle round passed through the front glass—likely the kill shot on the perpetrator. But here's why I love Harold; he zoomed in.

Fully visible were dozens, maybe hundreds, of bullet casings. Blood was everywhere. The store was wrecked—it looked like a bull on PCP had run through it—but that is not what caught our eye. He filmed them taking down people and *parts of people* from *on top* of the aisles of goods. All the people in the store had been beaten, ripped apart, and even thrown into the ceiling! We carefully watched every detail in slow motion, and it was clear that none of the victims coming out had a single visible GSW. That means all the bullets were aimed at the one person who wasn't using a gun—the perp who was still inside the truck stop at the time.

The video ended, and Harold and I looked at each other with big eyes.

We both knew this was a massive story! When has there ever been a shooting where *no one*, except for the SWAT team, escaped, and *everyone* inside was killed? And how does an active shooter kill people *without them having any bullet wounds*?

Soon, my investigation of the story hit a brick wall. I had documented everything we filmed and had run the story, but it fizzled out. Even though I had video of the bodies, the police claimed that people were trying to hide or escape, describing it as "a chaotic scene."

Whatevs.

It was BS, a company line, and they knew it.

Unfortunately, I received a lot of negative coverage on social media. Typically, at most news agencies, my bosses would demand I drop it. Not at CSN, though. My boss told me they would not run more unless I made my story "ironclad," but they liked the story and thought it was legit. Social media made it sound like I had somehow produced a "doctored" or "deepfake" video.

Something didn't smell right, though.

So, I had one of my tech-savvy news buddies run down the jokers who were posting negative comments on social media. He is one of my sources for verifying things on the internet. The guy, known only as "Spasmo," whom I have never met in person, did a thorough check and gave me the results—for a fee, of course.

Almost all negative reviews originated from spam accounts utilizing VPNs (Virtual Private Networks), indicating that the reviewers are not regular individuals. The likelihood of so many accounts being untraceable is virtually nonexistent, so I'm confident in saying none.

We, and all Americans, were being gaslighted—big time!

People high up in the government were trying to kill this story. So, I would be keeping an eye out for any more massive police gunfights.

———

Over a week had passed when eyewitness reports about "a war going on" started coming in. A raging gunfight—and explosions!—were being reported in the woods west of Colorado Springs.

Harold and I took the helicopter for this one. When we boarded, the pilot, Nora, had already spun up the rotors, so we were in the air quickly.

CSN is only a medium-sized news agency, so even with the largess of our trust-fund benefactor, operating a helicopter is expensive. So much so that even 9News had to enter into a helicopter-sharing agreement with 7News just to afford theirs. Our helicopter was not as fancy or costly, but we didn't have to share.

Our helicopter was a Robinson R44 Raven 2, accommodating four people (including the pilot). It could travel up to 348 miles at speeds reaching 126 miles per hour. While not as luxurious as theirs, it certainly got the job done. Additionally, it was "only" half a million dollars to purchase.

Looking out of my window, I could see a sea of cars crawling along I-25. Luckily, we were making much better progress in the air. As we arrived in Colorado Springs, we spotted a police helicopter hovering. It seemed we had finally found the crime scene—or what was left of it …

A church had been the epicenter of a war zone.

Police, fire, and EMS were swarming the scene, and the "just say no to the press" tape was already up. So, we hovered and watched.

Harold had a gift; he could get shots no mere mortal could.

We could see them bringing out two unconscious SWAT members and loading them into UCHealth's Flight for Life helicopter—LifeLine Two. One officer looked like she might be dead, as her head was at a weird angle and covered in blood.

"Hey, Nora, when Flight for Life takes off, follow it. I want to know where our mystery officers are headed," I said.

"You got it, Sammy," she replied.

We could see the church had partially imploded from most likely military-grade detonations; the front and back had enormous holes, and the whole church was starting to catch on fire. It had been boarded up, so it looked like some sort of standoff with SWAT had gone awry.

Movement caught my eye.

"Harold—"

"I got it!"

Harold zoomed his camera in at the edge of the clearing, far in front of the church.

"Oh my God, oh my God," Harold was saying.

I knew not to interrupt.

Harold and I had seen the worst of the worst in our ten years together. That he was pale as a ghost and saying *that*—scared me to the core …

I could feel my stomach lurch as Nora nosed the helicopter down and applied throttle. It was smooth, but I was still a bit nauseous from the sudden shift forward.

"Your officers are on the way to the hospital; you still want me to follow them, right?"

I glanced at Harold, and he nodded yes as he was lowering his camera.

"Yeah, thanks, Nora."

Night had fallen when the Flight for Life helicopter landed at UCHealth Memorial Hospital Central in Colorado Springs. Now that we knew where they would be (for a while at least), we diverted and flew back to the office.

The helicopter landed on the roof, and I heard the turbines powering down.

"OK, you guys are good to go," Nora said.

"Hey, thank you. You did a great job, Nora—as always," I said.

"Anything for you, girl," she said with a wink and returned to her instruments.

Harold and I opened the door and climbed down. We headed downstairs to the newsroom. I was beyond eager to see what Harold had gotten on that film.

He warned me before starting the video—

"I … uh … just … my God."

We both watched in horror as the police Crime Scene Investigations (CSI) took pictures and documented evidence. They quickly covered the evidence with tarps, but we had already captured the shot. We could see that the team—snipers, by the look of it—had been *torn apart.*

"Sammy, you and I have seen bomb blasts; this is not that. They were ripped apart, and my guess is that it was *this—*"

As the camera was zooming in, we saw the preeminent video of our careers, bar none:

Tentacles!

Giant, grey/purple tentacles with barbs and suction cups all over them. Big piles of them! Several were near the murdered snipers, and a line of them in the clearing. Hundreds of bullet casings on the ground illustrated this was undeniably a firefight against these creatures. One that SWAT lost.

When the video ended, Harold and I sat quietly for a long time. We both knew this was more than just a story.

Alien monsters had killed all those people.

Monsters are real now.

I felt sick and went to the bathroom to throw up.

———

Now that we knew where they were, we drove to the hospital to learn more about the officers. Of course, the hospital did not provide information on the officers and mentioned privacy and HIPAA concerns. That's OK because what they *did* tell us was that the officers *were* there.

So, this really did happen.

I had hoped what I saw was not real …

It was getting late, so we called it a night. Then we came back, week after week, for months.

I finally met one of the SWAT officers, a fit woman with her head covered in gauze. We knew this was the "dead" woman we saw at the church being loaded into the Flight for Life helicopter. Although she refused to talk with me, seeing her saddened me. Her head was wrapped, and what showed of her body was severely bruised and swollen. She was visibly still in extreme pain. What she must be going through, what she must have experienced …

Over the next several months, we heard stories of that same woman

—a woman who had grown half a foot in height and now looked like a giant pro bodybuilder.

That caught our attention.

Who loses fat and gains a hundred pounds of muscle while recovering from major trauma? And in just a few months, to boot? And no one gains six inches in height as an adult. We knew it was worth the wait when we finally got a picture of her. It was a crap shot, but it was there—

She was horrifying.

It wasn't that she was unattractive; in fact, she clearly was once stunningly beautiful, but over six feet tall and well over two hundred pounds of solid muscle. And she had horrible scarring on the whole right side of her face and neck that marred that DaVinci beauty. Judging by what we saw on that video at the New Era Revivalist Church, she should be dead, not potentially winning future pro-bodybuilding shows.

This was getting weirder and weirder …

———

We documented everything and even wrote a complete story about it, with all our video and documentation to prove it. However, until we got more, CSN was not willing to publish. Our first go-around at Perry's truck stop had made them a little gun-shy.

But Harold and I were not letting this one go. This was the story of a lifetime!

Months later, on a Sunday no less, I read a breaking news report from Long Beach, California, about a missing boat and several missing persons on the beach—

Could it be another alien monster attack?

I called Harold, who agreed it was worth investigating. Harold and I took the first flight to Long Beach Airport.

We arrived the day after the people went missing and made our way to the beach. There was a cordoned-off area at Bolsa Chica Beach.

We approached the officers guarding the scene and chatted with them. They were as "helpful" as ever.

Next, we interviewed gawkers—at least those willing to talk to us. We discovered the boat had disappeared with all its crew last night, just as a group of people had vanished by one of the fire pits. It was getting late in the afternoon, so we decided to go to the police station to ask more questions.

As we got out of the van at the Long Beach Police Department, a police officer with captain bars came over to us.

"Captain Ron Billings, how can I help you?" he asked.

"Well, Captain Billings, my name is Samantha Cox with Crime Scene News, and we can start with what happened here last night?"

"Currently, we are—" he motioned to his ear and raised a hand.

I saw Harold sneak off to the police scanner in the van …

As I watched the captain's face, he turned a dark shade and scowled. Something was up!

"They are fighting monsters on Bolsa Chica Beach!" Harold yelled from the van.

Damn it! We were just there!

"Let's go!" I yelled back.

As I turned, I felt a firm hand grab my arm.

"I'm sorry, Ms. Cox, but you must stay here," the captain demanded.

"I'm with the *free* press; let go of me!"

"No. You will both die if you go."

I stopped resisting, and he let go of my arm. Something about the way he said it stopped me in my tracks.

It wasn't "You *might* die." It was "You *will* die."

And he had physically grabbed me, a female member of the press. A male cop, a captain no less, risking his career to stop me from leaving …

"You have one chance to stop me, and only one—" I said.

I looked at the captain, and he looked defeated.

"Tell me the real story. I know about Colorado Springs and the tentacles."

I nailed it!

The surprised look on his face confirmed all my suspicions, and I knew this would be good. He had Harold put his video camera away and insisted that I not record anything. (I surreptitiously had a voice recorder going anyway.)

"OK, yes, these events are all related. The attack at Perry's truck stop, the church, and this attack …" His tale took a while, and even from far away, we could hear a war raging at Bolsa Chica Beach.

Every professional part of me was screaming to leave and go there. But another part of me—the part that wanted to live—begged me to stay. I could tell he was giving us just enough to stall us, but he was giving us a lot—

SCREECH!

A blue Tesla sedan skidded to a stop near us. I was amazed to see a giant, heavily muscled man in strange police armor emerge.

OMG, it's not a man—

It is her!

"Hey!" I yelled. (It was still noisy, even though she was close to us.)

"I'm Samantha Cox with Crime Scene News. Will you just tell me what is happening?"

What I saw next was horrifying.

She turned *inhumanly* fast and looked at me. The woman I met months ago, bandaged and scared, stood before me at over six feet tall and well over two hundred pounds of solid muscle.

"My God! What happened to you?"

I knew she was the same woman, or at least she *used to be*. I could see her thinking, and then she recognized me.

"Sorry, Samantha, but not now, I'm sure you can see I'm a little busy."

"Can you—"

KA-BOOM! BOOM, BOOM, BOOM!

In the distance, I heard deafening explosions and the sonic boom of supersonic jets—

The woman turned and walked quickly away. She was headed

toward the other mystery police in military-type armor. They had just emerged from a silver Tesla sedan—one with fire now engulfing it. The front of it had been in a significant accident, and EMTs were helping them with the smoke inhalation they must have had.

I could see Harold zooming in on their armor. They were covered in bits of grey and purple tentacle bits, purple blood, and—

Is that vomit?

Many officers suddenly cheered, so it must have been good news they heard over the radio. I turned back to the captain. Unfortunately, the captain had used the distraction to hurry off.

Oh well, we are off to the beach then …

———

Harold pulled up to the roadblock at Pacific Coast Highway and Warner Avenue. The police had blocked off both the PCH and the PCH frontage roads.

As we pulled up to the checkpoint, a military Humvee raced through without stopping. We could see the gunner sticking out the top, holding the grip of a mounted M-60 machine gun. Once we realized we couldn't get through the checkpoint, press pass or not, we did the next best thing: we got out and tried to get an angle down toward the beach.

I was looking through my binoculars while Harold filmed. (I'm sure he is zooming in.)

Harold was making gagging noises, which did not inspire confidence. I stared at Bolsa Chica Beach …

I could see the same tentacle monsters, or giant piles of them, where they lay—dead—on the beach. Heavy-caliber bullets or grenades had ripped them apart. One looked like it was hit with a missile or something—little pieces made a neat circle around a small crater where it must have once stood.

Then, I saw the gigantic pieces of what was once a mammoth creature. Giant quivering blobs of greyish/purple were everywhere. In them were partially dissolved people, giant tentacles (still writhing on the ground), and other unspeakable things. Even from here, we could hear alien mouths with flailing tongues screaming in alien ways.

Then there was the blood …

It was all over the beach, along with parts of people. The aliens' purple blood intermixed with the red blood of people, like what we saw at the New Era Revivalist Church many months ago. Only now, on a *much* larger scale.

I turned away from the scene and lowered my binoculars. I was trying not to have a panic attack.

The captain was right.

That would have been us if he hadn't delayed us from coming here. I tried so hard to hold it together, but I was crying and gagging at the same time as Harold was retching into a bush. He finished and started filming again, with vomit visible all over his shirt.

What a trooper!

We could still hear inhuman aliens shrieking, human screams … sporadic gunfire, and explosions. What we saw next, though, I can never unsee …

A giant ball of tentacles was rolling toward us—as the soldiers in the Humvee chased it. It was letting out a loud growling shriek as the M60 gunner fired into it.

Grrr-EEK! BRRRRAP! BRRRRAP!

I saw a soldier near us throw a grenade.

Shit!

"Grenade!" he yelled out—as I threw myself to the ground.

I wasn't the only one to hit the deck. The battle was *way* too close to us, and the grenade exploded—

BOOM!

I could hear the whisper of death as shrapnel flew over us, far too fast to see. We got up and saw what was left of the tentacle monster a few yards from a blackened crater in the sand. It was lying still with smoke rising off it, and its purple blood made a near-artistic spray design on the ground away from the blast.

A soldier yelled, "Clear!" as they drove off, probably looking for more creatures.

I never realized how glad I was that those soldiers were here. I can't imagine *trying* to find these monsters!

That is enough for one day, I thought.

I turned to Harold. That video would be all we needed, and now our editors at CSN would *have* to let us publish our story! It's just as scary as the other events—only even more so.

"Did you get it charging us?" I asked.

"You know it!" he replied with a big grin, as blood started streaming down his face.

"Harold—"

"Aw … dammit, that isn't good …" he said.

Before we saw the video, we needed to treat Harold's wound. Luckily, plenty of EMTs were nearby.

"Hey, we need help with a head wound!" I yelled at a nearby EMT.

He had just finished setting someone's broken arm in a sling and looked over. With a nod, he came our way.

"Thank you," I said.

He was a young man, probably in his mid-twenties, but he carried himself professionally.

"What happened?" he asked as he started getting out medical supplies.

"Grenade shrapnel, just the head, I think," Harold said. He looked a little pale, but I think it was more from the trauma of what we saw than from any blood loss.

"OK, hold still, and I'll clean it out and dress it. It looks like it just sliced across your skull and didn't go in," he said as he worked.

"You may want to steer clear of the ER until tomorrow," he added.

I looked at him strangely, and then it dawned on me! I don't know why I didn't think about that—the hospitals would be packed right now and doing full-scale mass-casualty triage.

So, instead of going to the hospital, we headed back to the hotel to watch the video. Harold had a big gauze thing wrapped around his head and had taken his bloody, vomit-covered shirt off; he looked heroic. He wasn't a big man, but at 5'8", he was a lean 180 pounds.

As a soft-spoken and intelligent Black man and a petite Asian woman, our team adeptly addressed racially sensitive topics, such as BLM protests and various claims of police brutality, without undue alarm. We made a great team.

Harold still should have gone flat instead of only ducking down, but I'm grateful he got the video. That grenade could have killed the lucky bastard!

But the video …

The creature rolled straight at the camera, clear as day, as if in a movie. We slowed it down and watched bullet after bullet hit it: little, and not so little, sprays of purple as each hit. Then, the grenade blast lifted it sideways into the air (does it have a side?) in a spray of purple blood. The video abruptly ends.

Harold and I looked at each other, then—also seemingly in slow motion—we looked at the camera.

The lens was cracked, revealing where grenade shrapnel had struck and likely damaged the camera as well. At least the recording was still operational, and the video was intact. Harold was fortunate that the camera absorbed the shrapnel instead of his eye. As usual, we downloaded and created backups. Then, feeling somewhat paranoid, we made thumb drives to carry with us.

Why am I being so paranoid?

Are you kidding yourself, Samantha? Just because you think they are out to get you doesn't mean they aren't.

The government has been hiding these events for long enough, and we'll go to press with this story as soon as possible. They can't stop something once it's aired, and good luck trying to "spin" this one!

This time, we would tell the story—

The whole damn story!

CHAPTER 3
NAVY SEAL

Two Years Ago
OST Denver Field Office—DENFO
Agent Lev

LOOKING AROUND MY NEW OFFICE, I absentmindedly flicked my Karambit knife around my thumb. Although I go by "Lev," I have also earned the nickname "Blender" because I'm exceptionally skilled with knives.

I used to be a Federal Air Marshal (FAM)—and technically, I still am. However, I have been assigned to the FBI under the "Overwatch Surveillance Team" pilot program.

No one in the government, including me, expected a run-in with the supernatural. When the government grasped the true nature of the threat, it clandestinely transformed our OST team into a covert unit to combat this new inhuman menace. I'm a crucial part of this team.

We ran headfirst into these extraplanetary monsters during our ill-fated raid on the New Era Revivalist Church (NER). The Big One, which later grew to an enormous size and attacked us at Bolsa Chica Beach, struck me with a tentacle and stung me. The "poison" transformed me into something no longer fully human …

Before the war on these monsters was won, my domestic partner, FAM James Grey, was on the losing end of a gunfight with these "SIMs".

SIMs are "Simulant Infected Monsters".

They are huge, fast, and inhumanly strong. With longer necks and limbs, they are giants with grotesque muscle mass and extremely low body fat. They are passable as humans but immediately draw the attention of those around them.

I am one of them now.

After James had been shot and supposedly killed, I revisited the destroyed NER. I guess I was trauma bonding with the site. That is where James and I were critically injured and, afterward, grew to love each other at the hospital. At the church, I came across a dog, Frank, that had also been stung and turned into a SIM.

Now, he was my service dog.

I also found out that James was only still alive—or I should say *revived*—because I had infected him during sex. Our shared "Alien STD" had saved his life. He was currently in an alien-induced coma and recovering in a hospital in Quantico, Virginia.

Now that we had taken on and defeated the extraplanetary menace, the teams and the FBI faced a more significant problem: putting this event "under the rug" would be almost impossible. Not many journalists showed up during the attack, although I did meet Samantha Cox from Crime Scene News again. I liked her, and she had a hell of a work ethic.

It was going to be very interesting from now on. I'm unsure how the rest of the government—hell, the rest of the world—will react to all of this.

When Samantha's story broke on Crime Scene News, we all assembled in BRIEFING (a large conference room at our field office) to watch. Signs in big, bold capital letters were posted in all the main areas of DENFO.

She had videos, interviews, and facts about everything: from the first event at a truck stop in Colorado Springs, the incident on board the plane with James, the NER massacre, and then the battle on Bolsa Chica Beach.

There was even evidence that the house we hit to kill the Reverend (he was the ringleader of the cult that summoned the monsters) was a battle, not just a fire. That was the battle that won the "war". We found the altar and book that, when destroyed, sent the Big One back to whatever plane of existence it came from. All the other monsters died immediately, and within hours, every part of them dissolved away as if never existing.

When the newsreel ended, we all looked at each other.

"Wow. I guess she nailed it," I said.

"Yeah, Lev, she sure did," Chayton said with a sigh.

Supervisory Special Agent (SSA) Chayton Blackwell was the Squad Leader (SL) in charge of our squad and reported directly to Special Agent in Charge (SAC) Robert Cho.

We all knew this would be a mess, but Samantha's thoroughness was impressive. She had tracked every lead and talked to every witness she could find, and her story was developed long before today. Plus, she had lots of videos of all of us, especially yours truly, as well as footage of the fighting and our vehicles and equipment.

Of course, other news agencies also covered the Bolsa Chica event. They investigated any previous "suspicious" events, but Samantha was the only one to have the whole story on the air so quickly.

"What are we going to do about her?" Morris asked.

Greg Morris was a special agent with the FBI, also assigned to OST.

"Nothing we can do, Greg. It's still a free country," Chayton said.

We all nodded. All of us knew that there would be more. Never before had there been a documented supernatural event that was true.

Until now.

There would be more supernatural events until we found out what caused them and put a stop to it. We knew it would be a shit show, but we had no idea how bad it would get …

Hours later, Justice and Homeland were already reporting a massive increase in Internet traffic and HUMINT (Human Intelligence —or people who know things). People were researching everything about the occult—joining extremist groups, churches, and anti-government movements.

Even though conspiracy theories were everywhere, we could focus on our work, and (for now, anyway) we remained unknown to the world. OST was still covert. Although we found ourselves in a different world now, the acceptance of the occult was still a hot topic.

People on one side were simultaneously claiming it was a hoax and that the government was covering up an alien attack. I'm unsure how people can follow anyone who gives them two mutually exclusive explanations for the same event …

The other side was worse—they accepted that the occult *was* real and wanted to know why the government didn't protect them. The blame game and finding heads to roll were in full swing in the government, as usual.

I have been around the government long enough to know how it ends. In the end, OST will be found out and exposed, and both sides of politics will blame each other, making it all worse by airing as much "dirty laundry" about the other side as possible. None seem to care that it would hurt the country, as long as they could harm the other party and maybe win the next election.

Sad and despicable, but reality.

Oh well.

Tomorrow, I leave for Quantico anyway …

———

So, it was mid-winter when I returned from my FBI course in Quantico to Denver, where OST was based.

The other OST teams were read in on the new job description via a classified briefing. Some, probably the smart ones, said "hell no" and were reassigned somewhere else in the FBI. Most, however, chose to join the fight.

OST was no longer "Overwatch Surveillance Teams."

Even though it was covert, and we were still officially called that, all teams were to become "unofficial" Occult Strike Teams. The government added a Quick Reaction Force (QRF) from need-to-know teams in Special Operations (SPEC OPS) as our "force multiplier."

Speaking of SPEC OPS, my next training course was a game changer—Navy SEAL school. No woman had ever completed the training, and I understood why. It's not a sexist thing; it's just that men are the physically stronger sex. They have gender and weight classes in sports for a reason—that is the reason. Unfortunately for that paradigm, I was stronger than any man.

Any human.

My eyes welled up—I missed being human …

That alienness was driven home as I wiped the tears away with the back of my hand and had to blink consciously. (I didn't blink or sweat anymore.) Already, I noticed that hot and cold no longer bothered me. It used to be that the "human" parts of me felt it, but now those parts just registered the feeling; it didn't bother me. I could go outside in the middle of winter wearing summer clothes and feel fine. Not that I did; I already drew enough attention. The last thing you want to do right now is to look like a monster.

People had gone from fearing me (plenty still did) to open hostility. One man even threatened to attack me unless I "stayed away" from his family—I was sitting at my table with Frank in a coffee shop at the time.

Still, I know how this ends for me as well. First, the unknown or unliked group is ostracized, then they are vilified, and then—

They are destroyed.

The day will happen when I become "Frankenstein's monster," and they will come for me. Not with torches and pitchforks—I'm far too scary for that. No, America loves their guns—they will bring those for me. But I can defend myself, right?

Nope.

Once the video comes out (and it always does with all the cell phone cameras), it will show me wiping out a bunch of people and undoubtedly killing some of them. They won't show the part where I warn them, try to stop it from escalating, and they attack me first.

No.

They will only show the part where I hurt those "poor, scared people" and use that to rally people to kill *anything* that is even *partially* alien. Humanity never changes. Deep down, we are elemental creatures when we are scared—we either run away from or kill what we do not understand. Calmness and rationality can only prevail if fear fails to take hold. That is rare.

Oh well.

One week on QRF, I was sitting in MESS, our "cafeteria," with Frank lying beside me. I was about halfway through drinking my hot black coffee—

Frank bumped my leg and barked once. Just once.

Damn, is he smart.

I didn't have to worry about when he needed to go. When he did that, it was the same as saying, "I gotta go relieve myself."

I left my coffee and took him to the pedestrian exit.

There was a Nuclear Materials Courier (NMC) agent at the port operator position. He was a new one named Berry Hillman.

"Hey, Berry, power poop time again," I said as I passed by with Frank.

He chuckled, and the interior door opened.

Waving, I walked into the sally port. This was one of only two ways in or out of our building. You either went through the pedestrian sally port or the vehicle one. Both had you locked between armored doors, and the machine guns would turn you into jelly if you were a bad guy. There were also holes above the door to let in gas, either CS or flammable gas. It is still, even after all these months, unnerving to know those machine guns can kill you at a moment's notice.

I was already used to being threatened by my employers, though. Every time we accessed a computer or database, it had a message threatening our jobs, finances, and freedom if we screwed up or divulged information to those without the proper clearance or need-to-know—just part of being an agent.

But having a machine gun pointed at you still sucks.

The outer door opened, and Frank zoomed to the grass. He was laying out the world's most giant turd.

"Jesus, Frank!"

He looked up at me sheepishly, then dropped his butt and slid it on the grass.

"How can I love you so much when you're so gross?"

He cocked his head. I know that is what dogs do when they are listening (I had been reading up on dogs now that I had one), but it sure looked like he was saying—

"Same here, freak."

I walked over, picked up his poop in a bag, tossed it in the outdoor trash, and reentered the building.

Frank and I had just gotten back to my coffee when the overhead page came on—

"Agent Levingston, report to BRIEFING … Agent Levingston, report to BRIEFING."

Hmm. Wonder what this is about?

Frank and I walked into the briefing room. It was large and contained all the AV equipment, an STU-III phone (for classified communications), and a large table with many chairs. Chayton was sitting there alone, waiting for us.

He was smiling; that is a good sign!

"Wow. This is my first briefing where you're smiling, Chayton."

He chuckled.

"I'm smiling for a reason. I'll get straight to it, James is awake."

I hugged Chayton. He was so startled he didn't know what to do, so he just patted my back. As I stepped away from him, he lifted a slip of paper.

"I know what you're going to say. Go to the airport; your flight to Virginia leaves in three hours."

———

I was the happiest person on the plane.

Once we were airborne, I went up front and chatted with the flight attendant.

This flight was surreal.

As a FAM, I defend the plane and everyone on it by keeping my cover. But this time, and probably every time from here on, I was not blending in. No one failed to notice me—I was like Beauty and the Beast.

The left side of my face—beauty.

The right side of my face—beast.

However, I never felt that a plane was better defended. I could kick some serious ass as a SIM-hybrid.

The flight attendant up front chatted with me for a bit, and then I returned to my seat. This time, there was no harassment or bigotry aimed my way. The plane landed, and we deplaned the aircraft. I always wondered why it was called boarding and deplaning—

Shouldn't it be boarding/deboarding or planing/deplaning?

Luckily, I'm paid as a federal agent, not as a philosopher.

I had left Frank in Denver. Until he got trained, he was a bit of a menace. He had already injured one of the NMC guys. Frank had jumped up to get petted and knocked a two-hundred-pound man into the wall.

Oops.

Luckily, I'll have plenty of time to deal with that when I return.

Making my way out of the Washington Dulles International Airport, I walked over and waited for my Uber. A few minutes later, I was on my way to the new hospital wing in Quantico. After all the usual security, I finally made it to his room.

I steeled myself to meet James again.

OK, I can do this. Just take a deep breath, I'm sure he's alright.

Opening the door to his room, I saw him. He was standing when I came in and turned. His face broke into a huge grin, and his eyes twinkled.

OMG—his eyes!

James was already a good-looking man, but his green eyes were possibly his best feature. Now, they were amazing! They were still green but almost the color of aquamarine and had the most dazzling, deepest hue I had ever seen. He was gorgeous!

I rushed forward and threw myself into his arms.

Oh no!

I looked up at him in a panic, but he was fine. He didn't even move when I slammed into him—

Wait a minute. I'm looking up at him ...

I stepped back and took a long look at him.

When I last saw James, he was six feet tall and about one hundred ninety pounds. After I became a SIM, I looked slightly down at him.

Now, he looked to be about my weight and musculature, but was a good six feet three inches tall. He had a slight increase in limb and neck length, as well as some deformation, but he still appeared human. His version of being a SIM-hybrid was less conspicuous than mine. Well, that and still having all of his face. Speaking of, he took a lot longer to heal than I did, so his scars were pale and hardly visible. I could still see the scar from the bullet right above his eyes, but it wasn't obvious.

How bizarre.

We hugged again and shared a long, passionate kiss. Then we sat down to talk.

"I'm so glad you're alive. I'm sorry I, um ... infected you," I said.

I feel so guilty.

He just laughed.

"Are you kidding me? I get a chance to be with you again. I couldn't be happier."

He always knew how to make me feel better.

"Thank you, baby ... How are you feeling?" I asked.

"Honestly? I have never felt better. I sleep and eat a lot, and finally have a six-pack." He raised his shirt to show off his abdominal muscles.

"Did they try and get you to do more tests?" I asked.

"Oh yeah! But guess what I said?"

"HIPAA," we said in unison.

Laughing, we shook our heads. We both knew there was no world where they did not share our medical results with the government.

"Well, it looks like Frank and I will be going to K-9 school before I even go to FBI training," James said.

He saw my surprised look.

"Chayton got me up to speed before you got here. I can't wait to meet our dog!"

James was beaming!

I was so happy to see him alive, better than new, and excited to meet Frank.

"When do you report?" I asked.

"We'll leave here in two days; I'll go with you to Denver and then leave with Frank. After finishing that training at the Federal Law Enforcement Training Center (FLETC), I return for a week, then it's off to the FBI training."

I nodded, but was sad I didn't have more time with him. Chayton had preemptively scheduled me for annual leave (our version of paid time off) so I could spend the two days with him here and another two back in Denver.

James saw my look.

"We have our whole lives ahead of us, lives we wouldn't have had if we hadn't become one of them," he said.

I nodded again. With that, we left the hospital and went to find a nice hotel …

———

Naval Special Warfare Center
Naval Amphibious Base
Coronado, California

I only had two days back in Denver with James and Frank before the day came when they left for FLETC, and I went to SEAL school.

When I landed in California, I boarded a bus with other Navy sailors to head to Coronado. Before long, we had arrived for Navy SEAL training.

All sixty-two weeks of it.

Usually, a mandatory service requirement in the Navy is followed by a battery of tests and evaluations before even being *considered* for SEAL training.

So, my "just showing up" put a lot of men in a bad mood about me.

They knew a woman was coming and figured I would be some wimpy hundred-pound DEI selection (DEI stands for Diversity, Equity, and Inclusion). On top of that, they would be annoyed by all the special consideration I would have to be given as a woman.

That was not going to happen—not on my watch.

I could hear them talking in the men's room when I came in. They all turned and looked at me—it was comical! Without a word, I undressed right in front of them and put on my uniform as they stared in amazement. Then, I turned to address them.

"Hello, everyone; I'm Patricia Levingston. If you want to piss me off—call me 'Pat' or 'Patricia.' Otherwise, call me Lev, Levingston, or the same the instructors will call all of us—worthless, oxygen thief, et cetera."

They were so shocked that none spoke, although I noticed most were grinning. These men were all badasses.

"I'll be eating, fighting, and bleeding with you. I don't need my own bathroom or any f—ing perfume. Clear?"

They all started laughing, and a few slapped my back (hands coming away bruised, I may add).

"Jesus, we were not expecting YOU!" one of them said.

Our camaraderie ended as the Navy SEAL instructor came in … his name tag read "WILLIS".

"Listen up, Candidates—!"

———

Over the next several weeks and months, we bonded. Our combined efforts were essential to meet each grueling milestone; no individual could succeed alone. Despite my advantages, none of us expected to finish training without learning to collaborate. The instructors were initially amused, then baffled and intrigued. I didn't tire like a human, and I was inhumanly strong and resilient. Their normal limits on recruits were pushed higher for me.

During our very first week came the infamous "drownproofing."

They would bind your hands and feet so you could only use your body to swim. Then they make you swim across the pool and pick up pool rings from the bottom—until you drown. When you drowned, they would haul you out and revive you. It was designed to make a human part-fish. Most did not complete this training and were washed out.

I realized that, even though I breathe, I don't *have* to.

Just like with pain, which I just "register" and not actually "feel," so too with breathing. When my body realized it wasn't getting air, it simply stopped breathing. It turns out that my alien parts don't need air, and my human parts need little, and somehow they store what's needed in my body. It took them hours, but they finally drowned me.

As they pulled me out, unconscious, I quickly came to on my own and violently flung one of the instructors away before I even realized it. Luckily, we were near the pool's deep end. I threw him halfway across the pool, and he landed with a splash.

Fortunately, Instructor Willis was unharmed. After watching him land, the other instructors started screaming at me and punished our entire team for my transgression. It didn't matter why; recruits don't put their hands on instructors.

Over the months that followed, we became elite warriors.

The limits to which my team and I were pushed were preposterous. Saying these are some of the toughest men in the world doesn't do the term "toughest" justice. I just hope they're part of OST's Quick Reaction Force …

Eventually, after nonstop training that made every twenty-four-hour day seem like a week, we were nearing the end of our training and about to be awarded the coveted "trident" of being a full-fledged Navy SEAL.

It was our last week of training, and we were at the explosives testing range, where we fired antitank weapons and grenade launchers. One of which was the Mark 19 GMG—Grenade Machine Gun.

The Mark 19 (Mk19) Automatic Grenade Launcher is an awesome weapon. We were taught how to load and fire it, maintain it, mount it to the top of a Humvee, and more.

Today, the instructors had something fun in mind. They had divided us into two teams …

"Candidates, today you'll engage the enemy (pointing to targets and vehicle husks downrange). The first team to successfully engage all targets from the Humvee in your AOR (Area of Responsibility) will get to eat dinner tonight. The other will clean the range, to include the heads (bathrooms)," Instructor Hamilton said.

In front of each team stood an Mk19 with 200 rounds of grenade ammunition. Next to it was a Humvee equipped with a pintle mount for attaching the Mk19.

As a team, we had drilled to mount the Mk19 and feed it ammo. However, my team and I had decided upon a different route for today —I just hope it works. Instructor Hamilton got ready to blow his whistle and start his stopwatch.

TWEET!

My team ran forward and grabbed the ammunition belt. They assembled the links to make one long belt while I went to the Mk19.

I could see Instructor Hamilton shaking his head.

We were already screwing up, in his mind. The weapon needed to be moved into place by several men, and *then* the belt needed to be fed into it and linked together. Now, we would have to unlink the grenades before loading the weapon.

In the blink of an eye, I picked up the Mk19 in both hands and jumped onto the hood of the Humvee. Then I ran up and got in the turret. I held the weapon down from the side of the vehicle as my team loaded the breach, and then I started destroying targets. I did not mount it; I just fired it like an ungainly rifle. I braced it with my left hand under it, and then held the right grip and hit the paddle trigger with my thumb. As fast as one fell, I was already on to the next target and then the next. Several seconds later, all our targets were gone. I smiled as smoke wafted out of the breach and the barrel.

I felt good!

There was a brief pause, and then I heard Hamilton yell, "Patricia, what the F— are you waiting for?! Help the other team, Blue Falcon!" (Blue Falcon stands for Buddy F—er.)

I shifted fire and helped the other team destroy their targets. When all were gone, I still had a few dozen grenades left on the belt.

"Patricia, do NOT let go of that weapon!" he yelled.

Hamilton walked over to me and climbed up onto the top of the Humvee. He sat right next to me in the turret.

"Jesus P, you're quite the machine! In fact, I'm *so* impressed that I want to shake your hand," said with clear sarcasm.

I looked at him, not sure where he was going.

"Do you see that target, way over there (he pointed to a bus at 1,200 meters, the furthest target away)?"

"Yes, sir," I said.

"When I tell you, you will fire—without stopping—all remaining rounds into that bus."

"Wilco (Will Comply)," I replied.

"Excellent. Now shake my hand."

I went to put the weapon down.

"Did I say to put the weapon down?"

"No, sir," I replied.

"Now, shake my hand. And don't break it, P!"

I did as commanded. I shifted the weapon into my left hand and shook his hand with my right. He gripped hard and did not let go.

"Weapons free!" he yelled in my face.

With one hand, I fired the Mk19. I realized what Hamilton was doing. I had to hold and fire the weapon *with one hand*. Simultaneously, I could not grip so hard that my other hand broke his. Still, about ten percent of the squeeze force happens to your other hand when holding something heavy with one hand. Try holding an egg in one hand and squeezing super hard with the other.

Hamilton's hand was that egg. The other hand held seventy-eight pounds of Mark 19 (about one hundred pounds with the grenades).

The Mk19 was slightly askew as I had to press the paddle trigger in the center with one thumb while maintaining a one-handed grip with the rest of my left hand. Fortunately, it tended to stabilize once it began firing.

OK, *this* was challenging!

Needless to say, this challenge degraded my accuracy.

A lot.

B-B-B-B-B-B-B-BOOM!

The last round went through the grenade launcher, and it was still. Smoke was wafting out of the barrel and breech. Downrange, some of my shots had hit, but most made a mosaic of everything around it.

"Hmm," Hamilton said.

"Nice shooting, P; next time, try hitting the target. We still need to work on your aim."

He let go of my hand. It didn't seem to faze him, but his hand was red and slightly swollen. He was going to need to ice that later …

"Change of plans; Team Alpha did not win because I had to tell you to engage and assist Bravo. You should have done that without asking!" he screamed.

"Now you all suffer. I feel more like swimming than eating now. Time to go for a swim, get your asses to the log!"

We all knew the log—every SEAL knows it.

Together, we carried that f—ing log everywhere. What sucks for me is that I didn't feel the physical pain or suffering the way they did, but I experienced mental anguish whenever I couldn't pull my weight or help more, especially when my actions caused my team to suffer. The instructors ensured I felt that pain alongside the rest of them, making me use every ounce of my abilities to support the team. I wasn't a superhero to them; I was merely a force multiplier and an asset to the team.

It was humbling, for sure.

I was proud when that trident was pinned to my chest—literally. The trident symbolizes the Navy SEALs and the rigorous training it takes to become one. As was tradition, they all took turns pounding it into my chest. When I returned the favor on each of them, I went excruciatingly slowly. I had mastered controlling my speed and strength at this point.

One of my most significant life accomplishments was that trident—not the physical trinket, of course, but what it symbolizes. I made it through training and became a Navy SEAL—and I was the only woman ever to complete the course. Sadly, since I was not a US Navy sailor, it was only an "honorary" title. Additionally, as an undercover agent, it wouldn't even be known to others outside of the SEALs. But it didn't matter—I had done it! I completed the training and learned to use my abilities to aid the team—a team that respected me just as I respected them. I realized that, for me, there will never be another course like this one.

Finally, I was returning to OST and James, and looked forward to applying what I had learned.

CHAPTER 4
FATHER LEIGHE

"FATHER LEIGHE, MAY I HAVE A MOMENT?"

That was Archbishop Marus Klein, and he always started the conversation this way. He was in charge but made everyone feel like they were speaking with a friend. He is a great man and always good-natured, even when he must go somewhere dark …

"Of course, Archbishop," I replied.

He smiled at my recognition of his rank. We used first names when not "at work," so I knew that when he didn't call me "Christos," it was business.

"I'm afraid it seems as though we may need your 'special' services again," he said.

"There's a woman in one of our churches in the States who claims that her daughter is possessed. The pastor of their church has investigated this claim using your new methods—I may add."

We remained silent for a long moment, as we both knew he would only be coming to me if the tests showed possession was not just possible but probable.

"Archbishop, I'm not only duty-bound to help but am also honored to be able to do so. Please tell me where this possession occurred, and I'll be on my way."

Archbishop Klein smiled.

"I have always loved how direct and how devoted you are. May God protect you on your journey, Father Leighe."

With that, and the usual envelope of information and orders, he left me to ponder my next mission.

I have served in my role for over eight years—one of the longest-surviving exorcists. Most people would find it difficult to believe in possession and exorcism, but I cannot understand anyone who *doesn't*. In addition to the ranks of our fallen, there is other undeniable proof.

The Bible is rife with "unexplained" phenomena. The parting of the seas for Moses, the trials of Jobe, the Ark… all written for anyone to read, and all "unexplained phenomena." But it is only unexplained in that God works in mysterious ways. He does or allows things to happen to test the mettle of those who believe. There are those members of evil cults who use subterfuge to bastardize the Bible into some genuinely evil and immoral ends. Some even believe that what they are doing is God's will or that supporting someone who is wicked and consistently sins, especially as their leader, is acceptable.

But they are wrong.

Jesus died to *forgive* our sins, not to have us commit new ones! Yes, some do not follow our faith, but they are still people—God's people, one and all. God does not make mistakes, and no human is a mistake. All are given free choice and free will. Those who choose the path of evil must be stopped.

Doing God's work will only happen here on Earth. Once you die, your soul goes to him to be judged. But He is not evil. And, although it may be hubris and blasphemy even to think it, He is the ultimate good and open to change.

Yes! I have thought the unthinkable! Could an all-powerful being learn?

How could an all-knowing being *fail* to learn, given that the humans He created were often unpredictable due to their free will?

This is where I, and others like me, come in ...

The following morning, I arose with the rising sun. Taking an Uber, I made my way to Fiumicino Airport, looking through the windows as we drove to Rome. I traveled light since other clergy would have the tools of the trade that I needed once I got there. After all, it would be a long journey from Europe, and I had to clear customs and security. Some of my "tools" could have created problems with that.

I didn't want to risk missing my flight, so I arrived earlier than necessary. After passing through security, I made my way through Fiumicino Airport to my gate. I was flying on Delta Air Lines with a connection at Hartsfield-Jackson Atlanta International Airport.

Now, the waiting.

After two takeoffs, two landings, and a short layover, I was boarding my flight to Sky Harbor International Airport in Phoenix. Settling into another middle seat, I lay my head back as we started down the runway. I was tired from my traveling, but my mind was thinking about my upcoming mission. As the A321 Airbus lifted into the sky, however, I instead remembered my very first exorcism eight years ago ...

———

"Father Leighe, I appreciate your swift response to my call for help," the woman said, her voice trembling with fear and determination.

Jeremiah and I had arrived to help them. We had trained together in the Vatican and were well acquainted with each other's tactics at this point. However, our excitement had to be tempered; we did not want these two to know we were there to perform our very first exorcism together.

I could see the woman's distress reflected in her young daughter's eyes, a silent plea for help. Cheryl and Monica—I still remember their names and faces.

"It's my husband, Lukas, you see ... he's not well. He's in his room in the attic and does not come out. All day, he mutters and dotes over that stupid book he found!"

Cheryl's eyes welled with tears.

"He hasn't eaten or slept as far as I know. When Monica opened the door and tried to talk with him, he screamed obscenities at her and slammed the door on her. But he was deep in the room and nowhere near the door; he closed it *with his mind.*"

She sat down with her daughter, and they both were quietly crying.

I had already read their pastor's report, which included their testimony: Over the past month, Lukas had become obsessed with the occult, growing increasingly withdrawn and cynical about the world around him. Then, about a week ago, he returned from a trip with an ancient book. He was excited and happy, and they thought he might have become the loving and caring father and husband he once was.

No such luck.

He went to the attic, bringing up supplies and everything he would need for his rituals. He told them he was not to be disturbed and would come down for them when he finished, but he never returned from that attic, and what was up there now was no longer a man—

It was a demon.

As a team, we ascended the steps. Jeremiah and I felt nervous but remained steadfast in our resolution. At the top, the murmuring and pungent smells of incense and sulfur couldn't shake our dedication. We could also detect something foul and sickly within, a scent reminiscent of stale vomit and rot. In perfect sync, I signaled to my apprentice, and Jeremiah flung the door wide open.

As I entered, Lukas turned on me—or what was once Lukas.

Lukas had shed all traces of his humanity. His eyes, once human, were now all-black. His skin, once healthy, was now leprous and covered in acne and boils, some still oozing pus. Long spines protruded from his naked body, and his fingers and toes had transformed into long, sharp claws. It was no longer human.

"Good evening, Father Leighe," the demon said with a grin, exposing sharp fangs.

"Good evening, demon. By what name should I call you?"

It laughed—an evil laugh devoid of any mirth.

We both knew of "the Great Myth".

I have always found the concept of knowing a demon's name intriguing. In every exorcism show, the exorcists gain control over the demon by learning its name. Yet, it knew my name—and still had no power over me. Knowing a name holds no extraordinary power; I wish it were that easy …

"I am Garandal—the poisoned," the demon growled.

Garandal, hmm.

Knowing a name had only one advantage: it helped me determine what kind of demon it was. This one I knew, even if it hadn't told me.

And it was not good.

The poisoned were a group of demons with many powers: the power of possession (which every demon has), limited telekinesis, venomous spines and bite, inhuman strength, and—most dangerous of all—the power to summon a Devil. Although the power needed (through sacrifice) was enormous, the poisoned could summon a Devil. However, it would need to convince many others (through disguise and guile) to join with it to summon the much more powerful being.

I could not allow this to happen.

It knew that we were there to banish it as we smiled at each other. Mine was a rictus as I prepared to go into battle. In contrast, its was a cruel smile of sadism—a trait that almost all demons and devils had.

"Now!" I yelled.

Jeremiah stepped to his right and drew a mini-crossbow as I leaped to my left and drew mine. The demon roared and lunged at Jeremiah.

The first bolt shot out of Jeremiah's crossbow, hitting Garandal in the shoulder. The poisoned were vulnerable to two things—blessed items (like our crossbow bolts) and fire.

AAKKH!

It screamed as the shoulder hissed and smoked—and then exploded in blood and pus. Its arm flew across the room from the pressure of the explosion. The demon streaked into Jeremiah and hit him with its remaining spiny arm. Jeremiah was flung across the room and into the wall. The plaster cracked and imploded as he fell to the ground in a heap.

The demon laughed maniacally and turned to say something witty to me. Suddenly, it did not feel like talking, though …

My crossbow bolt had found its mark. I could see just the finned end of it protruding from Garandal's mouth.

Its eyes bulged as I dived for cover—there was a luxurious padded reading chair just a step or two away. As I slid behind it, there was a loud "POP," and suddenly, there was gore everywhere. As its head exploded, blood, guts, bones, and putrid pus went everywhere. On the ceiling, the walls, and even the furniture. The smell was horrendous.

As I stood, I carefully stepped over to Jeremiah. I could see his chest rising and falling. I'm just glad he is unconscious—that is fortunate.

Quickly, I went to the book.

No great ritual was needed. I quickly produced a flask, not of holy water but of liquid butane (like what a lighter has). I put the book in the brazier that the demon had been using. Dousing it thoroughly, I lit it on fire. The house was old and had no fire detectors, so I opened a window.

Returning to Jeremiah, I could see he was starting to regain consciousness. His newly mottled skin was already beginning to ooze pus, and little spines were starting to sprout.

Crud, I can't get him out in time.

I was devastated that this family would be losing not only their father and husband but also their home. Quickly reloading my crossbow, I shot Jeremiah right between the eyes. Ironically, the "offspring" of the demon could not be as quickly killed as the demon itself—I would not have long …

It needed to burn, or it would fully awaken and wreak havoc on all living things. Since there may be witnesses, I quickly put on a jacket (over my white-tabbed shirt) and a handkerchief over my face. Then, I doused Jeremiah (and the headless Garandal, for good measure) and lit them on fire.

Running down the stairs, I turned to the mother and daughter and yelled, "Fire, get out!"

I saw them grab the family cat and follow me out the door.

"Tell the police your husband lost his mind and lit the house on fire, no mention of exorcism or me."

I turned to leave, but she grabbed me and hugged me. I could feel her sobbing as I gently pushed her away.

"I must go; the authorities will not understand what happened today. I will pray for your husband's soul."

As I pulled away from her, I ran to my car. Emergency sirens could be heard as I drove away from the neighborhood and onto the highway.

———

The thoughts of eight years ago vanished like a sailboat into the fog of memory as the plane descended. Sadly, I had an almost perfect memory, ensuring that event and others would haunt me forever. Taking these final moments in the air, I tried to rest …

I awoke as the overhead page announced our preparation for landing. Our flight arrived thirty minutes late but was otherwise uneventful. After being picked up yet again by an Uber, I made my way to Saint Mary's Roman Catholic Basilica in Tempe, where I would meet Mrs. Halston.

After an hour at the church, I heard someone say my name. Turning, I saw a pretty woman in her mid-forties with a freckled face and long auburn hair.

"Yes. How may I help you?" I asked.

"I need your help with my daughter. She's in a terrible state. I spoke with my priest, Father Namm, and he asked me to meet you here."

Hearing her plight made me remember the woman and her daughter from my first exorcism eight years ago.

"Is everything alright, Father?" She had a worried look on her face.

"Yes, yes. I'm fine. How may I be of service, ma'am?"

"Well, my daughter has been acting very strange. She keeps having 'blackouts' where she doesn't remember where she was or what she was doing. We thought, you know, maybe she was doing drugs or something—but she said that wasn't it. She, uh, um …"

I could see she was panicking. It was time to jump in.

"What is your name, if I may ask?"

"Oh, sorry, Father, I'm Joanne, Joanne Halston." She relaxed a little and gave me a weak smile.

"Joanne, is your daughter having trouble in school or her social life?" I needed to make sure it was a possession issue, not a parenting issue.

"Yes, I mean no—she gets straight As, and she is in a sorority at Arizona State University."

"OK. When did her troubles start? Can you describe these 'episodes' to me?"

"Well, she-um, well … she has seemed out of sorts. The only word I can use is … well, terrified!"

I stayed silent so she would continue. Since becoming an exorcist, I have learned much about interviewing and interrogation. The best way to get information is to get them talking and not interrupt—unless they go off-topic for a while.

"She said something happened the Saturday before last. They had gone to some sort of initiation for a new pledge. It was very late at night—but she is twenty-two and spends a lot of time on campus, so I wasn't worried about her. She was always the responsible one …"

She trailed off and stopped. So, I jumped in to keep her going.

"What is your daughter's name, Joanne?"

"It's Laura, Laura Halston."

I noticed her peculiar way of using names and moved on—

"Has Laura told you what happened that night?"

"No. She tries to, and then just … well … she can't talk! She wants to, but she can't!"

I betrayed no outward emotion, but I had jumped to attention inside! Not being able to speak, especially when it is about being possessed or about how you came to be possessed, is the hallmark of an actual demonic possession.

Joanne could not have known that.

"Mrs. Halston, Joanne, I know why you sought me out. Yes, I'm an exorcist. Yes, possession is a real thing. And, yes, your daughter *might* be possessed—"

I held up my hand to stop the inevitable emotional outburst.

"I need to talk with Laura first. It may be something much simpler than that, but we need to find out."

Joanne nodded her head.

"Thank you, Father. Thank you." She gave me a gentle hug and then turned to leave.

"Joanne—"

She turned back to me.

"Do NOT tell your daughter—or anyone else—about our conversation, and I'll be at your house in two days' time."

With a quick smile, she left.

I called the Vatican and told them we might have another possession and that I would need my "tools".

———

When I arrived at the Halston residence, it was midweek. Since it was still morning, her daughter was likely in school. I hoped so, as there was much to do before she came home. Saving Laura was a high priority, but the demon must be exorcised no matter what.

Sometimes, depending on how long they had been possessed and by what demon, people could be exorcised safely with the demon driven from its host. Other times, like eight years ago, the host could not be saved and died along with the demon. I started through my mental checklist.

Confidence is a big part of being an exorcist. With God's blessing of a fantastic memory, I've learned to pay attention to every detail, knowing I can handle whatever comes my way. Knowledge comes from details, and those make the difference between life and death.

As I walked up the walkway to their home, the details came.

The house was a three-story, costly, ultra-modern home. It was all stone and glass and fitted with Restoration Hardware fixtures. The lawn and shrubbery were perfect and well-maintained, and a Porsche Cayenne Turbo S and Mercedes S-Class were parked in the driveway.

I walked up the stone walkway and knocked on the door.

My arrival seemed to catch the man at the door off guard, his expression a mix of shock and confusion.

"Oh, uh, hi. What-a, what do you want, Father?"

"Hello, Mister—" I waited.

"Mr. Halston, Terrance Halston," he said.

Wow. The name thing seems to run in the family ...

"Terrance, I'm Father Christos Leighe; I was requested by your wife, Joanne."

"Oh? Hmm ... She hadn't told me. Ah, well, please come in, Father."

He stepped aside, and I entered through the ten-foot solid entry doors. The grand staircase and opulent furnishings were immediately apparent as I came in.

"You have a beautiful home, Mr. Halston," I said.

"Oh, yes, thank you. May I get you something to drink?"

"Tea would be wonderful. Milk and two lumps, if I may."

He looked at me, befuddled.

I laughed, and he smiled. I knew my laugh could be disarming and amiable.

"Sorry, too long in Europe. Sugar and cream, if it is not any trouble."

"No trouble at all," he replied.

A tall, thin, severe-looking man in a suit appeared, seemingly out of nowhere.

"Mr. Wallace, would you be kind enough to get our guest a cup of tea with ..."

He turned back to me, and I smiled.

"Two scoops of sugar and some cream, thank you."

"My pleasure, Father," Mr. Wallace said.

With that, he left to "fetch the tea."

Very interesting. Wealthy and with house servants.

Joanne walked in and was startled to see me, even though she knew I was coming today.

"Oh! Hello Father Lay …"

"Leighe. I pronounce it 'lay-he'."

"Yes. Oh, Terrance, he is here about Laura—"

Terrance's face adopted a peculiar expression. His features clouded, and he appeared angry. After a brief moment, he returned to normal. I feigned ignorance, pretending I hadn't noticed.

"Well, she'll be home this afternoon. What is this about, Father?" he asked.

From that moment, I knew that he was holding out on me. He knew something …

"Oh, I'm sorry, it is probably nothing, but Joanne wanted me to talk with your daughter. She's probably having some sort of young adult troubles. Nothing to worry about."

I smiled broadly and kindly, just the way I had practiced, to be disarming.

"Well, I have to get going then," he said.

"Busy man, I see," I said, still smiling.

"Yes, those bills won't pass by themselves," he smiled and left.

A short while later, I saw the Mercedes pulling out from the drive and speeding down the street. I turned back, and Mr. Wallace was there. I had not heard him, which is troubling.

"Father Leighe, your tea." He handed me a beautiful cup and saucer.

"Thank you, Mr. Wallace."

With a brief nod, he departed, and I feigned taking a sip.

"Joanne, I must see Laura's room … alone."

She stiffened slightly at that but nodded and led me upstairs. I left my untouched tea on the table, and as we walked, I chatted with her.

"Joanne, when Laura arrives, could you please let her know that a friend is in her room? You forgot to ask *her* name."

She gave me a quizzical look but nodded yes.

As soon as the door shut and I was alone in Laura's room, I began unpacking my bag and preparing. Before starting any exorcism, I learn as much as I possibly can about the people involved. Luckily, the Vatican has a robust investigations department, so I already knew her father was Congressman Terrance Halston and Joanne was a stay-at-home mom. Their only daughter, Laura, studied Computer Science and was in her junior year at ASU. She was a member of the Beta Zeta Sigma sorority; I had a list of all its members, starting with the sorority president, Dorothy Scranton.

I would need to question Laura in here, though, hopefully alone. If she *was* possessed by a demon, which is highly probable at this point, I wanted to limit Joanne's harm.

Not knowing what kind of demon it was would make it challenging, but most demons were filled with hubris and loved to talk—and I always let them. For such intelligent beings, they can be dim-witted about sharing information.

That is good news for me, though.

It was midafternoon when I heard the door downstairs open and female voices—Laura must be home. Luckily, I had finished my preparations in time. I heard footsteps, and then the bedroom door opened.

She had a big smile and was expecting a school friend. That all changed in an instant—

"What are *you* doing in *my* room?" she shouted.

I smiled and waited. It would not be long now …

"Waiting on you."

"You don't even know me!"

"Tell me your name then."

"It's … It's …" Her eyes rolled back in her head until only the whites were visible. That detail about demonic possession was something they got *right* in the movies.

She, or I should say the demon in her, started laughing—

"Foolish priest. I see you came alone. No helper today?"

Hmm. That is disturbing. How did it know we usually operate in twos?

"Nah. When it's what we call a 'lightweight' demon, they only bother sending one—usually a new one like me," I lied.

It laughed again.

"Nice try. You are not new."

Oh no, that is not good.

"Well then, I'm Father Leighe, and you are—?"

"No one to be trifled with," the demon replied.

"What kind of demon are you then?"

It laughed—long and hard.

"Oh no, no, no … I am neither a demon nor a devil."

It was my turn to be afraid. Outwardly, I was calm and had a smile. Inwardly, I was scared to death.

Not a demon?

They all had incredible hubris. So, this one saying it was not a demon meant it was something else. I don't have a plan for *something else.*

"Hmm … You *are* smart. For a human, anyway," it said.

She, or it, was gazing at me with great interest. I could see an intelligence behind the eyes that most demons did not possess.

It would appear I was out of options, so I hit the remote.

A blast of compressed air sent a mixture of holy water, garlic, and acetone (a flammable liquid) all over her. I didn't want to hurt her, but there was no holding back on this … whatever the hell it was.

With a bemused expression, it spoke, "Those won't work on me."

I swiftly drew my mini-crossbow and shot it in the chest. I had practiced with it and used it in combat numerous times. From beneath my robes—to a bolt in the chest—it usually took less than a second (hitting any part of a person at close range is an easy shot). The bolt's tip contained a tiny vial of sulfuric acid that, upon impact, combined with the potassium permanganate at the end of the vial to create a small yet powerful ball of flame.

For a brief moment, it looked dumbfounded. Then, it went up in flames and started shrieking!

AAIIIYA!

The inhuman shriek pierced my ears.

I dropped my crossbow, as it was empty and had done its job. Mercy needed to be given, not for the "demon" but for the poor woman, Laura. Drawing my handgun, a Glock 43 9mm, I shot her once in the head. She dropped to the floor, dead and on fire.

I grabbed the small fire extinguisher that I had brought and waited. As soon as I was sure the demon was really dead, I doused her with the white spray from the extinguisher.

Slowly, an unearthly red mist started coming out of her. It seemed to just ooze out of her pores and every orifice. The mist coalesced into a single entity, an alien amalgamation of indescribable horror, and began moving away from the body. I tried to recite my exorcisms, but it did not respond in any way.

The exorcism should have worked! Especially in such a weakened state.

The mist made its way toward the window. I tried shaking holy water into it and fanning it with my robes, but it did not respond to any ritual or device—or even follow the laws of physics.

There was one neat gadget that I had been wanting to try, though— a plastic bottle with a powerful, battery-operated fan. The design was to suck in any spirit that had a gaseous form, then spin the lid shut. There was zero effect, even when I put it right next to the retreating mist.

I was confused; it was telling the truth—this was no demon.

My Almighty, what is this thing?

It passed through the cracks and seals of the closed window and disappeared.

This was a first, and not in a good way. Laura was quite dead, and I had no proof of possession. There is a word for that in common vernacular—it's called murder.

I had sprayed her with a flammable acid, shot her with both a crossbow and a pistol, and lit her on fire. I'm pretty sure I would get the electric chair for this one …

Taking my cue from the monster within her, I went to the window and opened it. It was a beautiful fall day outside, as Tempe was typically quite hot. I grabbed my kit and crossbow. After climbing out of the second-story window, I jumped into a fern from the roof.

Dusting myself off, I ran for my rental car.

What on Earth was that?

————

I drove quickly, but not so fast as to draw police attention.

Once I was back at my hotel, I retrieved my "go-bag" for emergencies and fled. The bag had everything I would need for a quick getaway.

Luckily, one of my pastimes is planning for eventualities. I learned about "the seven Ps" from an army officer in my congregation and about PACE.

The seven Ps were this: proper prior planning prevents piss poor performance.

And PACE? Every essential plan should include four plans: primary, alternate, contingency, and emergency.

My primary and alternate plans were used against the demons and devils; the contingency involved retreat. And what about emergencies?

Well, that involved this—becoming a fugitive.

After leaving my rental car in the hotel parking lot, I ordered a Waymo. I wasn't sure how long it would take the police to put out an APB on my car, and I didn't want anyone to see me, so a driverless car was the way to go. Once I arrived, I knew I would be safe.

Archbishop Marus and I devised a plan for such an eventuality …

————

Crime Scene News—Denver, Colorado
Samantha

"You have to be kidding me," I muttered.

"Whataya got, Sammy?" Harold inquired.

"Get this, Harold: An exorcist from the Catholic Church is wanted nationwide for murder, arson, and obstruction of justice for fleeing the scene. He is a white male, 5'9" and 170 pounds, thirty-eight years old, with brown eyes and black hair. We have a picture as well. He went to

Congressman Terrance Halston's house in a wealthy neighborhood of Tempe to exorcise a demon from the congressman's daughter, Laura. He lit her on fire and shot her with both a crossbow bolt and a pistol round before leaving the scene."

He either isn't a real priest, or the exorcism did not go as planned, I thought.

I looked at Harold expectantly, and he just smiled.

"OK. When do we leave for Tempe?" he asked.

I smiled back and started looking online to book our tickets.

By the afternoon of the next day, we landed at Phoenix Sky Harbor International Airport. As Harold retrieved our rental car, I downloaded the directions to the Omni Tempe Hotel at ASU, where Harold and I had booked rooms for two nights. We picked up a Ford C-Max hybrid SEL, the economy model of the day, and tossed all our belongings in the back. After a brief ten-minute drive on SR143, we arrived at our hotel. The place was lovely; four stars were not our usual standard, but it was closer to our destination, so we decided to splurge a little. I hoped our bosses wouldn't mind the extra expense. We reconvened in the lobby after stowing our belongings in our rooms.

Our first stop would be the church of the dead daughter, Laura. If we couldn't find the exorcist priest, we would see the next best thing. We were on our way to St. Mary's Roman Catholic Basilica to talk with its pastor, Father Max Namm.

After a short fifteen-minute drive, we arrived at a modern and beautiful church. We parked and made our way inside. The outer façade was already impressive, but the inside was more so. I have always felt at peace inside churches, although I really don't know why.

A few minutes later, we noticed an older Korean American priest enter the main room. My press pass and Harold's camera were visible, making it clear that we were journalists.

"Father Namm?" I asked.

"Yes, how can I assist a member of our press?" He responded with a smile, and I could not ascertain whether it was said in earnest or in jest.

"We wanted to know what happened, not where he is."

I knew I didn't need a preamble; I'm sure news crews had already inundated him. I also handed him my card. He took it and read it with a strange smile.

"Ms. Cox, I remember your story quite vividly. Most amazing."

He was doing it again! Damn it, I can't tell if he means it or not.

"Then you know I'm after the truth, not to get your colleague arrested."

He considered what I had to say and waited before speaking again.

"I have your card, Ms. Cox. Let me see who can reach out to you at this number."

I thanked him, and we were on our way.

———

It was 6:30 a.m. the following day, and my phone was ringing. Most people would be mad about a call this early, but I had been up for ninety minutes.

"Samantha," I answered.

"This is Father Namm. I was wondering if you had time today to meet and chat a bit more?"

Intriguing, I thought.

"Of course. When and where?"

I had my notepad ready; it was always near.

"How about nine a.m. at St. Mary's Basilica? Does that work OK for you?"

"That sounds great, Father. We'll see you then."

He hung up.

That was a quick response from the Vatican, which is most intriguing. While I was on the plane, I did some research on our newest felon. He was a full Catholic priest who lived in Vatican City. He must have been flown all the way out to America just to do that exorcism. This was no small fish we were dealing with, so definitely not just some quack or pretender.

I did not doubt that influential figures from the Vatican were aiding the outlaw, Father Leighe; I was merely curious about their story. I called Harold to update him about our upcoming meeting, and two hours later, we met in the lobby and departed to meet Father Namm.

We quickly relocated the church. Thankfully, almost every car and phone now has a navigation system, and our nav system guided us directly to Third Street in Phoenix.

St. Mary's Basilica really was a beautiful church. I took a moment to look around at the details of it. The church looked like a Spanish mission style outside, and once Harold and I went in through the ornate double doors, we could see beautiful stained glass and sculptures of saints. An arched ceiling was high above us. There were many lit candles, with one large one near the main altar. Several people were genuflecting in front of the altar, and we noticed a gift shop near the stairs. There was also an offering plate right as you came in the door. I was not feeling charitable at the moment, however.

We stood off to the side, as I'm sure Father Namm would be looking for us.

I glanced at my watch—it read 9:02 a.m.

Harold and I patiently waited …

At 9:20 a.m., I was ready to leave.

"What the hell, Harold?"

"Careful, Sammy. You're blaspheming in the house of the Lord," he said in false admonishment.

"Harold, you and I are not going up anyway—"

"Good morning," I heard a man say.

We turned and saw that Father Namm had padded up to us. It is freaky how quiet he was.

This was awkward, as we were just misbehaving.

He saw our looks.

"No worries, the Lord has heard worse," he smiled as he said it.

"Sorry about that, Father; I'm not very religious after what we have seen," I said.

He nodded sagely and said, "No worries again, for I'm *extremely* religious after what I have seen."

Harold and I looked at each other. Neither of us was quite sure what Father Namm meant by that.

"Please, follow me."

He turned and started walking. We followed him to the back offices, through a cloakroom, and to a small study.

"Do not be alarmed," he said.

Harold and I looked at each other as Father Namm hit some hidden switch and pulled a bookcase forward.

"A secret passage, really?" I asked rhetorically.

How cliche.

"It is here for a reason. Please follow," he said as he turned and started down some stone steps. Overhead lights were on; it was not some ancient burial ground, just a regular set of stairs—in a hidden room inside a church study.

Not weird at all.

He hit another switch as we entered, and the bookshelf closed behind us.

"You know I'll include that in my story, right?"

"Of course—" he said, "you do remember where the switch is, yes?"

He smirked as he saw our expressions. He knew we had no idea how to get to the room, much less find the switch again.

Damn it. Oh well, it will still be a remarkable anecdote in the story.

After taking several turns (this place was a maze!), we finally arrived in a small, well-lit room. Sitting comfortably in a chair was Father Leighe.

"Holy crap!" I said.

"*Really*, Sammy?" Harold scolded.

Father Leighe just laughed.

"Sorry for the secrecy, but I didn't want to go to prison for the rest of my life if you had brought the police," Father Leighe said.

He nodded to Father Namm, who turned, nodded to us, and left.

"Please take a seat at the table and get comfortable. We have much to discuss for your story."

CHAPTER 5
BOLO

OST—DENFO

Agent Lev

WELL, *this is a new one.*

I had only been back at OST for two months, and it looked like I finally had something to investigate. Arizona State Police had issued a BOLO (be on the lookout) for a murder suspect. That wasn't unusual. What was remarkable were the charges and the suspect.

After printing the BOLO notice, I walked down the hall to see Chayton Blackwell. He had just been promoted to assistant special agent in charge (ASAC). Usually, I would go to my new first squad leader, Graham Hart, but he was home with sick children today. I guess even OIs can't stop sick leave.

"Hey, boss, got a minute?" I asked through his open door.

"Sure, come on in," he motioned to the seat.

Chayton has been with us since the beginning. When we fought the last OI, he was my TL, and I was happy to see him promoted. Although, he did not look like what you expected as an ASAC. He was an extremely fit Native American man—six feet two inches tall and

220 pounds of former Marine Recon and pro-MMA fighter. He had the cauliflower ears and facial scars to prove it.

I handed him what I had printed out.

Slowly, he read it, then spoke.

"So, a clergyman, Father Christos Leighe, doused a woman with flammable chemicals and then shot her with an ignitable bolt from a crossbow that lit her on fire ... Then he shot her in the head with a pistol and stayed to put her out with a fire extinguisher?"

He glanced up with an intrigued look.

"Yup, sounds like it," I said.

"Also, according to official testimony from the detectives, her mother had *asked* Father Leighe to perform an exorcism on their daughter?" he asked.

"Well, it's not exactly an OI, but it *is* still unusual," I said.

He nodded.

"I think you're right. Besides, things have been slow, so maybe I'll send out Second Squad to check it out."

He sat for a minute thinking and then grabbed the phone.

"SSA Tanaka, report to ASAC. Tanaka, report," he said, and hung up the phone.

As we were waiting, I thought about our "new" command and team structure. Since the entire OST division "officially" became Occult Strike Teams, we have changed to a more military-style organizational structure. We are still covert, but now all teams are strike teams.

Currently, we have five active squads, in addition to the six OST agents working in the MCC and the twelve NMC agents assigned to protect the office and vehicles during their shifts.

Each squad consists of six members: an SSA who serves as the Squad Leader (SL) and five additional agents. It is further divided into three two-person Fire Teams: Alpha, Bravo, and Charlie. Team Alpha always includes the SL.

Our squad, First Squad, was still on QRF this week. However, just because Second Squad wasn't on QRF, it didn't mean they were not still on duty; they were just on reserve. Therefore, QRF was saved for any emergencies, while the reserve was sent out on callouts.

"Hey, boss, you rang?"

David "Dave" Tanaka stood at the open office door. He was an unassuming man of Hispanic descent, approximately five feet nine inches tall, fit and muscular, weighing around 180 pounds. Like all of us, he had been hand-selected for the OST. His brown eyes glanced over at me.

"Hey, Dave," I said.

"Hi, Lev," he replied.

"So, Dave, have a look at what Lev found and let me know if your team is up for a little vacation to the desert ..." Chayton said.

Dave read the entire report and then responded.

"Sounds fun. Good eye, Lev. This is, for sure, weird as hell. When do you want us to roll out?"

"You up for going out tonight? Chayton asked.

"Why not? I'll let the squad know, and we'll head out when ready."

Chayton nodded, and Dave turned and left.

"I'm going to go grab some chow in MESS if you need me," I said, getting up.

Chayton threw me a mock salute, and I returned it.

I had finished my lunch and was sitting in MESS with Frank when I heard the overhead page.

"Agent Levingston to ARMOURY. Agent Levingston, report."

That was Chayton. ARMOURY, not BRIEFING.

Most peculiar, I thought.

So, Frank and I walked over to meet him there instead.

ARMOURY is the most secure area of the office, with only the SLs and above having access to it. So, I wasn't surprised to see Chayton still there, going through all the access steps and procedures.

I waved to Frank with the "shoo" motion; he knew that meant to get gone. With a little whimper of displeasure, he walked away. I heard the door swing open and followed Chayton through the heavy metal door.

Once inside, we saw rows of weapons, equipment, and even our "suits."

Those were ExoM battle armor suits. They featured an unpowered "exoskeleton" that absorbed about 70 percent of the load weight into the ground instead of relying on muscle. This enabled us to move more quickly, whether standing or crouching. However, crawling and getting up remained just as difficult as usual. The suits also included built-in Combat Application Tourniquets (CATs) and level three and four ballistic armor covering most of the body.

As I returned to the heavy weapons section, Chayton gestured toward a giant weapon.

"Merry Christmas, Lev. It isn't *yours*; it belongs to the government. But here's the world's only MOD X Mk19 GMG," Chayton said.

I looked him dead in the face.

"Don't ruin the moment, Chayton. This is special."

We both grinned. I could see a bow and a note on it: "To: SEAL Agent 'Lev' Levingston. Kill some f—ing aliens for us, Frogwoman!"

It was signed by Chief Petty Officer Melvin Hamilton.

I chuckled. Frogman was the slang term for a Navy SEAL. I was the first woman, so—Frogwoman it is.

Carefully, I examined the new addition to the ARMOURY: a standard MOD 3. However, it had been expertly modified with a semicircular drum magazine that held thirty-two rounds and fed the weapon evenly, ensuring it wouldn't be as off-balance as it lost weight from ammo expenditure. Along with the leaf sight, it featured a thermal optical sight, which can switch to infrared and magnify up to ten times. Additionally, a foregrip and a rear pistol grip were added; the paddle triggers were removed.

It was designed to be fired by a single operator, like a rifle.

"You have some scary friends, Lev," Chayton told me.

"Yeah, yeah, I do ..." I replied.

Not just the SEALs but also OST.

"Anyway, I thought you should know it's here—just in case we need you to use it."

"Wow. Remember when we were just police, Chayton?"

"Not really; it seems like that was long ago."

I nodded.

Not all our agents would get into SEAL school, and certainly not many would pass it. Nonetheless, the OST had a blank check for training, and the Nuclear Material Couriers (NMCs) also knew of many of the best training schools because they had taken them.

After a final inspection and function check of the MOD X, I put it in its cradle on the shelf; it was amazing. They had clearly taken my measurements; it fit me like a glove. Considering my inhuman strength, I could use it like an M-16 rifle, including one-handed, if needed. *That* was why Instructor Hamilton had me fire it one-handed.

"I'll get to take it to Buckley to test it soon, right?"

Chayton smiled. "Already planned for tomorrow."

I beamed with a broad smile. Buckley Space Force Base features several indoor and outdoor ranges designed to train its Security Police, Air Force personnel, and now its Space Force Guardians. I was eager to give it a try.

My SEAL training, plus what I had gone through in battle and recovery with OST, had turned me into a warrior. I had learned to expect combat and appreciate warfare's tools.

We left the ARMOURY, and Frank and I went to our dorm room.

While on QRF or reserve at the office, each of us had a "dorm" room. Each 150-square-foot room contained everything we needed for the week. I went to the small desk and turned on my laptop. It was time to do more research and learn about our enemies.

Between the horror and combat-related books in our MWR (Morale, Welfare, and Recreation) room and the endless reach of the internet, we spent every moment on duty training or studying. No supervisor had to force us or check on us. Everyone who survived the original OI didn't need to be told to be on high alert.

As for the other OSTs, who were just briefed on it? They didn't have to be told twice, either.

If we wanted to live and save our teammates, we had to learn quickly.

Another advantage of my SEAL training is that I conditioned

myself to need less sleep, so now I can train and learn more during the "extra" hours of my day. Not that I didn't still eat and sleep a lot; I just didn't *have* to. The most significant benefit was learning to use my newfound speed and power with control. I could now shake hands or pet a normal dog without causing injury.

Needing a break after a few hours of studying (reading about lycanthropes), I took Frank for a walk before he did his "one bark."

"Badezimmer"

Frank looked at me and immediately stood, tail wagging.

Since I was in SEAL school, the G decided to send James and Frank to the K-9 school. They returned, and a week later, James participated in the two-month FBI training. He then returned to attend other schools, while Frank remained at OST DENFO as a K-9 guard dog and continued his training with the other agents.

He had been taught German commands, which were customary in K-9 school. The dogs either learned German or Dutch, but our schools preferred German. This practice reduced the likelihood of commands being misinterpreted by the K-9. As we walked to the sally port, I thought about James.

James and Frank had returned from K-9 school, where they performed very well. I had been taking a course at the Online Learning Center about their school to learn about Frank's training and commands.

Frank had also been an eye-opener for his instructors. His abilities far outpaced even the famous Belgian Malinois (the most intelligent, talented, and dangerous dog breed). He could do everything they could: run obstacle courses, walk on ropes, climb ladders, jump and grab things, and the list goes on. However, unlike the Malinois, he could clear a ten-foot wall (versus a six-foot) and jump about forty feet with a good run (versus about thirty for the Malinois). Just watching the videos of him was amazing. I could tell Frank loved it, too; his tail was wagging a mile a minute. The other dogs were scared by him at first but eventually came around, and they all got along now. Which was good to know, so I could start trying to get along with Sampson, our other K-9 at the office. He is terrified of me.

It's hard to believe I had been gone for over a year. Training like I had seemed to take a lifetime, and then when it was over, it seemed like little time had passed at all.

The important thing was that I felt I finally had the skills I needed to battle the mighty aliens that we had encountered. I have no idea if it will be enough for the next ones, though.

The next ones.

There is a thought I do not relish.

Thankfully, we had only a small number of incidents while I was gone, and none were OIs. I let myself fantasize that there would be no more of them, but I knew that was too good to be true.

The other good news was that James had just completed his Tactical Surveillance Skills Training Program at FLETC and was scheduled to return next week. So, I get to see my domestic partner soon, after over a year and a half apart.

I hope he still recognizes me, I thought with a chuckle.

I'm fairly certain I'm safe on that; there aren't too many muscular women who are six foot one and 240 pounds with half a face out there.

State Capitol—Phoenix
Congressman Terrance Halston

"Congressman Halston, your wife is on line one; she says it's urgent," my assistant told me. He was one of my new ones, and I hadn't bothered learning his name yet. Without responding, I picked up the phone and hit the button for line one.

"Terrance here," I said. What I always say, no matter the caller.

"Oh my God! Terrance, come home quick! That man killed our daughter!"

I could hear her sobbing. I slammed the phone down and raced for my car.

"I'm out for today, emergency," I said to my shocked underling.

Running to my car, I ignored my coworkers' startled looks. Now that I think about it, I don't think they have ever seen me run.

Jumping inside, I hit the engine start button and slammed the Mercedes into drive. The tires fought for traction as I burned rubber through the parking lot. When I got to the gate, a Federal Police Officer (FPO) went to open the barricade, and he was not hurrying!

"Going a little fast today, Congressman," he said by way of greeting and warning.

"F— right off, my daughter has been murdered! Open the f—ing gate, now!"

The FPO stepped inside, and the gate opened.

I floored it onto the street, almost sideswiping another car. Along with others, their horns blared as I ran the red light and sped to my house …

As I pulled up, I saw emergency services packing the street outside our home. It appeared fire crews were working inside, and police cars and fire/EMS vehicles overtook our lawn. Of course, my annoying looky-loo neighbors were all outside gossiping.

Joanne ran over and threw herself into my arms, sobbing uncontrollably. I stroked her hair.

"Joanne, what happened after I left?"

"The last I knew, he was chatting with our daughter upstairs, then I heard a commotion, then I … I …" She started wailing in pain.

"Joanne!" I yelled at her.

"Then I heard her screaming! Then, a gunshot! Oh, Terrance, he killed our baby!"

She sobbed uncontrollably in my arms. As I stroked her hair to soothe her, I only had one angry thought on my mind—

The priest surely knows about my master now.

US Capitol—Washington, DC
House of Representatives

"Welcome, everyone. I would like to introduce Congressman Terrance Halston from Arizona. He is the chair of the House Subcommittee on Supernatural Affairs. Thank you all for joining us."

There was a smattering of applause as I took to the podium.

"Thank you, Congressman Newburg. If everyone would come to order, I would like to begin," Terrance said.

"Something is going on in the government that needs to be addressed. When our committee asked the National Security Council (NSC) to explain to Congress exactly what was happening with these so-called *supernatural events* (he sneered while saying this), we were told it was classified at the highest levels. Well, isn't that convenient? We have a truck stop shooting where people were killed—classified. We have an incident on board an aircraft where an air marshal and a flight attendant were killed—classified. We have an entire beach where hundreds were killed: federal agents, police officers, emergency responders, and even the military! Not to mention a good number of American citizens. And guess what?"

"Classified?" asked Congressman Newberg.

"That's right, Steve, classified!"

While this happened, a tall Polish man in a nice suit and tie was eating another antacid. He was sitting in the deposition chair and had already been sworn in.

"Well, I, for one, want to get to the bottom of this nonsense! We have videos, pictures, and eyewitness accounts of a gigantic monster. One from outer space or the planes of the Abyss. Hell, it could be from China for all we know … But, *amazingly*, there isn't a shred of physical evidence!"

Special Agent in Charge of OST, Robert Cho, had just finished chewing his antacid and rolled his eyes. Unbeknownst to him, Congressman Halston saw it from across the room.

"Well, we are fortunate to have the man in charge of the 'Occult Strike Team' here with us today. Since he felt it OK to roll his eyes at us while I was speaking, we are all curious to hear what you can tell us."

Everyone turned to look at SAC Cho. There was a pregnant pause that stretched on and on.

"Are you going to respond, Mr. Cho?" Congressman Halston asked.

"I'm sorry, your honor, but I have not been asked a question."

Halston's features darkened in rage, but it quickly passed. Then he smiled.

"Do you, or do you not, have intimate knowledge of all that transpired regarding these *alleged* occult activities?

"Yes, I do."

"Would you care to elucidate?"

"No. But I'll answer any and all questions to the best of my ability within the framework of my ability to do so."

Congressman Halston waited a bit before responding.

"Please, educate us on what this 'framework' is that you claim allows you to dodge our lawful questions."

"Very well. First, I'm not *dodging* any questions. However, the NSC has given me explicit instructions on what I can and cannot divulge."

"Mr. Cho, you *do* realize we can hold you in contempt of Congress?"

"I do."

Congressman Halston nodded with a smile.

"Good. First question: When did your office become aware of the 'supernatural'?"

Cho chafed at how Halston made air quotes with his fingers when he said "supernatural," but he knew he had to answer all questions truthfully and to the best of his ability.

"We became aware when an unprecedented force attacked Perry's Truck Stop and UA flight 436. A written report has already been submitted to the committee, including all dates and times."

"I'm sorry, what did you say? Can you describe these 'unprecedented forces' for us?"

"Aliens, creatures not from this Earth," Cho responded.

Several congresspersons made sharp intakes of breath.

Halston started laughing—big, hearty guffaws. After wiping tears of laughter from his eyes, he continued. Cho noticed several other members were laughing as well.

That is unusual.

Cho mentally noted which ones were laughing and which ones were looking at the ones laughing like they were insane.

"Mr. Cho, are you saying that *aliens* attacked us?"

"Yes."

"Hmm. So, if this was an alien attack, where are the aliens? Do you expect us to believe that it wasn't some monumental cock-up by the FBI that required military intervention to fix whatever crazy thing caused these deaths? And instead that it was *aliens*—really? With no proof of their existence?"

"I do not."

"Excuse me, Mr. Cho. What do you mean 'I do not'?"

"You asked me if I expected you to believe it was aliens and not a 'cock-up' by the FBI. Clearly, I do not think you will believe anything I tell you. To answer your question, with respect, of course."

Halston turned bright red. Some of the committee members laughed.

"Mr. Cho, are you trying to land yourself in contempt?" Terrance yelled.

A long pause …

"No."

"Can you please tell us what creatures attacked the plane and the truck stop?"

"I cannot."

There were audible gasps. This response was not something a congressional subcommittee was accustomed to hearing.

"Can you tell us what attacked the beach in California?"

"No."

"What can you tell us, Mr. Cho?"

"Anything not classified need to know, eyes only, NSC—"

"Mr. Cho, for the last time, I'll have you in contempt if you do not answer our questions!" Halston interrupted. Halston was getting angrier and angrier. "Are you aware that a Catholic priest murdered my daughter during an exorcism?" he nearly shouted as he spoke those words.

"Congressman Halston, I'm aware, and we are looking for the suspect now. I'm truly sorry for your loss. But I'm unsure how a quack murderer is relevant to the supernatural."

Halston suddenly became calm.

"Thank you. I do appreciate that. However, without tangible, hard evidence of any supernatural creatures' existence, the onus will be on the FBI to explain what happened. Considering your inability to answer the most basic questions of this subcommittee, I'll move to hold you in contempt … I'll also make a motion to have the committee visit your OST headquarters and have full access to your personnel and records. It's time to get to the bottom of this bogus 'supernatural' charade."

Halston slammed the gavel.

"You will make yourself and your office available to the committee. Consider yourself in contempt."

SAC Cho visibly shrugged and said, "OK."

"Dismissed," Congressman Halston said.

———

Hellious

The subcommittee went well.

Hellious was pleased with Terrance Halston's performance. Although we could not yet obtain the location and capabilities of this new OST group, we were getting closer.

It had already possessed the college girls, and they were on their way to their next assignment—fall break. With direct control of the congressman as well, it would soon possess more members of both the House and the Senate. It didn't need to control the idiots in the "Freedom Party," as they were already dedicated sycophants of

Halston. So, there was no need to possess them; they effectively did what I wanted anyway—by supporting Halston.

Halston backed an extremist party that had the potential to gain significant power if they could secure their president's election during the next cycle—or even sooner if everything aligned with my plan.

Besides, I already had another operation in play very far from here, far from America's reach and influence.

OST DENFO
SAC Robert

"Wow, Robert, you really pissed them off, didn't you?"

"Yes, Madam President. I believe that I did," I replied.

POTUS chuckled.

"Good. I can't stand that 'Freedom Party' or that Halston clown. They seem to want to dig into everything and screw it up five ways from Sunday."

"Yes, they do. I'm concerned, though—"

"Ahh, don't be, I can make the contempt crap go away."

"No, Madam President, I mean about them wanting to see the OST office and look at all records, equipment, and personnel. No offense to them, but that is kept secret for a reason. These congresspersons don't even have real Top Secret clearance checks. You and I both know they can leak this information or cause a lot of damage to the operation."

There was a long pause.

"Yes, you're right. You'll not divulge the location of the OST Headquarters or anything about its capabilities. You'll not release details of any creatures or the Hybrids that work for you. I'll handle any heat that comes your way."

"Thank you, Madam President."

"Keep up the good work—goodnight, Robert."

"Goodnight, Madam President."

The line went dead on the STU phone, and I pressed the button to terminate the call.

Sitting in the briefing room at OST DENFO, I contemplated the true nature of today's interview. Subcommittees consist of politicians, and they often have ulterior motives. After some deep reflection, I made a decision and sent out a PA to the office.

"ASAC Blackwell, report to BRIEFING. Blackwell, report."

A few minutes later, ASAC Chayton Blackwell walked in.

"Sir?"

"Have a seat, Chayton; it looks like we have another monster to deal with—Congress."

"Ugh. Glad that is you and not me."

"Don't be—because it's us now. Let me fill you in on the players and what I think they are really after."

———

Chayton and I had finished the briefing and were making some small talk when we heard a light rapping on the now-open door. We turned to see one of our newest agents standing there.

"SAC Cho, you have a letter addressed to 'The Supernatural Investigators for the FBI.' We assume it is for you," Agent Melissa Woods said.

"Thank you, Special Agent Woods."

"No problem, sir," she said, handing me the letter and then turning to leave.

"A moment, Agent Woods?"

She turned and stood erect, not at the position of attention, but still a bit formal. She was about five feet six inches tall and a fit 150 pounds, a Black woman with a bald head and deep hazel eyes—quite the looker, although I did not indulge in thinking that way.

Agent Woods came highly recommended. She was smart as a whip, had excellent training scores, and already had some significant busts to her credit.

All in only three years with the FBI.

I was glad to have someone so exceptionally qualified, but knowing she was on First Squad was bittersweet. It meant she was replacing one of our dead agents.

"Melissa, I haven't had the chance to formally welcome you to OST. You're assigned to First Squad, Team Charlie, correct?"

"Yes, sir."

"Good. I'm impressed by your past work and look forward to your help at OST. Have you met Special Agent Morris, your TL, yet?"

"The giant? Yes, I have," she said, smiling.

"Great! Well, I know that team is top-notch now. Thank you, and welcome aboard."

"Thank you, sir."

She turned and left.

"I think I'll go see how Second Squad is doing if you don't need anything else?" Chayton said.

I nodded, and he left. After Chayton departed, I popped an antacid and slowly chewed it. As I walked out of BRIEFING and into the central vestibule, I paused to read the names on the wall for the hundredth time:

TO THE BRAVE MEN AND WOMEN WHO GAVE THEIR LIVES DEFENDING OUR COUNTRY:

Special Agent Larry Skaggs, Federal Bureau of Investigation (DOJ)
    Federal Agent Donald Newburg, Nuclear Materials Courier (DOE)
    Federal Agent Jim Phillips, Nuclear Materials Courier (DOE)

I desperately hoped not to see any more names on this wall. Knowing Melissa was replacing Larry, who died on Bolsa Chica Beach during the last OI, struck me hard. I turned and made my way to my office. Whenever I felt my dedication waning or started to feel tired, I would step out and look at that wall. That was all the motivation I needed. We would become the best at what we do, so I wouldn't have to add any more names to that damn wall.

I flicked open my switchblade knife and unsealed the letter. It was strange to get a letter; almost everything is via email nowadays. I took a sip of coffee and started reading—

Dear Supernatural Investigator/G-man,

I'm writing to inform you that you have another supernatural creature on your hands.

Father Christos Leighe—wanted fugitive—has met with me.

After hearing what he had to say and seeing irrefutable proof of the reality of possession—by demons and devils, no less—I'm convinced of their existence. Before the events of Bolsa Chica and Colorado Springs, I would not have believed any of this. However, after watching monsters attacking us and being killed by the US Army first-hand, I'm what you might call a "true believer."

The purpose of my contact with you, super-secret-G-people, is two-fold:

First, I want an exclusive on the story of whatever the hell this new creature is and how you will stop it.

Second, Father Leighe would like his name cleared of any criminal wrongdoing.

If this is acceptable to you, we should meet. I have included my business card.

Sincerely,
Samantha Cox
Investigative Journalist
Crime Scene News

. . .

Well, if this day gets any better, I'll be crapping rainbows.

This was a sticky situation, and I absentmindedly fiddled with her card as I thought about what to do. If we contacted and collaborated with her, we would be accessories after the fact for a wanted fugitive, as the FBI, no less.

Hmm. What else can I do?

It occurred to me that we would have to work with the US District Attorney to clear Father Leighe of any charges and figure out what we could give Ms. Cox for her non-classified story.

Another easy day, I thought glumly.

I went to take another antacid, then realized I had just had one.

Oh well, it can't hurt to at least hear her out.

Second Squad is already in Tempe looking into the "exorcism gone wrong" of Father Leighe anyway, so I may as well let their squad leader, Dave, know …

I picked up my phone to call him.

———

Tempe
SSA David "Dave" Tanaka

Never in my wildest dreams did I imagine being "read-in" to a unit confronting the supernatural. The evidence of the OIs that had occurred was so compelling that it shattered my disbelief, leaving me in a state of shock. The sheer magnitude of what we were facing was beyond anything I could have imagined.

When we all saw the news about an alien attack in Southern California, we knew this was for real. Already, it was a "9/11 or JFK moment" for everyone in America and the rest of the world. Everyone remembered where they were and what they were doing when it happened.

Some thought it was a cover-up for something the US of A had done terribly wrong.

Some thought it affirmed their religious concepts of the "End Times".

However, many were adrift in a sea of confusion, not knowing what to think and waiting for their preferred media to guide their thoughts.

After seeing what we saw, none of us in OST could deny their existence. Any disbelief had been shattered, and we were now faced with a reality we could not ignore. Besides, all we had to do was shake Lev's hand if we had any doubt.

We watched her crush an apple to pieces in that hand—and she didn't even strain to do it. That is one scary woman, and I'm glad she is on our side. Her strength and abilities were a comfort in the face of the unknown.

I'm just thrilled I got to meet the legend, finally.

She had returned, successfully, from SEAL training and was even fiercer now. And now could shake people's hands like a normal person. Except for having the strength of a strong man's grip, you would never know she could crush every bone in your hand.

As her squad was currently on QRF, mine was sent to the desert to examine the "exorcism" and determine its merit as a possible OI. We arrived in Tempe last night and got an early start this morning.

Second Squad's Alpha Team consisted of Steve Robinson and me. I also had Jeffrey Doyle and Alfie "Al" Wilson on Bravo, along with James Dixon and William Barker on Charlie.

It has now been well over a year since the one and only OI has occurred (so far). The back-and-forth in high government has been raging, and the calls for answers have only increased in that time. Plus, we have been kept busy going after doomsday cults and crazies. So far, though, no actual occult activity has occurred.

Our new assignment is to investigate the murder of Laura Halston. As of now, we just have what the police knew—that Mrs. Joanne Halston had asked an exorcist to examine if her daughter was possessed. The man she called to help, Father Christos Leighe, had subsequently brutally killed her daughter and fled the scene.

He was now a wanted fugitive.

Could exorcisms be real, also? I never thought I would have a job this crazy.

My phone started ringing. Fortunately, Steve was driving, so I reached into my pocket to check who was calling. It was the boss, SAC Robert Cho.

"Tanaka, go ahead, sir," I said.

"Good morning, Dave. I have an update for you. It turns out I have an admirer, Samantha Cox from Crime Scene News, who reached out to me. She is with our favorite fugitive—Father Christos Leighe."

I silently waited for him to continue.

"They want to set up a meeting with you. Also, she wants an exclusive story and to have Christos cleared of all charges."

"Not asking for much, is she?" I said rhetorically.

Robert chuckled.

"Yeah, let me work on that, but the offer is a go; I talked with POTUS directly, and—if they prove extremely helpful, as in full cooperation, then she will make it happen. Let them know that. But they are to give us *complete* assistance, or there is no deal."

"Understood, sir. I'll ensure they understand and let you know if they are in or out."

"Sounds good; good luck, Dave."

"Thank you, sir."

The line went dead. Seconds later, the shared contact for Samantha Cox popped up, and I saved it on my G-phone. I called the number, and she picked up on the first ring.

"Samantha Cox."

"Good morning, Ms. Cox. I'm Special Agent Dave Tanaka, FBI. I was wondering when and where you would like to meet."

"As soon as you can. But how do I know you won't arrest Father Leighe as soon as you see him?" she asked.

"Well, he is a wanted fugitive, and we must arrest him—unless he becomes a CI (Confidential Informant) for us. I need you both to know what is going to happen. When we meet, I'll present him with an immunity deal from the DA. In return for his *complete* assistance and help, all charges will be dropped."

There was a long pause.

"Yes, Ms. Cox, you'll also get your full exclusive, same deal for you—complete cooperation in exchange for your story. You can tell the whole story, but all agents' identities and government building locations will be redacted. Plus, as needed for national security, we must also redact certain parts of the story as necessary. The details are on the NDA and written contract. Does this work for you both?"

I waited patiently as she muted me. I'm pretty sure she was talking to Father Leighe. A minute or so later, she came back on the phone.

"Yes, we are in. Let's meet at St. Mary's Basilica; how about four p.m.?"

"That works. We'll see you at four."

"You aren't double-crossing me, are you?"

"No. If you want, you can read the contract and then bring out Father Leighe. But we need your help, and you need ours. This is your best option, honestly. Otherwise, you don't get the access you want, and Father Leighe will eventually be apprehended and go to prison."

There was another long delay.

"OK, see you at four, Agent Tanaka."

The line went dead.

I texted my other team members to inform them of the developments and to let SAC Cho know the meeting time and place.

With a quick U-turn, we headed to St. Mary's Basilica. Meanwhile, Team Bravo was headed to the local police stations, and Charlie headed to ASU, where the late Laura Halston was a student.

I wanted to get to the church early and do some surveillance there to ensure it wasn't some weird trap. I didn't think it would be, but we had to plan for all variables.

CHAPTER 6
SECRET SERVICE

Georgetown—October—ASU's Fall Break
Ritz-Carlton Hotel
Dorothy

THE COOL BREEZE tickled my skin.

I wore my sexiest Missoni dress and my long blonde hair combed up in an elegant chignon—ready for a night out in Georgetown with my sorority sisters.

This tanned and taught body will be a serious asset tonight, Hellious thought.

I knew the demon was controlling my mind, but when it took over, I had to do as it commanded. For the hundredth time, I willed myself to remember being possessed.

The worst part was that it was making me a monster AND a criminal—and there was nothing I could do about it! Plus, I won't remember anything from my possessions, just a "blackout" with no memory at all. That "felony blackout" that most criminals say happened? That was going to be me. Even if I lived through this, I would probably end up in either a padded room or a jail cell.

Damn you, Demon!

Careful, I control you now.

SMACK!

My face stung where I had slapped myself, really hard. I fell into tears and hated this thing for making me feel out of control. The other girls turned to look at me in fear.

That's better; now let's get us some men in nice suits to take you away from that awful man who hit you …

As I straightened up my makeup, I looked around me again. All eight of us were standing outside, waiting for the limo.

It was surreal.

Even though we all looked like we were ready for a fantastic night out, our expressions were filled with terror. We knew that would change once we arrived at Degrees Bistro. There, the monster would make all of us look happy and approachable. That's why we wore expressions more suited for a funeral than a trendy nightclub. We all noticed that Amanda was nowhere to be found, and Laura—

OMG, poor Laura!

At least she was free of this horrible nightmare.

I took a moment to survey the other women as we climbed into our limousine. The girls and I looked fabulous. In our twenties and with a substantial financial boost, we looked like a million bucks. Together, we probably *were* worth a million dollars!

The unspoken indulgence of mani-pedis, massages, and facials. The endless hours spent on our hair, eyes, nails, and skin. All the workouts and tanning … then there are the costly clothes, jewelry, and accessories—

They don't have a chance, *laughed Hellious.*

I really hate you!

I know. *Hellious laughed longer this time.*

After a short drive, we were dropped off by the limousine at 3100 South Street Northwest in Washington, DC. The Ritz-Carlton Georgetown was truly impressive, with all the glam and glitz of a high-end hotel. Once the bellhops got the doors for us, we all headed inside.

We were pretending to be celebrating Chloe Russell's engagement. The allure of a group of extremely hot, young single women—celebrating a bachelorette party, no less—would be too much temptation for the men of the Secret Service detail.

Degrees Bistro was one of the hottest pickup spots in Georgetown. Everyone (with money) went there. The men dressed to impress, looking good, being well-groomed, and showing they had money and power, or that they worked for those who did, such as the Secret Service detail staying at that hotel.

Of course, we had a reservation in the "Living Room" (the lounge next to Degrees Bistro) and walked in, already partying it up. Chloe had a diamond tiara on her head, and we were already acting a little tipsy. The men in the room immediately noticed.

This is going to be fun! And easy, commented Hellious.

We had a large booth with an adjoining table. After settling into our seats, Peter (my assistant) brought in a big cake with candles. He turned and gave me a tight smile.

Peter.

His reward for all his hard work?—being killed by me to become one of us. I knew I had no control to stop it, but I still felt the shame and the rage for what this monster made me do. Forcing a smile, I turned my head away. I couldn't bear watching him.

Bottle service kept the champagne coming, but we didn't eat. The thing in us wanted us at our best, so we couldn't have a flake of cake stuck in our teeth, could we?

It was working.

Several men and one woman in the Secret Service detail were looking our way and getting ready to break the ice with us. After a few minutes, three men and a woman approached us. The woman came straight to me.

"Hey, congratulations! I'm Heather. We wondered if we could join you and the woman of honor?" Agent Heather Butler asked.

Nice trick, using the woman to break the ice, I thought.

Suddenly, I could feel the full weight of the monster in my head. It was in control, not me. I felt disassociated as the beast took complete control of me.

———

"Hell yeah! We were wondering when you sexy peeps would join us," Hellious said.

I gave the woman a mischievous smile. She smiled back and sat next to me.

Knowing everything that was happening, but "sharing" the experience with Hellious being in charge was, in addition to being horrifying, also surreal. Hellious controlled me, but sometimes I was allowed to act on my own. We were two minds sharing my body.

That's correct. Sit back and enjoy the show.

As the other men mingled with the sorority sisters, the rest of the detail came over and joined in—except for one.

He sat apart from the team, watching and pretending not to know the other guys. This agent was going to be a problem. He was watching and sipping what looked like a light beer, and he was quite sober and did not join the others.

I bet he is their leader—

I felt a hand on my thigh, and the woman, Heather, leaned over and spoke into my ear—

"Let's just watch the show for a bit; laugh while the guys make idiots of themselves," she said with a wink.

She was close to me, and I could smell her perfume—it was a pleasant floral smell. Her hair was short and black, and she had deep brown eyes. She had scooted closer to me to whisper in my ear and was now watching the others with me.

Her hand stayed on my thigh, however.

Oh, come on! You are not making me do this! I'm straight—I like men, not women! Dorothy chimed in.

(Laughing) I'm impressed; you're the first human to join me while fully possessed. Sit back and enjoy!

Heather leaned into me and smelled near my neck.

"I like your perfume, is it Bond No. 9?"

"Wow! It is!" I lied.

"What is yours?" I asked.

She leaned over and exposed her neck to me; I felt an overpowering urge. Grabbing her shoulder, I leaned in very close to her skin.

"Wow, nice grip you got, girl!" she said.

Clenching my jaw, I could feel my teeth cut into my gums as they lengthened, but it stopped suddenly as I regained my composure. Instead, I took a deep breath of her intoxicating scent as my lips grazed her neck. I could feel her tighten up and then relax. She made an almost imperceptible moan, and I pulled away suddenly.

"Yeah, it's OK," I said, grinning.

We locked eyes as she purposefully inched her chair even closer. Her hand, still on my thigh, squeezed gently. A couple of the guys gave us a look like, "Really, you already bagged the hottest one? Heather, you're a bitch." She just smiled and gave them a look, saying, "Yup, way ahead of you all."

Inside, I was disgusted. I have nothing against homosexual or bisexuality, but I have never found women attractive in a sexual way. Just my luck; this demon would make me be with a woman. I felt sick. The only thing worse than rape is knowing it was going to be consensual by her but that I didn't get a say in it. This demon was going to have me raped by a gender I didn't even want to have sex with.

The night went on, and everything was going well. Some men had already filtered off to take the girls to their rooms. Heather had surreptitiously moved her hand under the table toward my crotch. Wearing a dress with no undergarments, she started using her fingers. I moved to stop her.

"We are in public, Heather. I don't need someone taking pictures," I said.

"Well, there are no cameras in my hotel room—"

The implication was quite clear.

I smiled, took her hand, and we got up. Holding hands, we walked to her hotel room. She was beaming, and I could tell she was extremely excited to have sex with such a beautiful young woman—she was about ten years my senior.

We got off on the fifth floor and went down the hall.

"Mi casa es su casa," she said, opening the door.

It was a standard hotel room. Government agents have to get a cheap G-rate, but they usually have high hotel club status from all their traveling. So, the room was a nice upgrade, but not up to my usual standards.

As soon as the door shut, she was on me. Her tongue was deep in my mouth, and her body was pressed against me—

Hmmm. It appears Dorothy is pushing back again ...

This demon seemed to be enjoying itself, using my body to do it. The whole time we had sex, in many imaginative ways, the demon was loving it. However, it prevented all my true feelings from showing.

Heather and the demon were enjoying my rape.

I didn't blame Heather, as she didn't know any better, but I'll watch this demon die if it's the last thing I do!

(Laughing).

We were lying naked in the bed together now, cuddling, post-coital.

"Can we try something?" Hellious asked.

"Of course, baby. Anything you want," Heather said.

I smiled and reached for my purse.

NO! Please don't hurt her!—

She will be one of us soon, no worries, my pet.

I reached into my oversized purse and pulled out a thin, waterproof tarp.

Heather's eyes narrowed. We already had sex, and *now* I was bringing out a tarp? She was slipping back into cop mode, I could tell. In another moment, though, she clearly decided to think with her libido instead of her head.

"Hmmm. So, you're a squirter?" she asked with a smile.

"Oh, gushing is an accurate term, yes."

We laid the tarp over the bed and lay back down. I went to nibble on her neck while she was pinned under my body. Her excitement was building as her blood pulsed from her neck.

She was moaning in ecstasy as I drained her of every drop of blood. Not that, as a "demon," I needed it; my only requirement was for her to die, so I could easily possess her. Something about the taste of blood satisfied me, however.

After finishing, she lay in a pool of blood, and we were both covered in it. She was bone white and dead. Then, she jumped out of bed as if nothing had happened, and her skin quickly returned to its original color and looked as healthy as ever. There were not even any bite marks on her.

"That was fun! Let's get this place cleaned up. You and I have work to do," Heather said.

———

SSA Matthew Ellis

One of the things I like to do off duty is to practice what I do on duty.

So, I quietly sat watching my team. Even in a bar, we have an SOP for how we move as a team. Well … some things get in the way of the protocol. When I saw a group of beautiful college girls come in for a party, I had a feeling my team would find them irresistible.

And in seconds, the bachelorette party had gotten my team's attention.

I could see Heather making the introductions and the team's usual nightclub MO. This should be interesting.

Smiling as I enjoyed my nonalcoholic beer, I observed my team in action. They were performing exceptionally well with the sorority sisters. I also noticed how easily the attractive young woman allowed herself to be charmed by Agent Butler. The men were having an effortless time as well.

There was something not quite right about the entire situation, though. I rose to the position of TL for the vice president's (VPOTUS) detail because I truly embraced the job. Most of the agents relished the status that came with being Secret Service agents, but I couldn't have cared less. I sipped my beer and tried to discern what was troubling me. The throbbing in my temples had returned; I supposed it was time to retake my Rizatriptan medicine. I struggled with high blood pressure and migraine headaches because I couldn't turn off my "cop mode".

What is wrong with me? Why can't I be happy for them? What is nagging at me?

One of the pretty women looked over at me as I sipped my beer, the one with Heather. She looked at me with a look that implored, "Help!" Then, in the blink of an eye, she was a different person.

What the hell?

There was a disconnect happening. Time was on fast-forward, and there they went … My guys were hooked and reeled in. I watched, fascinated, as the girls escorted members of my team up to their rooms.

Something was terribly wrong.

I pulled out my phone.

My instinct was to call my team members and have them come to me for an emergency meeting, but I knew I might just be being paranoid (as usual). Instead, I typed a long text to my best friend, Sharon. Although she didn't work in the government, we had known each other for over a decade, and I trusted her—

WHOOP

I heard the little text-sent sound.

I don't know why I sent it, but I felt a sense of foreboding. I told her about the weird looks of the women and how they had seduced my whole team. When I saw Mark Woods leaving with a woman half his age, that's when I knew—

Mark was a good agent, but the least fit person on my team. And God help me for saying this: he was ugly as sin! It looked like he was taking his hot daughter out of a party, not going upstairs to have sex with her.

OK, this is officially an enemy action. Eight women (I counted them) who look that pretty would not pick up on ALL my agents!

I typed another text—this time in all caps. My BFF Sharon knew that if she saw that, I would be in trouble and couldn't get help from my agency.

Other agents thought I was unnecessarily paranoid, like the time a young, comely Shin Bet (Israeli Intelligence) agent tried to get sensitive information from me on one of our details.

When I report that a beautiful woman, half my age, is flirting with me and gradually asking more direct work-related questions, revealing information about me that she couldn't possibly know, and that she is a contact for a foreign agent, they simply respond by saying I'm imagining things.

Well, now my whole team was being seduced by women who would not typically give them the time of day. This *definitely* was an operation of some kind.

Taking a last look at my text, I confirmed it contained everything I had witnessed and was thinking. Should I really send this to my friend in case things went wrong before I could figure out how to stop it? When I sent this one, there was no going back; it was a big deal to trust a civilian with this. I debated sending the text … but finally hit send.

WHOOP

Sipping my beer—the same one I had all night—I enjoyed its flatness and lack of flavor. This is what kept me sober; I needed to see what my team could not. Their guard was down because they were off duty and drinking, but mine stayed firmly up. We are not supposed to drink while armed, and I'm not. My Heineken Zero had no alcohol because I prefer to be armed, always.

One of the last women remaining took a good, long look at me.

She wore the same passive, distant expression, then giggled at something Michael Jenkins had said. They walked off together, hand in hand, toward the elevator.

Again, Michael was not a good-looking man. He had the personality of a toaster, and I had never heard a funny word from him in three years.

We *are* in trouble, and I don't even know how.

The last of my team left for the elevators. A solitary man, obviously a personal assistant to one of the bachelorette party girls, picked up what little remained of the cake. The different girls had walked off with all the champagne, and I noticed each had a bottle as they left. I also noticed that none of the girls ate the cake—or anything at all, for that matter.

I paid the bar tab and headed to my room. Heading to the ninth floor, I watched the elevator door shut. A slim hand reached in to stop the doors—one of the last remaining women from the bachelorette party, the engaged one.

"Hi! Sorry," she jumped on the elevator.

"No worries," I said.

As the door started to shut again, I suddenly put my hand out to stop it.

"Oh, no! I forgot to pay my bill!" I said.

I jumped out of the elevator and turned to watch it close. The woman, a cute twenty-one-year-old with dimples and a diamond tiara, was smiling at me, but the smile did not reach her eyes …

As the doors shut, I could still see her eyes boring into me.

I went straight to the concierge.

"Good evening, Mr. Ellis; how can I help you?" he asked.

"I need a favor."

"Of course," he quickly responded.

"I have a bit of a stalker. Normally, I would be flattered, but she won't take no for an answer, and I'm married," I lied. "Can you tell her I headed to another bar?"

He smiled, "Of course, sir."

"Can you call me a taxi, also?"

"You are a taxi, sir," he said, then chuckled.

I gave him a severe look; I was not in a joking mood.

"Just kidding, of course," he added.

I saw him pick up a phone and tell a driver that he was needed. Five minutes later, my taxi arrived.

"Take me to the nearest train station," I told the driver.

"OK," he replied.

We were off, and I was in full tactical surveillance mode. I held my phone up, hitting the camera app button, and then video mode, selecting the camera facing me (and out the back of the cab). I hit record.

Sure enough, the same young woman came outside and looked right at my cab as we pulled out into traffic. As soon as we got a few blocks away, I said to the driver—

"Hey, change of plans; I want to go to my friend's house first to get a few things. Can you go down this street to the end?"

He looked at me with annoyance but turned down the side street.

"Just take another right at this street."

He turned down another street into a cul-de-sac.

"This house is it. It may be a while, so let me pay my tab, and I'll call another cab."

He parked, and I paid him with my credit card.

"Thank you."

I watched him drive off. Now, I would make my way back on foot, turning and doubling back as I went (to look for a tail).

Finally, I made it to the hotel. It was one a.m., and I quickly went to the elevator and then to my room. No one followed me or waited in ambush, so I quickly showered and got ready. Then, I lay down for a nap—fully dressed, armed, and prepared for the day ahead. I drifted off to sleep, knowing my door stop (with a loud alarm) was wedged under my door.

Chloe—The Possessed

I watched the elevator doors shut and smiled as he stared back at me. This one was smart; he knew something was wrong.

There was no need to chase him; I knew he would have to join his team in the morning. Besides, everyone except him had been successfully targeted. Even now, I can feel the number of people under my control—both direct and indirect—swelling. I will get Agent Matthew Ellis; I just have to be patient.

I am curious about this one, maybe I should see where the human goes.

After taking my beautiful host back to the lobby, I decided to observe his tactics. He was waiting for a cab so, when he was ready to leave, I walked outside to watch him.

I didn't plan on chasing him, but he would be more tired—and an easier target tomorrow—if I made him a little more paranoid. He was filming me from the backseat as I watched him. I smiled malevolently at him as he pulled away, and I then walked back to Degree's Bistro.

No longer needing Chloe, I diverted my attention to my true self—my mist form inside Dorothy. I required the direct use of another body for a separate mission. Only one person outside the sorority had read my book, and I was glad that Peter took the time to read it before giving it to Dorothy. I am also pleased that he is fluent in Italian...

Hellious

The morning sun was coming into the lobby as I sat there with my new host, Peter. I had left Dorothy's body and taken his. She was still mine, of course, but when my mist entered a new body, it was the only one that was physically "me." I could only subsume a host that had read the book, or was involved in the summoning, so I could not go into anyone "risen" by my undead, only ones I had physically, personally, killed. My only tangible form is the mist, but I would mold this host body into one of my "natural" human forms. My human form—only possible in the body I was physically in—was beyond irresistible.

I would do that soon enough, but for now, I am waiting to watch my sorority leave.

A few minutes later, I heard the women coming into the lobby.

"Damn, girl, you look a little hungover today," Dorothy said, greeting Ella Jones.

"Yeah, I blacked out something fierce when I got back to my room," Ella responded.

"You and everyone else," Dorothy added with a look of concern.

The sorority sisters would still be valuable, so I needed another person to approach a new target—one that would grant me immense wealth and power.

It was vital for me to remember that when not directly controlling a human, they only remembered "blackouts" and did not remember anything while I controlled them. That's why I switched who I actively possessed regularly. The girls knew they were probably being controlled, but any time they tried to run away or tell someone, my powers controlled their subconscious and stopped them.

It was 8:30 a.m., and I had watched the SS detail leave thirty minutes earlier, so our little sorority group had succeeded admirably. Only SSA Ellis remained human—the others on the Secret Service detail were now under my control. Soon, they would meet with the vice president to "protect" him.

Oh, the irony. I chuckled to myself.

Additionally, Congressman Halston was making significant progress in trying to learn about the enigmatic "OST" group. The government established this task force specifically to address supernatural issues, such as me, and locating and dismantling them was a top priority. That is why I intended to kill the vice president and take control of him. With several key congresspersons already under my influence, I had a high likelihood of success in tracking down this OST group. Once the Freedom Party joined forces with the possessed, they would have the votes and clout to enforce the defunding and prosecution of the OST team. Moreover, if I could seize the vice president, I could use him to gain access to the president.

The sorority's limousine pulled up. I chose the limo again in case the humans opted to check the CCTV or speak to the hotel staff. It helped maintain appearances.

They piled in, and the limo pulled out into traffic, heading to the airport per my instructions. The sorority had done admirably. Except for Dorothy and Amanda, I let the rest become "inactive." Amanda had stayed behind at ASU, as she had work to do …

As I can only directly control a few people at once, I needed to let some of my possessed be more passively controlled. I gave my plans some more thought as I walked into my hotel room. None of the possessed did anything substantial without my say-so. Dorothy, however, was someone to watch. She was the first human who did not black out under complete control.

Fascinating.

It was time to switch my primary attention to the Secret Service. I wanted to keep Dorothy and Amanda under my direct control to watch the sorority sisters, so I only directly controlled Heather on the Secret Service detail. Even with my multifaceted mind, there were limits.

I decided to visit Agent Ellis in one of my natural human forms, so I molded my current host body. Although my authentic self was a terrifying mist resembling my proper form, with my mist inhabiting one of the dead humans from the summoning, I became transcendentally beautiful. After I finished my transition, I walked into the bathroom.

"Irresistible," I said, looking in the mirror.

That mist is the best beauty product on the market. I chuckled.

———

SSA Matthew Ellis

After my phone alarm went off, I hit the button to silence it.

0600.

With only four hours of sleep, I got up. Making coffee, I wanted a full hour to figure out what to do. I'm not a paranoid person, but I'm also well-trained and not stupid.

What was with those women?

Wealthy and connected young women would not be interested in "The Help".

I noticed that each one wore what seemed to be thousands of dollars in clothing and jewelry. Young women like them would likely be pursuing the wealthy and powerful, or at least those directly connected to them, not Secret Service agents.

So, they were after my team—

But why?

This was what was nagging at me. I didn't have a motive—yet. The absence of an apparent reason for these women's actions was like a puzzle with a missing piece, driving me crazy.

OK, one decision was made.

For better or worse, I knew I couldn't keep this to myself any longer. I needed to tell someone. I sent another long message to my friend, Sharon, feeling a wave of relief as I hit send—

WHOOP

After relaxing for a bit, I joined my team for breakfast. It was the usual hotel fare: eggs, omelets, potatoes, cold cereal, pastries, and so on. Nothing fancy, so I opted for eggs and potatoes, coffee, and toast with jam for dessert."

Something was still nagging at me.

"OMG, those women were amazing!" said Brian Atkinson.

"Oh yes," said Heather Butler, looking satisfied.

Listening carefully to the agents' banter, I realized something: None of them remembered the women leaving their rooms. In fact, they all remembered fantastic sex and then nothing else until they woke up this morning. None of them seemed different, though.

I guess I'm just paranoid, I thought.

We finished up and checked out. Getting into our blacked-out Chevy Suburbans, we convoyed to the VPOTUS residence. I relaxed and thought—

Maybe it was just a sorority dare?

———

We pulled into the VPOTUS compound.

Several uniformed officers and our plainclothes agents were visible. After checking in with the officers at the guardhouse, we headed down the road, pulled around the circular drive, and parked. Then, we disembarked the vehicle and headed inside. We followed protocols (all classified, of course) and went into the VPOTUS' primary residence.

Taking up positions, we waited until called.

After a routine day of short trips, the VPOTUS returned to his residence. A "static" detail of agents and police guarded him while we were not there. He had no more trips until tomorrow morning, so we went to our new hotel—the Embassy Suites in Georgetown.

The large, rectangular stone building reminded me of a government building. Of course, many buildings in DC looked like that. As we all went inside, the interior was immediately familiar. This was not our first time at this hotel.

No sorority girls were there this time.

"Hello, checking in?" the man at the hotel check-in asked.

"Yes, two keys, please," I said.

He smiled knowingly, as he had checked me in many times before.

"Here you go, Mr. Ellis," he said, handing me the cards.

"Hey, boss, we're all going to go out to get dinner. Do you wanna come?" Heather asked.

"No, thank you. I'm just going to order room service and get some sleep. You all have fun."

"You got it, boss." Heather turned and went over to the other agents, who had already checked in.

Turning from her, I headed to the elevators. Even though I wanted to go with them, I was exhausted. So, my big evening was to clean up, eat some barely edible takeout, and go to bed.

At least I was finally at ease about my unfounded concerns. Nothing untoward had happened, and everyone seemed to be acting normally. I was exhausted and hoped to catch up on the sleep I didn't get last night. Opening my door, I walked in. As usual, I went to "clear" my room. I'm unsure when I developed the habit, but since I did it everywhere while working, it was natural to do it in my hotel room without thinking. Each suite had a living room, then a bathroom and bedroom, in that order, as you went from the entry door to the back of the suite.

I'm glad I can finally relax. The last twenty-four hours have been rough. I went to the bathroom next—

Something is wrong.

At first, I couldn't place it—then I took a deep breath. I smelled perfume.

Drawing my firearm, I went to look in the bedroom. My intake of breath was audible—a naked woman was in my bed.

And what a woman she was!

Dressed in nothing but almost nonexistent lingerie, she was—by far—the most beautiful woman I had ever seen. An alarm was going off in my head, but I wasn't sure what to do.

"Are you going to shoot me, Matthew?" she asked, with a tight smile and eyes that sparkled in amusement.

Crap, she knew my name. This was personal.

"Maybe. I haven't decided yet." My pistol didn't waver.

It was aimed at her chest—her flawless chest, with the most beautiful breasts I had ever seen. I couldn't help but stare as she sighed contentedly and stretched.

OMG, she is beautiful on a level I never dreamed of—

"W-what do you want from me?" I sputtered out.

She got up and walked over to me. Everything was moving and jiggling perfectly, and I couldn't help but become aroused. She walked right into the barrel of my gun.

Whispering in my ear—

"I want you to shoot into me, but not with your pistol …"

Her perfume and musk were overpowering and delightful. I could feel myself floating with pleasure.

BAM!

It was over in a split second—my gun was in her hand now.

Oh crap!

"You don't need this," she said, tossing it onto the bed. Stepping in, she exposed her neck.

"I am plenty vulnerable," she purred.

I couldn't help myself—it was like she had a spell on me. I kissed her neck in ecstasy and felt her almost naked body grind into me. She turned her head and kissed me deeply. Her perfume had a delightful smell, but her mouth—

It was like kissing a predator; I could taste and smell rotting flesh. I gagged as she pulled away and laughed. Seeing my chance, I lunged for the bed—and my gun.

With inhuman speed, she grabbed me by the neck with one hand and lifted me off the ground. I couldn't breathe and struggled in her grasp with both of my hands on her hand. As I tried to peel her fingers off, it felt like I was grabbing metal bars—nothing moved.

She smiled and purred as she leaned forward and spoke in my ear.

"You will be one of my favorites. Smart and capable, what is a woman not to love?"

As her head moved away, I punched her in the face as hard as I could. Being suspended in the air like I was, it didn't have full force, but it was still a vicious strike.

She just giggled.

I noticed her face didn't so much as move, much less have any damage. My hand, on the contrary, felt broken, like I had punched a brick wall.

"Oh, you like it rough! Why didn't you say so earlier?" she purred.

Hundreds of razor-sharp teeth suddenly appeared as her lips lengthened horizontally.

I knew I was dead.

What was this thing?

I was in ecstasy again as she nibbled on my neck. Lightly and then with great force.

It felt *so* good …

CHAPTER 7
FUGITIVES AND FREE PRESS

St. Mary's Basilica

SSA Dave

STEVE and I parked on the street near St. Mary's Basilica. NMC Agent Charlie Simpson would stand guard over our Tesla while we were inside. We had cased the perimeter for a while and saw nothing suspicious.

Several people were inside, but no service was happening. By design or luck, there would not be a service at our four p.m. meeting time, either. After clearing as much as possible (ensuring no signs of surveillance or operatives), we settled in to wait.

At 3:40 p.m., we saw Samantha and her cameraman from Crime Scene News. They were also looking around, but mainly for us. They sat down near the Via Assisi gift shop, and I motioned to Steve. We got up and walked over to them.

"Hi, I'm Dave Tanaka. We spoke on the phone, and this is my associate, Steve Robinson," I said, and Steve nodded.

"Hello, Dave. This is Harold; he works with me—where I go, he goes," Samantha said.

Harold nodded as well.

"OK. Let me show you something—" I said.

I sat down across from them and handed them the NDA/Sensitive Information forms and the Confidential Informant (CI) contracts.

"These forms are for all three of you. The immunity agreement only needs to be signed by Father Leighe. Once they are all signed, we are off to the races. However, the forms stay in my sight. So, once you finish reading, it is time to meet Mr. Leighe."

She nodded, and they spent the next several minutes reading.

"I'll grab us coffees; what do you all want?" asked Steve.

"Black, please," I said.

"Same for us," said Harold.

Samantha nodded.

"Four blacks, coming up."

Steve walked off to City Central Coffee shop, just a hundred meters away; I watched Steve from the corner of my eye, while keeping my attention on the contracts.

Sitting quietly, I observed our new friends, remembering their appearance and mannerisms.

Understandably, it took them a while to read the forms. Steve came back a few minutes later with our coffees. Halfway through my coffee, I saw them signing the forms. Then they pushed them over and looked at me.

"OK, time to meet the man of the hour," I said.

"The pleasure is mine, Agent Tanaka."

I turned at the sound of his voice behind me; it was incredible. He had the deep, sonorous voice men coveted and women would swoon over. His pleasant demeanor immediately put me at ease.

That's a weird charisma that guy has, I thought.

He proffered his hand, and I shook it. Taking a seat across from me, he was ready to start the process of becoming a CI.

"If you can read over the NDA, CI, and immunity agreements, we can get to work, Father Leighe," I said as the priest sat.

He carefully read the forms and then signed them.

"Here you are, Agent Tanaka, and please, call me Christos," he said, sliding the forms to me.

"Well, Christos, so much for the easy part. Let's go somewhere private to discuss our next steps. We'll all stop these monsters together. Although I know there is some compulsion, I truly appreciate all three of you for helping us. This OI, sorry, Occult Incident, is a tricky one," I said.

They nodded in appreciation.

"It is never too late to go to church ..." Christos said.

I stared at him for a moment and then got his meaning.

"That would work well. I assume you have a room here in mind," I said.

He nodded.

"OK, let's go kill a monster ..."

It was past dinner time when we hashed out everything they knew and added in (nearly) everything OST had learned. Their help was invaluable, so I called SAC Robert Cho—

"Cho," he answered.

"Hey, boss, CIs are signed on. We just had a great convo about our newest 'not a demon' OI. Turns out the priest did have a chat with the monster. It was immune to exorcism, and this was his first time facing something that wasn't a demon or devil. Yes, we have new intel on those now too—"

"Oh, *that's* just great. Now we have demons and devils in addition to OIs?" Robert asked.

"Yup, I knew that would make your day," I said, smiling.

I could almost hear the crunching of antacids while I waited. A minute later, he spoke again.

"OK, I'll relay to the other squads what you told me. Do we have additional intel?"

"Yes, Christos has the list of the sorority girls associated with Laura. She was the one possessed by the OI creature that he killed."

I paused.

"I'm sending the list now, along with all the intel we have from

Christos and Samantha Cox. Robert, I don't know what it is, but Christos mentioned that when he killed Laura, an unnatural red mist emerged from her. He said nothing could stop it from leaving, and he tried everything."

"Swell. Thanks for the information, and keep on digging. What do you need?"

Dave thought for a long moment.

"If we are going to surveil the entire sorority, I'll need more agents. Otherwise, we are good for now … I do have one favor to ask—"

"Shoot," Robert said.

"I never thought I would say these words, but … considering what you had us read in the MWR room …"

There was a pause.

"No idea is too weird at this point, Dave," Robert said.

"Christos said that garlic and holy water did nothing to it. But I still want to try wood-core bullets for our Glocks, just in case it is some kind of vampire."

No hesitation or laughing.

"Absolutely. I'll have them made, and a courier will bring them to you. Just give me the drop location," Robert said.

"Thank you. I don't know whether to hope they work—or to hope they don't."

"You and I both, Dave."

He hung up.

I took everyone to dinner at Phoenix City Grill. I chose this restaurant because it was busy enough, with tables spaced far apart, to prevent eavesdropping. However, it was still quiet enough for us to hear each other talk.

As we ate, I reflected on everything I had learned. We needed to interview the sorority with Father Leighe. I knew Samantha would insist on joining, so she and Harold might as well come along. Besides, I had no other leads here in Tempe or Phoenix.

As I pondered, I absentmindedly spun my fries with my fork in the ketchup.

"You know, boss, that is not how you eat French fries," Steve said.

I chuckled.

"Yeah, Steve, I know … I was just thinking that the only leads we have right now are the sorority girls … sorry, women."

When I said "girls," Samantha looked askance at me.

"Sister is the correct term," Sammy said.

I nodded.

"So, Father Leighe, sorry—Christos, I know exorcism doesn't work, but fire and bullets seemed to end the host pretty quick …"

He grimaced a little but nodded yes.

"If it isn't a demon, what does everyone think it may be, or what may or may not work on it?" I asked.

I was grasping at straws, but there was little else to do. Besides, I was starving and wanted to eat my steak. Christos spoke first.

"As for the host body of the possession, and we have determined possession, it seems to 'die' normally."

"OK, so it's possessed by a mist? You said nothing stopped it?" Harold asked.

"Yes, and these 'incidents' … what do you call them again?" Christos also asked.

"Occult Incidents, or just 'OIs.' We call the entities monsters," I said.

"Fancy verbiage," Sammy said as she wolfed down a large serving of lasagna.

Damn, that woman can eat a lot for such a little thing.

"By the way, I ordered wood-core bullets for our Glocks; it's worth a try," I said.

Christos nodded, Harold and Steve kept eating like famine victims, and Sammy looked at me with interest, her fork suspended mid-bite.

"Tell me more about these bullets," she said.

"I wish I could; they're being made now. Once we have them, I'll give you one."

She smiled, "I'm surprised. I figured that would be, you know, *class-e-fied.*"

I chuckled.

"We both know you were going to take one when I wasn't looking anyway."

"That's true," she said, nodding.

She finished her meal while the rest of us were only halfway done.

She could keep up with the NMC guys, Hell—maybe even Frank, with how fast she ate.

Washington, DC
Hellious

Good luck, I thought, chuckling as I contemplated this "OST" group pursuing me.

Already, I had taken congresspeople, but I had one additional target in mind—a man who perfectly matched my ambitions. I knew he was one of the few people on Earth who would not just join me willingly but eagerly! His power would add to mine, making me unstoppable.

I didn't just desire to rule America and make everyone there my undead slaves; I desired to rule this *world.* I would move on to other worlds after that, of course.

The only thing that brought me more joy than the suffering and death of the humans was their terror! I wanted all to run screaming from me while they watched their fellow people become my undead. One, by one, by one …

Smiling, I contemplated my next target—how should I approach this man?

He would be in Seattle, Washington, for some business venture, and I would meet him there. His security team went with him everywhere, so I decided the best route was to show up as something irresistible to him—something he would let walk past his security team and to him.

My proper form would obviously not work, as it was beyond horrifying. The mere sight of me could easily cause him to have a heart attack. After all, he *was* eighty-four years old. However, my other "natural" human forms were ones of unsurpassed beauty! It did not matter if I was male, female, or androgynous. So, I chose my androgynous form for my flight to Seattle. Snap! Crunch! My bones were noisy as I shifted into my new form. Once it was completed, I knew that no human could resist the allure of my unbridled sexuality—or the sound of my voice.

I was *literally* irresistible.

One thing I found particularly fascinating was what they called "the internet". I marveled at the humans' stupidity, for they had created the ultimate weapon of their own destruction!

My intelligence was immense compared to theirs. In just a few days, then weeks, I absorbed more knowledge than most would in their entire lives. My mind was multifaceted, allowing me to think with multiple perspectives simultaneously. I utilized this ability to read and learn, like dozens of Einsteins. While one group practiced weapons or tactics, another could be learning computers or flying a plane. Anywhere on Earth, I could access all my minds at once, similar to the human Internet and Wi-Fi.

And all of them were part of "me".

There are so many things to learn and do! If I weren't such a sadist, I could spend an eternity learning everything humans had ever done, learned, or experienced.

As it was, I would be an excellent ruler of them all.

Unbeknownst to them, I could also enter the mind of anyone I possessed. I could *directly* possess only a small number of individuals, and those entities grew more powerful in my presence. Indirectly, I could command perhaps a few dozen additional beings at a time. I could see and control them, but they were only slightly more robust and resilient. Even with my intellect, though, there were limits. An unlimited number of undead would obey any straightforward commands I issued, but I could not "see" through their eyes. For now, I wanted only those I could control, as there was a risk associated with the ones I did not fully control; they would be left without guidance. Then, they would revert to their primal urge to feed and reproduce.

I booked a private plane using a false ID I had just created and a credit card given to me because of my fake high credit score. It was a private plane in a private airport without security checks—a perk that is only available for the rich and powerful.

I couldn't care less about wealth for appearance's sake, but I had done my research on human thought. This man would recognize me as a powerful, rich, intelligent being who would aid him in his quest for limitless power.

At least some humans understood their place: as rulers and controllers of those beneath their contempt. They would have a special place in my hierarchy.

I smiled.

Hiring my security team was also easy. I offered them a fabulous paycheck and a sign-on bonus, but only for those with the highest degree of what humans call "Special Operations" skill sets. They picked me up in an armored luxury SUV—a "Bentley," they called it—and took me to the private airport hangar.

Many humans spend their whole lives desperately trying to become millionaires. I did it in one day. Now, I am already a multimillionaire many times over. And by many times, I also mean many *people,* all of whom I controlled.

Humanity's chance of survival is exceedingly slim.

I had the sorority to thank for summoning the most powerful creature yet from our plane—me. What was genuinely terrifying for them was that *my* Master would soon be on its way as well …

Washington, DC
Sharon

Sharon was terrified.

Her friend, Matthew, never texted her about work. The fact that he had sent more than one text, the second *all in capital letters,* told her he was in trouble.

His last text was the worst.

The party night texts were terrible enough, but he sent one more yesterday afternoon, saying nothing untoward had happened. I was relieved.

Matthew and I had known each other for a long time. We even dated back in the day, but found we worked better as just good friends. The good news is we were BFFs and could lean on each other during hard times. For him to send those texts meant that everything was *not* OK …

This morning, I sent him an "Is everything OK?" text.

"Sorry, I was just being paranoid. LOL. All is good," he responded.

My features went pale, and I put down my coffee—even my hands were shaking.

LOL was code.

Matthew *hated* the LOL acronym! He told me he would only use it if he needed help, and at that point, I should contact whoever I needed to. Absent-mindedly, I twirled the spoon in my coffee as I thought about what to do.

Who do I even contact?

I can't go to the Secret Service; he told me his team was somehow compromised. After "The Incident" two years ago, when aliens attacked for the first time, I was more open to believing crazy stuff. Plus, the most unflappable person I know is Matthew. If he needed help, then he *really* needed help!

There were rumors online (thus, to be taken with a grain of salt) that a secret organization in the federal government dealt with the supernatural. I pondered … while stirring.

"The FBI," I said out loud. Startled by my own voice, I jumped a little.

Get a hold of yourself, Sharon.

OK, time to write a letter.

With a deep breath, I sat down at my computer and wrote a letter to the FBI. I included everything he sent me, copied all the texts and a photo, and printed it. I placed it in an envelope, sealed it, and put the tagline "Supernatural hunters: Critical event has occurred, open immediately" on the outside.

Then I just sat for a long time. It was my Saturday off, and I thought long and hard about who to give it to. Was the FBI even the right choice? If this turned out to be nothing, it would make him a laughingstock or possibly even cause him to face disciplinary action.

But I knew it wasn't. I can count on one hand the number of times in over a decade that he reached out like this—using only my thumb.

Decision made, I Googled the closest FBI office and went to get ready.

Matthew, I hope this reaches someone in time.

I got in my car and headed to the FBI office. Last night, there was a light dusting of snow, so the streets were a little slick in spots, but I made it to the FBI building and finally found some paid parking at a meter.

I shouldn't be here more than two hours, I thought, as I fed the meter with my credit card.

Walking into the J. Edgar Hoover Building, the first thing I saw was security.

"Good morning," I said to the security officer.

"Good morning, ma'am. What is the nature of your visit?" he asked.

"I have a threat to national security to report."

He immediately got that "uh oh, another crazy person" look. I laughed.

"Don't worry, I'm not crazy. I have information about an attack reported to me by Agent Ellis that needs to be routed to the right people. I'm only delivering a letter."

He visibly relaxed a little, then nodded and motioned to the magnetometer.

I placed my purse on the X-ray belt, along with a tray for my keys and other items. Then I walked through—it did not beep. After clipping on the visitor badge he gave me, I grabbed my stuff and went into the lobby to wait.

And wait … and wait. An hour later, a man in a suit looked around, saw me, and waved. I waved back and stood as he came over.

"Good morning, Sharon, is it?"

"Yes."

"I'm Deputy Assistant Director Eric Mitchell. I was told you have information about an attack?"

"I do. Do we have somewhere more private than the lobby?"

"Of course, come with me, please."

He turned and started walking. I struggled to keep up with his stride—he was tall and had long legs. After a few turns, we arrived at a small office.

"Please, have a seat," he said.

I did; the seat was surprisingly comfortable.

He sat at his desk across from me, the desk between us.

"So, tell me about this threat," he said.

He had the bored expression of someone who had listened to many crazy people in this chair.

I explained everything that occurred and stressed the importance of getting the letter to the right people as quickly as possible. His features changed from bored to genuinely interested as I spoke.

"Shouldn't this go to the Secret Service?" he asked, once I had finished.

"No. Matthew is in charge of the VPOTUS detail and is concerned about his team being compromised. That is why he contacted me, a civilian, to come to the FBI instead."

"OK. Typically, I would escort you out and have a good laugh, but given the strange events that occurred two years ago … I'll pass it on to the appropriate agency."

"Thank you, Mr. Mitchell."

He nodded and walked me back to security. We waved, and I headed back to my car. There were twelve minutes left on the meter; I got lucky.

CHAPTER 8
VPOTUS

OST DENFO

SAC Robert

KNOCK, Knock, Knock

I saw one of the NMC Agents, Thomas Hussain, standing at my door.

My door was open, but it was customary to knock before barging in.

"Come in, Thomas. How can I help you?" I asked.

"Letter delivery," he said, holding up a letter.

"Been getting those a lot lately," I chuckled.

He smiled and handed me the envelope.

"Have a good day, sir," he turned and walked out.

This is getting weird.

After that last letter, I hoped for good news—no such luck. Opening the envelope, I started reading. My dread got worse and worse as I read. Finishing the letter, I thought about what to do. There was no choice, not really.

Any potential threat to the POTUS or VPOTUS was to be reported immediately; that was not optional. I walked to ASAC Chayton's office, and he looked up as I entered. I handed him the letter.

"What do we have, boss?" he asked.

"Hopefully? Nothing. But you need to find out and tell me. Look up everything about this right now, priority one. I need a brief ready for when I call POTUS in a few minutes," I said.

"On it," he replied. He sensed this was serious and was already calling agents for help as I headed to the briefing room. I walked in, put up the "Classified Briefing in Progress" sign, and turned on the Secure Terminal Unit (STU-III). We used these for any classified conversations, and this one certainly was. I hoped this "Sharon" turned out to be a kook; otherwise, we were in a terrible situation. I waited for Chayton's report …

After getting all the facts from Chayton, I dialed the secure line to the president's office on the STU.

"Office of the President, Olivia Jordan speaking."

"Good morning, Olivia; this is SAC Robert Cho. Message POTUS 'code AMBER' immediately, please. I'll wait on the line."

"Yes, sir." And with that, the line went mute.

I waited for only about a minute.

"Robert, what is happening?" the president asked, by way of preamble.

"Madam President, we have information that the VPOTUS detail may be compromised," I said.

"Skip to the meat, Robert," she said.

"OK, a concerned citizen was contacted by the VPOTUS detail's lead agent. He told her the team had been compromised. The way it is described, it could—I want to stress *could*—be a complete takeover of the detail by another OI monster."

I heard a sharp intake of breath.

"Oh … That is not good, Robert."

"I know, Madam President. I'm starting to wonder if this new crea-ture can … well, I never thought I would say this; maybe it can possess multiple people. If so, VPOTUS is in danger from his own Secret Service detail."

"Humph. Thanks for giving me an easy one, Robert!"

I chuckled.

"Most welcome, Madam President, but I'm going to need your input on this one. If my team moves on the Secret Service or our own government in any way, it will, well, become your problem in a hurry."

Quiet ensued—we were both thinking: This *is* a tough one.

"I need more, Robert, you know that. What you have given me so far is hearsay at best," she said.

"I expected that, Madam President. Here is the intel we have so far: A photo from that night clearly showed a KSM (Known or Suspected Monster), a member of an ASU sorority. Our new CI, Father Christos Leighe, provided details regarding his exorcism of one of the ASU sorority sisters, Laura Halston. After he killed her, a red mist emerged and escaped. Therefore, the likelihood that the OI has compromised the entire sorority of ten, now nine, women is extremely high. Furthermore, the odds of those women being in Georgetown purely by coincidence, alongside the Secret Service detail, are almost zero. Additionally, in what world does a group of attractive twenty-somethings invite *every* agent up to their rooms? We also tracked their movements: they flew into DC that day and returned the next morning. Their sole purpose for the trip was to attend an event at the Ritz that night, where the detail was located. It was a bachelorette party for one of the sorority sisters, Chloe Russell. I did some digging, and Chloe is currently married to Jonathan Russell, who is MIA from his employment and whose whereabouts are unknown. Consequently, I would estimate with 95 percent confidence that the OI has compromised the VPOTUS detail. They had ample time to infiltrate the detail that night, and the privacy of the hotel rooms would support that hypothesis."

Another long pause. Finally, POTUS came to a decision.

"I'm sending you QRF-Oscar; I want you to brief them and use non-lethals if possible to secure the vice president from his residence. My God, if we are wrong about this ..."

I waited.

"I trust you, Robert. Last chance before your neck and mine are on the line. Is this a go, or do you have doubts about this?"

"It's not 100 percent, but it rarely is. A civilian reporting … but her details, including SSA Ellis's texts and a photo of a known KSM, are compelling. We can't afford to take the risk, in my professional opinion."

"OK then, I'm implementing CODE RABBIT. Godspeed, and go save our vice president."

The line went dead; I had my orders.

———

CODE RABBIT.

That code meant POTUS was moving to an undisclosed location immediately. Only her personal protection detail would know where. She would communicate via STU cutouts, and one member of her team was an IT specialist extraordinaire, so I knew she would be safe. Continuity of government was safeguarded, especially if we couldn't get to VPOTUS in time. Considering that the next person in line to the presidency, after VPOTUS, was the Speaker of the House, who was good friends with Congressman Halston, we had to succeed. If this thing knew how to possess people and could take over an entire SS detail, VPOTUS would be a good target. I'm sure it would move on to POTUS after that, so I'm glad she implemented CODE RABBIT.

The downside of her implementing CODE RABBIT is that the same compromised detail would now bolster the security of the VPOTUS residence. Both they and the regular residence security detail would be waiting for us.

Who else in government was under its control already? With enough people in the correct positions, it could effectively take over our government. What would it do next?

OK, this isn't a one-man problem.

"QRF to BRIEFING, QRF report," I said over the office PA.

In under five minutes, the whole squad had assembled in BRIEFING.

"OK, let's get started," I said to them.

"QRF-Oscar is inbound to Joint Base Andrews."

I saw everyone's relaxed postures immediately change. Everyone sat up straight, and their eyes got bigger. They all knew this was something significant. I saw that Lev was smiling—these were her people coming. The military QRF assigned to support OST operations were all elite SPEC OPS warriors.

"We have reason to strongly believe that this new OI has compromised the VPOTUS Secret Service detail."

Everyone was paying complete attention—no gasps, as many of us had previously seen and battled OIs.

"We are setting up an OP. Your squad will join QRF-Oscar and secure VPOTUS from his residence. Non-lethals on the SS detail, lethals as backup. I hate to say this, but it will be a serious black eye if we are wrong. But if we are right … crud, it sucks either way. But we must try and save VPOTUS; the president already gave the order."

Looks of dismay were passed among the team members. Our worst nightmare is having to go up against our own. That nightmare just came true.

"Alright, Graham, mobilize and prepare First Squad. All the intelligence we have regarding the OI will be on your iPads, and QRF-Oscar will meet you at Joint Base Andrews. You will set up your battle plans with them there and go operational as soon as possible. Any questions?"

"Boss, how many troops are we getting?" Graham asked.

"That's up to Naval Special Warfare Command. Usually, we would be allowed one or two eight-man squads from a platoon; they will be from SEAL Team 8 DEVGRU. But this is happening fast, and we'll take whatever they give us."

Graham nodded and turned to us.

"OK, First Squad, prep for move out, then meet me in the armory at (looked at his watch) 0930. Let's go," Graham said.

Everyone moved out with a purpose.

After everyone but Chayton had left, he turned to me.

"Boss, I have additional questions …"

———

Agent Lev

I hurriedly got ready and then eagerly headed to ARMOURY. Seeing my fellow SEALs would be a treat, and I looked forward to working with them.

Once we were all inside, we headed straight to the ExoM suits, like we had practiced.

The ExoM suits had integrated armor, a passive weight-bearing system to carry more gear, many pouches, holsters, ammo mags, a gas mask that could be put on without removing the helmet, auto-deploying tourniquets for each limb, and other first aid gear. We all helped each other get them on.

Then, Graham issued our usual weaponry: FN SCAR rifles with built-in targeting computers. IR and regular lasers assisted the computer in delivering an accurate first shot, and the 40GL, tucked under the rifle barrel, could fire a single 40mm grenade. Those were slung over our backs. Additionally, a Glock-18 pistol that could empty its 33-round magazine in under one-and-a-half seconds was secured in our leg holsters.

All of us were taking out the FN 303 launchers instead of MP5s this time.

FN Hershal made the FN 303 for law enforcement and the military. The top mounting Picatinny rail held our usual Thermal scopes (Infravision and up to 10X magnification), plus flip-up iron sights. It fired from compressed air at 3,000 feet per second, and the bottle was good for up to 110 shots. With a 15-round drum magazine loaded, it weighed only eight pounds, and the tiny drum magazines weighed under a pound each. Luckily, these weapons should be used chiefly at closer ranges, as the maximum range on the FN 303s was only 100 meters.

I placed my extra magazines into quick-access pouches on my chest. With the loaded weapon and six spare drum magazines, I had a total of 105 rounds. Hopefully, that would be sufficient.

It could fire six different types of rounds. Ours were loaded with PAVA/OC powder, designed to inflict non-lethal kinetic damage while delivering a powerful blast of OC pepper spray. FN also developed an experimental round featuring a built-in capacitor and a web of small prongs that extended upon firing. It would begin discharging on contact and continue that discharge intermittently for several minutes, much like a Taser. Hopefully, this would prove effective with the two rounds loaded alternately in the weapon. We knew the Secret Service agents would lack gas masks or heavy body armor, but we remained uncertain about their capabilities if they were possessed.

We also placed a handheld stun gun in one of the pouches for close-combat scenarios.

"Agent Lev, come get *The Gun,*" Chayton said with a grin.

"NLs, I assume?" I asked, walking over to him.

He nodded.

Usually, that weapon would destroy the VPOTUS's residence and those inside it. However, the new Mk19 Non-Lethal Short-Range cartridges fire using a telescoping cartridge case to make them non-lethal (NL). I prefer the police term "less lethal," as I doubted it could guarantee that *any* target, directly hit, would live. The barrage of rubber "bullets" from each shot would act like a giant shotgun on whatever it hit.

I also knew the other 32-round drum held the deadly HEDP explosive rounds—just in case. That would be in my combat pack. Now that everything was issued to me and secured on my armor, I headed to the garage.

Even after all this time, the other agents stared in wonder as I walked out carrying a weapon that, loaded, weighed over a hundred pounds, as though it were a tenth of that weight. I placed it lovingly into my car and secured it.

"Lev, you need help; you treat that like it's your baby," said Bob.

Robert "Bob" King and Melissa Woods were the new First Squad members.

"That's because it *is* my baby," I replied with a smile.

"OK, let's get going, guys!" Chayton yelled out.

Since our battle at Bolsa Chica, OST now has six modified Tesla Model S cars. The other three were already deployed with Second Squad, and the Model X (MX) would remain with the new QRF Squad at DENFO. After securing everything in our cars, we got ready to move out.

We drove to our hangar at Centennial Airport, with five-minute intervals between each car. Once we were all there, our usual airman loadmaster got busy loading the vehicles. All three of our Teslas were heavily modified and armored.

After locking down the cars and marking them "secured and ready," we entered them and put on our seat belts. The C-130 pulled out of the hangar and went to the runway. After a short wait (for takeoff clearance), we rolled down the runway and into the air.

———

Joint Base Andrews—Virginia

A few hours later, our C-130 touched down at Joint Base Andrews. The plane's loud rattling lessened after it landed, and the engines powered down to their ground speed. Minutes later, we heard a hangar door shut as the plane stopped and a ramp lowered into a large room.

While our vehicles were being unfastened from their moorings, we stepped out to meet with QRF-Oscar. That designator was for us; it meant whoever they assigned to us from the Special Warfare Group. In this instance, it was SEAL Team 8—or, it appears, one eight-man Squad from that Team.

The loud, familiar banging of our feet echoed in the spacious hangar as we walked down the C-130 ramp. I could see one of the SEALs approaching us.

"Welcome, OST; we have been read in on your training and capabilities. For non-soldiers, it's pretty good. I'm Lieutenant Taylor, commander of SEAL Team 8 and the OIC (officer in charge) for this operation. I apologize we could not get more SEALs for this OP with such a short timeframe," he said.

"I'm Graham Hart, OST First Squad Leader," Graham said, shaking Taylor's hand.

"Larry Caldwell is with me on Alpha Team. Levingston and King are here on Bravo, while Morris and Woods are on Charlie," he added.

"This is First Squad. Cole and I are Alpha; Brooks and Price are Bravo (waves); Carr and Reynolds are Charlie, and Evans and Lamm are Delta. Now, let's go over to the sandbox—the map on the table," Taylor said, gesturing toward it. He continued speaking as we all walked over to it.

"First of all, I want to thank you all for including us in your monster hunt," he started.

"However, only your Bravo Team will be joining us on the raid."

I looked at the rest of my squad. Their expressions were mixed, but there were no comments of disagreement.

"That works; Teams Alpha and Charlie will look for more OIs in the area while you conduct your OP, lieutenant," Graham said.

"Very good," Taylor replied.

All of us joined the briefing, even though only OST's Bravo Team —Bob and I—were joining in the raid. Bob King was a former Army Ranger. Even with the training the other team members had, the SEAL commander probably did not want them screwing up his OP, so Bob and I were the only ones he wanted to go with them. That makes sense, as we were already adding two unknowns to a team that had worked together for many years.

Besides, the other teams *did* have work to do. They would try to discover how far this "mass possession" went, beyond just the Secret Service detail.

We assembled at the table with a well-laid-out map. He was using plastic blocks for the buildings, keeping them to scale.

The table, which also contained little black die-cast cars, was covered in a detailed diagram. He also had a box of little green army men, the same kind we all played with as kids. A box of little pink plastic pigs was for the Secret Service.

Cute.

I noticed all the little army figures being used were additionally colored or marked to represent individuals on our team.

"First, SEAL teams Alpha through Delta consist of two men each.

Charlie and Delta will serve as our sniper teams for this mission. Alpha will lead the way into the residence, and Bravo will follow. We will conduct a standard front-to-rear clear until we reach VPOTUS, code name—PAPA. Lev, you will accompany Team Alpha, which consists of Petty Officer (PO) Cole and me, " he gestured toward him. " Bob, you're assigned to Petty Officers Brooks and Price on Bravo."

He paused to ensure Bob and I were still with him.

"OK, so our sniper teams will remove the Secret Service Counter Sniper (CS) teams after Bravo disables their landline and comms. Thanks to POTUS, we have that capability. After disabling the CS teams, we'll remove any exterior guards and maintain the two sniper teams on the A/B and C/D sides; that should give us cover fire in the event of a combat extraction of VPOTUS. Charlie Team will have A/B, and Delta will have C/D so that every side will have eyes on it. Teams Alpha and Bravo will extract PAPA. Make damn sure you come out on side A/B if you want cover fire from the Gator—" He saw Bob's curious look.

"The Gator is our heavily armored Expedition. We'll also be using two SEAL Desert Patrol Vehicles (DPVs). And, as OST was kind enough to lend us one of their NMCs, Agent Bachman, he will protect our extraction and provide cover fire from the Gator as we exfil. Remember, each SS we disable on the way in is to be zip-tied and gagged until extraction with PAPA—then we just use non-lethals and move on."

He stopped for a minute and looked at all of us. He wanted to ensure we had everything. His team was paying attention, and he was pleased to see that we were as well.

"OK, we have limited intel on the interior of the residence—sucks for us, but we go with what we have. The primary extraction plan is that we zap the guards, grab PAPA, and come out the front. EVAC in the Gator. Sniper teams will EVAC in the DPVs."

He paused and continued.

"Gator is out front, side Alpha," he said, moving a plastic crocodile into position.

"If we need to exit from any other side, the sniper teams will provide cover until we can reach the Gator. If the Gator is a no-go, the alternative is the DPVs with the sniper teams." He moved the small black dune buggies to their designated positions.

"EVAC of PAPA is the objective. All units will have that as priority one."

We nodded our heads in agreement.

"OK, if all goes to hell, the contingency is to hole up in the safe room with VPOTUS. If that happens, we call in the cavalry. The whole world will show up, and we'll be the bad guys. Secure PAPA and surrender to the military unit designated "EAGLE'S NEST" only. POTUS has already set them up to come in should our extraction fail."

He paused again.

"Emergency plan is to go lethal and exfil or protect PAPA at all costs. I cannot stress enough—we must get PAPA away from any SS. We must assume they are all possessed at this point. Damn, that is weird to say!"

The team all chuckled.

"Alright, it's open to questions now, but make it quick," he said, with a glance at each member.

No questions. Just nods all around.

"OK, the mission is a go."

———

VPOTUS Residence—0200 hours

The first Secret Service "agents" at the guardhouse were the easiest. They were part of the Secret Service's Uniformed Division, which meant they were federal police, not agents.

Pop, pop, pop …

A short barrage of FN 303 rounds took them out, and we had them gagged and zip-tied—both hands and feet bound together—in record time. Moving down the road, we quietly made our way to our next targets.

The SEALs had their own gear, but Bob and I were wearing our

ExoM armor. We had each borrowed a set of the SEALs' Night Vision Goggles (NVGs), which, by pure luck, fit with our helmets. I made a mental note that our armor needed those.

"Darkness falls," said Bravo Team. The landline and external comms had been disabled; we were a go. At the same time, Charlie and Delta Teams took out the counter-sniper teams on the roof and the house's exterior.

So far, so good.

Their DPVs went on electric power (they were the new "hybrid" model), and we drove them to where the sniper teams were, then quickly made our way to the front of the residence. Two "roving" agents came around the building, and we shot them from about fifty meters. Tying up the downed SS agents as we went, we were ready to breach. One of the SEALs ran a tiny fiber-optic camera into the door gap to see inside.

Two SS agents were in the grand foyer; they did not notice the camera. I knew there were two because PO Brooks held up two fingers.

Brooks put away the camera, and he and PO Price got ready to open the double doors wide. LT Taylor and Bob were prepared with the FN 303s. I wasn't shooting because I was carrying a hundred pounds of Mark 19 in my hands, and my weapon was not quiet. Brooks did a finger countdown, and they threw the doors wide open.

The two SS agents were caught flat-footed.

They reached for their guns as they were peppered (literally) with PAVA/OC powder rounds. The alternating electric stun rounds made them jerk uncontrollably as they fell to the ground. We rushed into the grand foyer—and grand it was.

This place is enormous.

We covered the foyer entries while Brooks and Bob secured the SS agents. They also took their radios from them. Hearing their comms was a priority. Between the federal police and the agents, we all now had their radios.

Our limited intel came from POTUS's memories of her visits to the residence, so we knew he spent time in the study next to his bedroom and the safe room. We would have to act quickly to prevent him from accessing that space, and we had one more hallway to navigate.

Again, using the flex-camera, we peered around the corner. Two agents were at the end of the hall. Brooks held up two fingers, then flashed his hand out quickly.

Crap, that meant one of them spotted the camera.

Everything seemed to go into slow motion as I lunged around the corner. One agent lifted his arm to talk into his mic as the other drew his firearm. As I sprinted into the corridor, their attention was on me. I felt FN 303 rounds fly past me—all hits on them and none on me.

Good job, guys.

They fell, and the SEALs rushed forward to secure them, but it was too noisy.

"Contact!" was yelled from inside.

I sprinted and went through the closed door. As the door shards exploded inward, the agents covered their faces and eyes. This was precisely what I had hoped for. Again, several FN 303 rifle rounds hit them at the same time—serious overkill.

A pale-faced VPOTUS stared at us in alarm as our team flooded the room and took up positions guarding the doors into the room. I approached VPOTUS

"Sir, we are here for your protection. CODE JUDAS."

The president had briefed us that he would know what to do if he heard that. That code meant the president had ordered extraction from his compromised detail.

"Oh no," he said.

Now, all we needed to do was get him back down the hall, through the foyer, and outside to the Gator.

Easy.

"CODE Armageddon! I repeat, CODE Armageddon!" came over my stolen Secret Service radio's earpiece.

We all had one of their radios, with the ear mic in one ear.

Damn. We missed one somehow.

We were also briefed on that code. It meant the residence had been breached, and enemy forces had the vice president. The remaining agents would secure the perimeter to stop our escape now until they could eliminate the enemy forces within.

And we were those enemy forces.

Not good, not good at all.

One of the doors to our right opened, and an SS agent came through; he had an MP5K. Before he could use it, he was hit with over a dozen FN 303 rounds.

Pop, pop, pop …

They didn't faze him as he fired a long, deafening burst into PO Price.

BRRRRRRAP!

The two "secured" SS agents also jumped up. Tearing their hands and feet free from the flex cuffs, they bit off their gags in one bite and smiled at us.

It was a trap!

The agents no longer maintained any pretense of being human. Their mouths were elongated to reveal hundreds of razor-sharp teeth, and their hands had long, dangerous-looking talons coming from each finger. They charged the SEAL Team.

Without saying a word, we all went lethal—

I saw Price drop as the barrage of bullets shredded him, even as I brought up the Mark 19 GMG. The SS Agent who shot Price was faster than expected, but not as fast as I am.

I fired a short burst, maybe three rounds, into him.

B-B-BANG!

The firing of the grenade launcher was quieter than usual but still quite loud. Dozens of plastic balls hit him at once, and he was shredded all over and slammed backward into the wall—I had not been expecting that. Whatever "he" was now, it was no longer human. It looked at me and smiled. The wounds were horrific. Blackish material was splattered on the wall behind it, where dozens of rubber bullets had gone *through* it.

But it wasn't dead yet.

BRRRAP! BRRRAP!

A hail of bullets from two of the SEALs shredded its head and torso—they were pissed it had killed one of their own. This time, it did die. Its shredded body dropped to the ground; its head was barely recognizable as ever having been human. Simultaneously, the other SEALs took out the other two undead SS with bursts to their heads.

BRRRAP! BRRRAP!

I grabbed VPOTUS and yelled, "Safe room!"

The VPOTUS pulled me toward a bookshelf. Hitting a hidden switch, the bookshelf swung open like the door to a bank vault. Meanwhile, I heard LT Taylor over our radios.

"Go lethal, I say again, go lethal—" LT Taylor said into our mics.

"Moving to the safe room with PAPA, contingency protocols," he added.

We ran into the room, and VPOTUS reached up to hit a switch. More of the undead SS agents poured into the room we were just in, and we traded automatic fire as the giant metal door swung shut.

That's weird. Why would they risk hitting VPOTUS like that?

In the sudden quiet, the SEALs were reloading their MP5s as I switched out the giant drum magazine on my Mark 19. Now, it had the usual high-explosive dual-purpose rounds loaded. Capable of piercing vehicle armor before exploding, it was equally at home against vchicles and as an antipersonnel round. I would have to be careful where I fired it.

"OK, confirmation received, EAGLE'S NEST is en route," LT Taylor said over the radio.

"Yeah, and hundreds of police," Brooks added.

PO Cole was checking on Price, whom we had dragged inside before shutting the door. As LT Taylor turned to talk to him, Cole spoke the words we all dreaded to hear—

"Price is KIA," he said. Price had been killed in action.

"We are safe as long as that door is shut, yes?" VPOTUS asked.

"Yes, sir. We hole up here and wait for EAGLE'S NEST. You will be safe as long as that door stays shut," LT Taylor said.

"Whew. That is good to know," VPOTUS said.

Then he reached up and flipped the switch to reopen the door—

———

Hellious

I can't believe how efficient these humans are! I am impressed by this group. They will be a fine addition to my growing army of undead.

As I flipped the switch to open the door back up (also breaking it), I registered shock on the Navy SEALs' faces. Wildly, I lunged forward and bit down, hard, into the SEAL closest to me. My razor-sharp teeth ripped out half of his neck in one bite.

The others did not hesitate; they turned and emptied rounds into me with little effect. When I possessed a body directly, it had much more power. The host I currently had was still stronger, faster, and a lot tougher than my other possessed undead—

What the—?!

Suddenly, I was flying out the door as if hit by a truck.

———

Agent Lev

Everything just went sideways for our OP.

Jesus, this undead thing messes with your mind.

I knew we were dealing with undead because my "non-lethal" rounds went through their bodies like butter. As did the SEALs' bullets. Also, black gunk flew out wherever they were hit.

No blood.

I am far from a qualified mortician, but their lack of blood, combined with what looked like rotten, dead tissue spraying out, led me to believe they were no longer alive—just animated, maybe? Our mission wasn't to kill monsters—it was to save VPOTUS. Now, it seems we were too late, as it was a monster now.

BRRRRRRAP! BRRRRRRAP!

"It" being the vice president of the United States.

Oh crud.

I realized I couldn't fire the Mark 19 in here as the door swung back open. Although it's supposed to arm only once it has "spun enough"—between fifteen and twenty meters—if it did arm in the safe room, it would kill us all. Knowing my relationship with Murphy (luck—usually bad), this would be the first time it activated at close range.

So, I ran forward as the monster—that was once VPOTUS—leaped forward and bit down on PO Cole's neck. I hit the beast full force from the side, and it flew out the door, along with a spray of blood and a giant chunk from Cole's neck. Bob grabbed Cole, put his hand on his ravaged neck, and yanked him out of harm's way.

As VPOTUS landed ten yards away, I yelled, "FIRE IN THE HOLE!"

PO Brooks and LT Taylor dove to the sides of the door for protection as I squeezed the trigger.

B-B-BURP!

As grenades came out of the Mark 19's barrel, I saw several undead SS agents firing their MP5s at me. Even in combat, they had their mouths open in a huge grin with a hundred teeth showing, but my first target was the VPOTUS. Even as bullets were smacking into me, I hit him dead in the torso with three rounds as he started to stand up.

They tore into him and knocked him down again.

I realized he was within the twenty-yard arming distance; the grenade had not spun enough to explode. However, it still made for a nasty 68mm bullet. Realizing my mistake, I aimed for the back of the room and fired another short burst—

B-B-B-BOOM!

Two of the undead SS agents were directly hit and exploded like supernovas of gore; the remaining rounds hit the back wall and exploded. The explosions shredded the other vamps and everything else in the room. Furniture, undead SS agents, and whole sections of the building were ripped asunder. And all that explosive pressure and shrapnel also came into me. Even as a SIM, I couldn't get out of the way in time.

I felt enormous pressure as the blast waves hurled me into the safe room's back wall, and everything went black …

———

BRRRRRRAP! BRRRRRRAP!—

I snapped awake to the sound of gunfire.

From my training with the SEALs, I knew I recovered incredibly quickly from unconsciousness. Still, I could sense I had taken *a lot* of damage. Thankfully, I didn't feel pain anymore—because, as I looked down, I could tell I was seriously injured.

As I lunged to my feet, I saw the two remaining SEALs in a fire-fight with new undead SS agents who had shown up. The study was no more. In its place was the ground zero of several powerful explosions. A whole section of the wall had been ripped open, revealing the hallway where the other undead agents were.

Bob was giving Cole first aid, and it didn't look good. However, the thick walls of the safe room protected them.

"FIRE IN THE HOLE!" I yelled again.

The two SEALs, Brooks and LT Taylor, ducked behind the walls as I leaped to the edge of the door. This time, I *would* have cover, so I fired one-handed around the wall.

B-B-B-B-B-BOOM!

The Mark 19 flew out of my hand as I registered *a lot* of damage to that arm and hand. But it was much worse for them—a shower of undead blackness, debris, smoke, and dust filled the room.

Fortunately, I was a SIM. So, at least I still *had* a right hand, though it was pretty messed up. I left my probably damaged Mark 19 wherever it had landed in the safe room. Pulling out my Glock with my left hand, I joined the others as we maneuvered around the corner with our weapons and eyes alert. There was now a large section of the house on fire—whatever was left of it. As we watched and waited, the only sound was the crackling of the flames; nothing more came at us.

Suddenly, we heard machine gun fire from the DPVs outside, and then Charlie came over the radio—

"Hostiles eliminated. Be advised that our arrests are imminent. Charlie and Delta are going out of commission."

We could hear the bullhorns outside now and knew that Charlie and Delta were being taken into custody.

"OSCAR, this is EAGLE'S NEST. We are on-site and demand your immediate surrender. Please advise the safety of PAPA," came the message over our radios.

Oops.

"SEAL Team 8, OIC Lieutenant Taylor here. Be advised that PAPA was a hostile and no longer human—he was eliminated. We are in the safe room; fire signal for surrender," he said.

A few moments later, a grenade was launched into what was left of the burning study, and green signaling gas poured out of it.

"SEAL Team 8, we surrender, coming out now!" LT Taylor said on the radio.

I holstered the Glock as the SEALs lowered their weapons on their slings. Then, raising our hands as high as we could, we emerged through the smoke and fire to a sea of uniformed officers—there must have been over a hundred. Luckily, my Mark 19 was still lying somewhere in the safe room along with PO Cole, who had bled to death.

"Turn around, keeping your hands up high … Drop to your knees … Drop to the ground … Hands out to your sides, all the way out …"

They came forward and put us in cuffs. For some reason, maybe because they didn't know what to make of me, they put two sets of cuffs on me.

The party was over.

CHAPTER 9

CONGRESS

Joint Base Andrews—Virginia

Agent Lev

OUR VEHICLE, a paddy wagon for transporting prisoners, made its way with sirens wailing. There were no windows to look out of, and we did not know where we were being taken. POTUS had sanctioned the mission, so hopefully, we were not on a one-way trip to a prison camp.

The sirens turned off, and we could hear a garage door opening and closing. The latch clanged, and the back doors opened.

"Jesus, guys, save some for the rest of us!" said PO Jason Evans as the doors opened.

His smile evaporated when he saw only four of us.

"Where are Jack and Derek?" he asked.

Taylor just shook his head.

"Mother F—ers!" he yelled.

"SITREP," LT Taylor said. He was asking for a situation report.

Evans calmed immediately. As he was uncuffing us, he gave us a SITREP:

"Charlie and Delta are green. Agent Bachman is also here, safe and sound. All our weapons and equipment have arrived in the other vehicles. We are fully operational. Transport is being loaded now. The destination is still undetermined, but anywhere that isn't here will do. Additionally, we have already been debriefed by OST; I never thought undead could be real," PO Evans said.

He had just a hint of terror in his voice, unless I was imagining it. The look on his face revealed it, though.

"OK, team, let's reload and rearm. I want to be wheels up in fifteen minutes or less."

He looked over at me and nodded once. I nodded back. Then, I went to help the team prep for EVAC.

"Lev and Brooks, get your asses on the bird and have Corporal Campbell fix you up," LT Taylor ordered.

"And Lev—"

"Sir?"

"Quit bleeding, you're making a mess."

He turned and walked away to finish the loadouts and prep.

We all knew that the powers that be would soon open an empty prisoner van and try to shut down any flights in or out of the area. So, we had to hurry—the "where to" briefing would occur once we were airborne. Immediately after we finished stowing our gear, we belted in. Seconds later, we exited the hangar doors and went to the runway.

"ATC, this is Tango Sierra, requesting permission for takeoff."

The pilots' comms were on our channel as well.

"Tango Sierra, this is ATC, permission granted, runway Two Lima."

"ATC, we copy, runway Two Lima, out."

I could feel the big C-130 as it gathered speed and slowly lifted into the air ...

The medic worked on us nonstop throughout the entire flight, first tending to PO Brooks, who had a GSW to the arm. He had approached me first, but I shooed him away.

By the time he returned to render aid, there was a small pool of blood under me. I had multiple GSWs and dozens of pieces of shrapnel in me.

Many more bullets were stuck in my armor. My face was a bloody mess, quite literally—I had an annoying piece of shrapnel that kept bleeding into my left eye. I had already removed the more significant pieces stuck in me and was busy cleaning and dressing wounds when he got to me.

"You should not be alive, much less walking and talking, you know," Corporal Campbell said as he started removing shrapnel and dressing wounds, shaking his head. He wasn't wrong; the GSWs alone should have killed me, not even counting the bullets the armor stopped and the shrapnel over my entire body. He finally got the shrapnel out from over my left eye, and suddenly, I couldn't see because of the blood.

"Dammit! Hold still a sec," he said.

The blood finally stopped flowing, and he rinsed the blood out of my eye.

"Hey, Lev," Brooks yelled over the noise of the C-130.

"Check out this photo; I sent it to ya …"

He had on a big grin.

"Lev, the walking dead!"

I looked at the photo on my phone as we all chuckled; I did look like a character in *The Walking Dead*. Every part of me had either bullets or shrapnel in it, or both. Plus, I was covered in dust and debris, undead blackness, and dark-red blood.

So, I would not be sending that photo to James … ever.

LT Taylor came over to us as we were about to land.

"Hell of a job, Lev. If you ever want to be on one of our teams, you just let me know—"

I nodded.

"Thank you, I wish I could," I said.

He nodded back.

"Maybe after OST …" he said, walking off.

I felt good that I helped the SEALs destroy the enemy, but I was furious they had killed two of us. Now, we are headed to God knows where to do God knows what. I'm sure SAC Cho has a destination in mind, though.

———

Washington, DC
Congressman Halston

I was fuming.

My assistant had just called to tell me the entire VPOTUS detail, including the vice president himself, had been killed. I needed that man, and now we have lost him! Add in that the cowardly president went into hiding, and I was in a foul mood. Thinking hard about what to do next, I picked up my phone and called the OST DENFO on a secure line.

"OST, Agent Berry Hillman, how may I help you?" answered a man.

"This is Congressman Terrance Hallston; I need to speak to your SAC immediately," I said.

"Sorry, but all senior staff are currently unavailable."

"*Really*. And when will they be available?" I asked frostily.

"Above my pay grade, no idea."

"No idea—*sir*," I said to him.

"You don't have to call me sir," he replied.

I slammed my phone down to disconnect the call.

So, this Cho fella wants to play games and be charged with contempt of Congress? I can make that happen! Before calling my colleagues, though, I had to think hard about what to do next—

RING, RING

Another damn phone call!

"What?!" I answered angrily, picking up the receiver.

"Um … Ah, sorry, sir, but you told me to call when I got news."

It was that new, dim-witted assistant of mine again.

"Go ahead," I said.

"They have now arrested the perps, and they are on their way to FBI headquarters currently. Oh, also, the DA just granted full immunity to that Christos Leighe guy. He and that Crime Scene News team were given CI status."

I heard the headset make little popping sounds as I gripped it extra hard.

"*What* did you just say?"

"Well, sir, I said—"

"It was rhetorical, moron!" I screamed, slamming the phone back down.

I got up and walked to my car. I was headed to the J. Edgar Hoover Building, the FBI headquarters. The OST team that had just attacked the VPOTUS residence was arrested and was now being taken there for processing. I wanted to be present when they arrived.

A small group of us were waiting as the police vehicles arrived in the bay. I was eager to finally see these SEALs, and I was sure some of the OST agents were with them. Well, now I get to encounter these guys face-to-face. The door opened, and my smile faded away. The van was empty, and my face turned crimson.

We need to watch your blood pressure, Terrance; it could be the death of you.

I knew the creature possessed me, and I didn't care. It wanted the same things I did—unchecked power and a lot of it. I took a deep breath to calm myself.

What do we do now? I demanded of this creature within me.

Nothing. Go back home and make legislation to take to the committee and demand answers. OST just killed the vice president. Use that. Make OST fugitives and try to shut their operation down. Do what you must.

I nodded to myself. No monster was needed to make me hell-on-wheels to find and destroy OST. I had plenty of reasons already—they were working with the man who killed my daughter.

I would be heading back to Tempe now. From there, I would craft more legislation to pursue these despicable criminals.

Soon, I would make them all pay.

———

On board the C-130—at 30,000 feet

Agent Lev

"Oh, no," that was all SAC Robert Cho said when I provided him with an After Action Report (AAR) from a secure line during our flight. Typically, the SL would handle that, but we were just one team from OST—and I was the TL.

"Lev, I understand that your team did what it had to. There was nothing more you could have done—" Robert added.

I knew the "but" was coming.

"But after killing an entire Secret Service detail along with VPOTUS, we just gave Halston and company a lot of ammo to come after us. The optics are beyond horrible when viewed from the outside. Already, I can see Halston's written admonishment: 'SEAL Team and OST destroy VPOTUS's residence, killing VPOTUS, and all Secret Service agents on his detail. The fugitive team escaped with help from other government agents.' You know he will come after us …"

I could hear chewing on the line; I patiently waited.

"I'll deal with Halston's group. Your team—including the SEAL Team—is already en route to Tempe. We have determined, God help me for saying this, a nest of monsters is there. An entire sorority of them," Robert said.

"Clarification. You did say a sorority of them? All young females, I assume?"

"Is that an issue for you, Lev?" Robert sounded surprised.

"Not at all, it's great. Makes target acquisition easier," I said.

There was a pause.

"Lev, you're the scariest person I know," Robert said.

"Yes. And I want our enemies to know it as well."

I said it with a frostiness I didn't know I had. The last two years had changed me, and I wanted my foes *dead*. My bloodlust *was* a little scary, even to me.

"Jesus … I'm so glad you're on our side. Tell the team 'good hunting' for me. You'll link up with Second Squad and their CIs when you land," Robert said.

"We have CIs now?" I asked. It was my turn to be surprised.

"Yes, that is correct. You'll meet them when you land. Anything else, Lev?"

"No, sir," I said.

"Good luck and happy hunting."

The line went dead. We had our orders.

I called James.

"Hey, sexy," James answered.

"Hi, baby," I said.

The other SEALs smirked, and I flipped them the bird, only to realize the finger was dislocated and broken.

"Hold on a sec," I said, pulling my hand down. I snapped the finger back into place with my teeth, then flipped them off.

They shook their heads—

"F—ing bad-ass!" I heard SEAL Evans say.

"Are you alright?" James asked.

"Yeah, babe, just a little frag and such, nothing too serious. You know the drill—seriously wounded but combat-capable," I chuckled.

There was a long pause.

"OK, I'm glad you're alright. Can you express my thanks to the other SEALs for me?"

"Of course. All is good; talk later."

"Copy that; stay frosty, Goddess."

I hung up and put my phone away.

"How's the wife?" SEAL Carr asked.

I looked down, ensured I had the fixed hand (the other one was *really* messed up), and lifted it to flip him off as well.

Everyone laughed.

Corporal Campbell had finally finished patching me up. He talked to me as he was putting away his medical gear.

"OK, Lev, now make sure you take off a few weeks for bed rest. No heavy lifting or sudden movements," Campbell deadpanned.

Everyone, including me, laughed. We all knew that wasn't going to happen.

"Thank you, Campbell, I appreciate you," I said.

"No problem, sailor," he winked, grabbing his field kit as he walked away.

Now that I was patched up and had given my AAR to Cho, I shut my eyes for a quick combat nap. The military had taught me how to catch forty winks almost anywhere. My senses still tingling, I drifted off.

———

Luke Air Force Base—NW of Phoenix
Naval Operational Support Center
US Navy

We landed at Luke Air Force Base.

As we taxied down the runway to our hangar, we saw a phalanx of police cars with their lights on through the front windows. The flight deck was open to the rest of the plane, as we didn't exactly need to worry about terrorists on this flight.

Uh oh. Again?

As we rolled to a stop, we assembled at the cargo door at the aft of the aircraft. We left our weapons secured; we would not use them on police officers. The door came down on its hydraulic hinges, revealing several dozen police officers with weapons drawn.

Suddenly, several blacked-out SUVs pulled up between us and them.

Men in expensive dark suits emerged and approached the patrol sergeant. Following a heated discussion, the sergeant shook his head in resignation. He then turned to his assembled officers and said something we couldn't hear. The officers lowered their weapons and holstered their sidearms.

One of the suits walked up to us with a stack of papers.

"Good afternoon. I hope you had a restful flight," he smirked.

Smart ass. Nothing about a C-130 is "restful".

"We just had a lovely discussion with the officer in charge. They were here to arrest you, obviously. However, this executive order overrides your new *alleged* felony status," the man said.

He handed us the stack of orders, and I gave them to LT Taylor. Each member took one.

A quick skim revealed that it was an executive order stating that no agency or person would "Impede, obstruct, arrest, detain, or otherwise hinder OST operations in any way. All federal, state, local, and tribal agencies are hereby ordered to give OST full, unobstructed, and unimpeded access to any and all information, transportation, personnel, and resources. This is in effect until rescinded in writing by the Office of the President of the United States."

It was signed personally by the president.

Dayyam. That would stick in some people's craw, but it also made my day.

Unlike in TV cop shows, the Air Force Security Police simply shrugged and continued with their day. They were not at all bothered by the executive order; a few even came over to chat with the SEALs. We couldn't disclose what was happening, but they had figured it out—it wasn't difficult. They expressed gratitude to the SEALs for their service and wished us all good luck in our mission.

We were on our way.

Unimpeded, I may add.

———

Halston Residence—Tempe
Congressman Halston

CRACK—TINKLE, tinkle

It turns out that in the phone versus window challenge, both lose.

My cell phone shattered, and my window cracked. I had thrown my cell phone into the window after talking to the DA. There was nothing I could do about their CI status and immunity deal. Adding insult to injury, POTUS had also just signed an executive order. That order, signed by POTUS herself, meant there would be no chance of changing the DA's mind on this one.

I looked at my cracked window and the pieces of my phone on the floor.

Temper, temper, Hellious chided me.

"F— you!" I said aloud.

Only laughing could be heard in my head. And it wasn't mine.

I knew this monster may hear my thoughts, but I didn't give a damn.

This OST group had to be stopped. Not only could they get in the way of my rise to power, but they could kill my golden goose.

How do you like being called a goose? I addressed the monster.

Humph. No answer.

My plan to derail Cho in the next subcommittee meeting, which I had already scheduled, just went down the drain. Although Congress approved many things and the president had limited authority, she still possessed authority over the executive branch, so the executive order ultimately protected the OST.

I started pacing in my ornate study. I had designed it like one of those old libraries with paneled mahogany wood and fine antique fixtures; it always felt like old money.

Hmmm, what to do?

I snapped my fingers—I had it!

The legislative branch could override her executive order with new legislation. This would ensure that all executive agencies fell under the Committee on Supernatural Affairs' purview.

Also, to have legislative authority, we would need to be voted in as a full committee.

This was not going to be easy, as the president would surely veto anything we sent to her to be signed, requiring a two-thirds majority vote. The coward had gone into hiding, so we couldn't even get to her or her detail now—OST must have tipped her off.

I stopped my smile short. *Wait a minute!*

Yes, that means they know about me and mass possession. And they probably know about you as well.

Crap.

Well, it is time to get to work, then.

I went over and sat at my desk. Picking up my landline phone, I called Congressman Liam DeMarcus, the Speaker of the House. Now that VPOTUS was dead, DeMarcus was next in line to succeed the president. We already had several key congressmen and senators on board. Imagine everyone's surprise when a dozen or so voted for a sponsored bill they normally would oppose!

"Liam here, what's up, Terrance?" he answered.

"It is time for the subcommittee to be voted in as a full committee. Then, immediately after, to vote on our bill for unlimited congressional oversight of all government agencies. We'll call it the 'Laura Act,' named after my murdered daughter," I said.

"I like it! I really am sorry for your loss, of course, but that'll give us more weight come voting time. Anyone who goes 'on the record' against our bill will, obviously, hate children and America and love harboring criminals—just like our bitch president. We can sell that to some who might not normally vote our way."

"Yes, let's make it happen—and fast," I said as I hung up on him.

Liam was a cad, but he would make things happen. While he was doing that, I nursed a forty-year-old Scotch and thought about what to do next. The committee would happen; we had the votes. So would the law on agency oversight.

POTUS's executive order truly was a massive abuse of presidential power.

Unlimited and unfettered access to all federal agencies? Forgiveness for mass murder and destruction? Unrestrained authority? Hell, I wouldn't be surprised if we got a lot of legislators on board who *weren't* possessed.

I smiled and enjoyed the burn of the liquor as I rested my head on my three-thousand-dollar leather chair and napped.

Being rich does not suck.

———

FBI Headquarters
Doctor Neil Jeffries

Knock, knock, knock

I looked up, and it appeared that Jamie was dressed for casual Friday, but it was Monday.

"Neil, your stiffs are here," she said.

Jamie was our receptionist; she was always so matter-of-fact about things.

"Thank you, Jamie. I'll be down soon," I replied.

She walked back out.

I continued eating my sandwich, which included sliced bologna and "processed cheese food spread." I always wondered what was in that. Maybe it contained some of the same ingredients as my embalming fluids?

Hmmm.

I was curious to find out, but it would have to wait. The first bodies, or pieces of bodies, were arriving. OST's body count was something else. There were active-duty military units with lower body counts.

As I finished my sandwich, I pulled up the OST AAR. While it loaded, I looked around my Spartan office. My diplomas hung on the wall behind me, and a picture of my wife and children rested on my desk. It dawned on me that I had never truly bothered to decorate beyond that. My work always seemed to take priority. Now that the report was open, I began to read ...

This time, they had taken on—

That can't be right.

I reread the report, as I couldn't believe what it said.

They had deliberately killed the vice president of the United States! And, for good measure, his entire Secret Service detail.

Wow.

I locked my computer, got up, and headed toward the stairs going down ...

Walking to the morgue, I whistled like a school kid—boy, I would hate to be in their shoes right now …

I put on some light jazz and got to work.

Although I was the FBI's lead coroner and could have had another doctor perform the autopsy, I took particular joy in being the first to autopsy these new aliens. This was not the first time aliens had used people to become monsters, either.

I shuddered as I remembered an angry OST agent named "Lev."

Although she was scary enough as a SIM-hybrid, the other ones — the "full SIMs" I autopsied —were even more powerful.

Scary ass world we live in now.

As if we didn't kill each other enough as people, now we had aliens to do it.

Oh well—

I went to the large sink and prepped myself for the autopsy. Then, I walked over to my first new "alien."

"Let's see what's inside you," I said aloud.

What remained of the Secret Service agent lay on the cold metal examination table. I stood next to the corpse, a bone saw in hand. As I pushed it down on the dead SS agent's chest, I knew, from years of experience, that I had to push down somewhat hard for it to cut through the thick sternum and manubrium bones that protect the heart and lungs.

SKREECH!

Black goo splattered all over me as the saw went clean through him and into the table, sparking on the metal.

I quickly pulled it back up—it had gone through him like warm butter.

Unlike those TV shows where doctors seem to "forget" to wear their personal protective equipment, I had mine on. My face shield, white lab coat, and gloves were now covered in foul-smelling black muck.

"Well, *that* is gross," I said aloud.

Oh well, I guess I don't have to worry about staying clean anymore.

I continued carving a little more carefully this time. I activated my voice recorder—

"Subject is a Secret Service agent," I said as I examined the body tag.

"Name is Matthew Ellis. The cause of death is explosive trauma, shrapnel from grenades, and numerous GSWs. Cutaneous skin appears normal, but internal organs are—"

I looked closer.

Wow.

"Internal organs show signs of extreme decay. Organs appear to have been dead for many weeks or even months; I won't know until labs come back. The subject also has no blood volume. The body was exsanguinated *in the past* before being 'killed' by OST."

I turned the recorder off and sat on my stool, looking at my flayed-open corpse. It was missing an arm and a leg, both of which had been blown off.

"Matthew, what did they do to you?"

———

US Capitol—Washington, DC—House of Representatives
Congressman Halston

"Thank you all for coming; the Subcommittee on Supernatural Affairs is now in session."

That was Congressman and Speaker of the House Liam DeMarcus. He gave a short cough and then continued—

"The votes today are regarding the establishment of a full Committee on Supernatural Affairs, formed from the subcommittee, as well as the passage of the separate 'Laura Bill' to accompany it, should the first vote succeed. You all have the amicus briefs and have been given the opportunity to debate both bills in our last session. We have had the time to read them and discuss what the bills entail. Through your diligence, these bills are now ready to be voted on; today, you will go on the record. We must ensure accountability for our government's actions. Before we vote, I would like to introduce the sponsor of one of the bills, the 'Laura Act,' Congressman Terrance Halston."

There was clapping, and I took to the podium.

I had no notes, thanks to Hellious' perfect memory. We decided to make my message even more poignant, because it came from the "heart".

"Ladies and gentlemen of Congress, I stand before you today, childless …"

I did my best to convey a sincere expression of deep sorrow; it wasn't difficult.

"The creation of this subcommittee was to get to the bottom of what the government was doing, specifically the executive branch, without any input from Congress."

I saw "yes" nods from many, including some unpossessed congresspersons. That was a good start.

"The subcommittee needs full legislative authority. Today's 'yea' votes will do that. We all want to be accountable to the American people for our government's actions, and I believe that is true on every side of the aisle …"

I am starting to see more yes nods.

"We took the time to bring in the leader of this unofficial group— the 'Occult Strike Team' leader, Special Agent in Charge Robert Cho. And what did we learn? Nothing. He stood in contempt of Congress and refused to provide any details on these supposed 'aliens.' More- over, the FBI presented no physical evidence that these creatures existed at all."

I saw some incredulous looks and knew I needed to dissuade any thoughts of aliens being real.

"I want to show you all something—"

Motioning to the man controlling the sizable overhead projection screen, he dimmed the lights. The projector showed scene after scene of the visual evidence from phone recordings and voice recorders. By the time the video ended, the evidence was conclusive—aliens *did* exist and *had* attacked us.

The lights came back up.

"So, that is pretty compelling, no?" I asked.

There were many nodding heads, with the Freedom Party nodding "no," while almost everyone else nodded a confused "yes." They knew my feelings—that the "aliens" were a farce to cover up government incompetence of some kind.

"This evidence shows that aliens are, in fact, real," I said.

I deliberately paused, then motioned to a man in the audience.

"That is Doctor Charles McMillian. He is an expert in both computer science and artificial intelligence. Please, let's welcome the good doctor."

I applauded, and a few hesitant others also clapped. All of the Freedom Party members clapped enthusiastically.

"Please, Doctor, can you tell us more about the video we just watched?" I asked.

He already had a mic on so that all could hear him.

"Yes, first of all, everything you just saw is fake," he said.

There were audible gasps.

"I generated everything you just saw from input I gave to our proprietary AI—which is even better than the versions available to the public. The ability to cover up or create large-scale events with disinformation and deepfake videos is here. Today. You all just witnessed that."

"Thank you, Doctor, please be seated," I said.

"Now that I have your attention, it begets the next question. If we can prove what is fake, how can we prove what is real?"

Again, I waited.

"By investigation, of course. By compelling our government employees, the same ones running this illegal 'shadow organization,' to explain exactly what is occurring and what they are doing. SAC Cho—"

I motioned to him, as he was sitting in the audience, though he was not allowed to speak unless called by the committee.

"He has refused, under oath, to answer the committee's questions. He would not share any valuable information about the 'monsters' or even about the organization itself, including its purpose and activities.

When questioned, he claimed that everything was classified. Well, that's exactly what Congress inquired about—the classified information!"

I took a moment to get my composure. I was acting, of course.

"Who is on OST, where does it get its enormous extra funding, what weapons do they have, where is their office, what is their official charter, what reports have they submitted so we can know what they are actually doing?"

"Nothing!" I yelled.

"That is the answer we got. It is 'need to know,' and Congress doesn't have that need, even when questioning a government employee under oath. That needs to change today. All I'm asking is to make the subcommittee a full committee and to compel OST to explain to Congress what it is and what it is doing. And what it has *already* done. They won't even tell me why my daughter 'had' to be murdered ..."

I took a deep breath.

"Before we vote, I want you to know this *is* personal to me, not only as a patriot who wants Congress to have accountability but that the executive branch should as well. This OST group killed my daughter ..."

It's a bit of a stretch, but since Father Leighe is a CI now, that is technically accurate.

"And the vice president of the United States! They attacked and killed his entire Secret Service detail. They even used a fully automatic grenade launcher and a SEAL Team to destroy his residence."

I paused for effect.

"Do you think it is OK to keep letting them run amok unchecked? Let's immediately disband this dangerous entity. I think we should at least control that funding and know what we are sending that money to, don't you? We are being kept in the dark on purpose! The ascension to the full committee will give us that authority to investigate. Also, let's suppose POTUS wants to put out executive orders that provide OST full access to ALL government resources and absolve them of *any* criminal activity; what then?"

"Well, she already has!" I yelled emphatically.

"So, it is up to us to stop her! There is no agency in the entire government with that much power, and we can't even ask who they *are*? What are they *doing*? … Please, we all know this is too much power without oversight. That is all I'm asking. For me, you, the American people, and … and for my daughter …"

There was genuine clapping from most, along with a standing ovation from the Freedom Party and the (now fourteen) possessed congresspersons.

The projector came on again and showed all the damaging information on OST. The same information in the PowerPoint was in the packets that each congressperson was given before the first debate. It included every incident that had occurred since OST's inception.

"Alright, everyone, it is time. On the matter of the creation of the full 'Committee of Supernatural Affairs,' how do you vote?" asked Congressman DeMarcus.

After the usual and painfully slow process, the votes were tabulated.

Of the 429 voting members of Congress (6 of the 435 could not vote), most of the results were as expected, but a surprising number of the unpossessed favored the first bill independently.

The final tally was 301 yeas and 128 nays. The bill passed the House!

"Next up—the Laura Act. On the matter of passing the Laura Act, how do you vote?" asked Congressman DeMarcus.

It's the same slow, tedious bureaucratic process.

Final tally: 290 yeas and 139 nays.

All the possessed voted "Yea," while all but twenty of the unpossessed voted "Nay." So, my impassioned speech and the previous debate got us some additional "Yea" votes.

But that was enough.

We likely would have lost if it weren't for the congresspersons under Hellious's thrall. We needed 286 votes for each, not for the passage into law—we only needed half for that—but to secure the two-thirds necessary for the president's inevitable veto.

Now we had them.

The bill was on its way to the Senate. If only we controlled the Senate majority leader, we could fast-track it into law.

Oh wait, we do …

———

SAC Robert

I listened in awe as the votes were cast.

My awe was at our leadership's immense stupidity. Nowhere in today's vote or the preceding debates did anyone ask about the validity of the interviews and evidence the government *provided* them. They were shown one 'deepfake' video and now just assumed everything was false unless Congress investigated it.

I shook my head and had another antacid.

Part of me *hoped* they would "fire me" from OST. As a career federal employee, my pay would not change for at least two years, and even then, it would still be high. Besides, I was eligible to retire from the FBI in only two more years, anyway.

I sighed.

I knew I couldn't do it, even if they did dissolve OST. My country and its people needed me, not just as a leader but to keep them alive! I would not turn my back on my agents, either. Many had given their lives, and the others were putting theirs on the line. The least I could do was buffer them from this bureaucratic BS.

Oh well, back to work then.

It was time to fill in OST on the machinations of the highest levels of the US government. I'll fly back today and be in the office tomorrow to brief everyone.

For however long OST lasts.

CHAPTER 10
TEMPE

Luke Air Force Base—NW of Phoenix
Naval Operational Support Center—US Navy
Agent Lev

WHEN THE POLICE VACATED, the USAF loadmaster released the moorings on our car.

We knew the executive order wouldn't last, so we were on the clock. I hadn't slept much, but there was work to do. Being a SEAL (I consider myself one; I earned that) allowed me to stay up for days on a mission if I had to, and it looks like I must. After saying my goodbyes to the SEALs, who were returning to Virginia for another OP, they told me they hoped to see me again someday.

The other two teams on First Squad, Alpha and Charlie, were still in Virginia looking for more mass possessions, so our team was on its own—until we met up with the Second Squad, anyway.

Que sera, sera ...

I looked again at our Tesla, which was white this time.

I have always been told that white hides dirt better. I wonder what it will look like later?

As usual, Bob climbed into the passenger seat, and NMC agent

Anthony Bachman got in the back. The moorings were off the car, so I stepped on the brake, and it shifted into drive on its own.

Man, this thing is weird.

The C-130's cargo door was already fully open, so I carefully drove down the ramp into a mild late fall day in Phoenix.

Our first task was to connect with the other OSTs and discover what we could learn from our new CIs, which should be fun. Bob called Dave, the leader of the Second Squad, to arrange a meeting place.

"Make it a diner, Bob," I said.

"Hell yeah," said Anthony in the back.

"Meet us at a diner, Dave," Bob said into the phone.

A few minutes later, he hung up, and I entered the address Dave had given us into the Tesla's navigation system. It started routing us immediately.

We drove to a diner near ASU's campus, the Phoenix City Grill.

I backed into a parking spot in one of the back rows of the lot. We wanted to minimize looky-loos, so I deliberately double-parked as the lot was less than half full. Not in an obnoxious way, just with the tires on one side slightly over. That way, it looked like I was a lousy parker, not an A-hole.

Anthony stayed in the car. We would bring him a to-go order; that was always the deal.

Bob and I walked to the diner.

The weather was lovely—fall and winter bring down the temperature in the desert—and it was an overcast morning, which also helped. We looked for tails and any sign of surveillance, memorized the exits, looked for available cover, and watched windows and rooftops.

And that was just to go for breakfast.

The diner had a cute bell that dinged when the door opened. The patrons were used to the sound and ignored it, but the young woman at the check-in looked up. They already had Halloween decorations displayed; I had forgotten all about the holidays.

"Good morning, table for two?" she asked with a tired smile that changed to one of shock when she looked up at me.

"No, ma'am, we are meeting friends, thank you," I replied.

Ashen-faced, she nodded as Bob and I looked around.

We saw Dave and Steve at a big table. Next to them, a large, comfy corner booth was empty, but we never sit in booths because they are a deathtrap for the people on the inside. Trying to respond to an emergency is hard enough while sitting in a chair, much less having to slide out of a booth. No one else in the diner looked out of place. I could see the restrooms, the door to the kitchen, the door we entered, and one emergency exit.

So far, so good.

I thought about those sweet days before I was a cop and a soldier, back when I just came in and sat down without a care in the world. Dave saw us and waved. I waved back, and we went over.

As usual, people tried not to stare—and failed. Luckily, I was used to this by now.

Samantha's eyes widened in recognition as I sat down. Bob sat next to me.

"Oh wow, it's you!" she said.

"Yup, in the flesh. It's good to see you again, Samantha. I apologize we couldn't talk the last time I saw you; I really was quite busy …" I deadpanned when I said it.

There was a pause, and then she chuckled.

"Yeah, I did see that!" Samantha said.

I smiled.

"Well, now that you're 'read in' on OST, I can tell you—that was an amazing story; I admired your bravery and tenacity."

"Oh wow! Thank you! I rarely hear that from law enforcement when I do an 'expo' story."

"You tell the truth; that's what's important. It doesn't hurt how disturbingly accurate your reporting is; you're quite the journalist. Anyway, we had a little run-in at the VPOTUS residence, but what about you all …" I trailed off.

I wanted to know what she knew.

She gave me a knowing smile, chuckled, and responded to the unasked question—

"Yes, I'll answer your question on what we have learned. But first, VPOTUS is all over the news! So that was you?"

"Yes—Bob, I, and some SPEC OPS guys."

"Wow. The press is short on details, but massive explosions and gunfire aren't something they can cover up. The other news agencies are having a field day."

She had a bummed look, and I knew it bugged her not to be reporting on it.

"Don't worry; no one will be able to trump your story, especially when OST says it is officially verified."

Dave and Steve gave me "what the hell?" looks.

"Guys, we know she will have details she could only get from us. If she cites us as an on-the-record source, we get to fight the lies in Congress right now. (SAC Cho had just briefed us on events at the Capitol.) Besides, we all know she'll tell the whole truth, right, Samantha?"

"Hell, yes. And please, it's just Sammy to people I know."

I nodded.

"Oh, my manners—" Dave said, then continued, "This is Sammy and Harold, and Christos, Father Christos Leighe—"

"Former fugitive, now converted," Christos added with a charming smile.

"So ... VPOTUS?" Sammy asked.

"Turns out the Secret Service were all undead. They were waiting in ambush—"

"Hi, folks; who ordered the steak and eggs?"

I stopped mid-sentence as the waitress returned with the table's orders; they must have ordered before we arrived. After she finished putting down all the food and drinks, Bob and I placed our order. She turned and left, and I continued my tale.

They all quietly took in the news. Sammy ate like us SEALs—she wolfed down an omelet like nobody's business. Sammy put down her fork and swallowed.

"OK, so these things are 'undead'. They sound like vampires," Sammy said.

I nodded.

"Hmm, they *actually do*. The rotted insides, no blood, the ability to camouflage as 'normal' humans and then change into those things … Yeah, that does sound about right. But, from what we have read about vampires, they are supposed to be deathly allergic to sunlight. We know the Secret Service detail was operating in daylight the day after Agent Ellis said the team was attacked," I said.

Sammy perked up; I could see her in full "reporter mode".

"Any chance you can expound on that?" she asked.

"Of course. Sammy, you're part of the team now. Yes, we still must be careful what we say to regular civilians, but we all must share our intel if we want to stop this OI," I said.

I noticed she did not ask for clarification, so she already knew what OI stood for. That is good.

"SSA Ellis was the agent in charge of the VPOTUS detail and was worried it had been compromised; that is how we knew to go there. Looks like he was right. Also, if we fail against this OI, you won't need to worry about your story. No one will be alive to read it."

That cast a gloom over the table. Bob's and my food arrived, and we all quietly ate our meals and got refills of coffee.

Dave spoke first, "AAR on our end. Christos here is an exorcist. He has successfully exorcised many demons and even a devil—"

I didn't think anything could surprise me anymore; I was wrong. He saw the dumbfounded look on Bob's and my faces.

"Yes, those are real too and have been around *for centuries.* Christos's run-in with Laura, the congressman's daughter, allowed him to speak directly with our main OI monster. It didn't give a name but said it was not a demon or devil. Christos can confirm this—"

Christos saw Dave look at him and nodded; he knew he was being asked for a debrief.

"The monster that possessed her was brilliant; it knew things it should not know. For example, exorcists usually operate in pairs, and the monster already knew all about demons and devils. Additionally, holy water and garlic had no effect. Demons hate those things, and I believe vampires are supposed to as well," Christos said.

"From what we read, yes," I said.

"Exorcism and prayer had no effect. And when I killed Laura ..." Christos had a forlorn look when he said that. "When I killed her, the monster came out of her body as a reddish mist. The mist was impervious to anything I tried and left through the window's cracks. I never saw it again."

"OK, so we know what works and what doesn't on them. The main monster possesses the undead, and they can expand into an army of undead that can hide as normal humans. Am I missing any details for the report?" Dave asked.

"Doesn't sound like it. Glad this is another easy OI," Bob replied.

We all nodded and drank our coffee. Everyone was thinking hard about what to add. It wasn't just Sammy's story or Christos's innocence anymore. If we failed, we would all someday be one of them.

"OK, I'll send what we have. We can always add more later," Dave said, breaking the silence.

"Our current operation is this: we have eight of us OST now, or twelve with the NMCs, but they must guard the cars and equipment. Team Bravo is going to the police stations to see what they can get, and Charlie is doing the same at the ASU campus now. Charlie is going to have a harder time of it. Civilians are always worried about releasing anything sensitive without a warrant; litigation in America is killing us. So, I think our best bet is to surveil the sorority. Considering what Christos told me, combined with what you said about the entire detail being taken over, I think there is a high probability that the whole sorority is possessed."

We all nodded in affirmation.

"Well, I'm out on any tactical surveillance OP for obvious reasons. What are your orders, Dave?" I asked.

Dave thought for a minute.

"I'll have you, Bob, and Anthony be my new Delta Team. You'll be QRF for me and stay near campus. Research anything you can online or in the area, but be ready for a quick response when I call you," he said.

"Wilco," I said.

"Father … sorry—Christos, Sammy, and Harold—you're with Steve and me as Alpha Team. We are going to find one of these sorority sisters to capture. Perhaps we can extract some useful intel from one of them. Meanwhile, I've already asked the FBI to send a team to assist Charlie Team with tactical surveillance on the sorority at the school. They did a good job recruiting some of their younger agents. We are calling their team *21 Jump Street*. As soon as Charlie gives me a solitary sorority sister we can capture, we'll swoop in, and, um, well, technically, we'll kidnap her," Dave said.

Yeah, our ops get weird.

We knew our best chance at getting one of the sorority sisters alone was to capture her that night. We finished eating, paid the bill on Dave's G-card (government credit card), and were on our way.

Bob had booked us a two-bedroom suite at the Tempe Westin. That gave us a base of operations near the campus, and Bob and I needed to crash for a few hours. After checking in, he and I would sleep for a few hours while Anthony guarded the car. After Bob got up, he would switch out so Anthony could crash.

Our room was excellent; it had everything we needed, so I brought my overnight bag into the bedroom. While Bob waited in the living room, I went to take a shower. We always kept one person ready, just in case, especially with this enemy. It was probably hunting us as much as we were hunting it.

Putting my loaded Glock on the sink next to me, I turned on the water in the shower and climbed in. I didn't look to see how much was hot and cold, as neither fazed me in the least. I finished quickly, climbed out of the shower, and toweled dry. Throwing on my clothes, I put my holster into place with my Glock 18 in it.

This Glock was a remake of the old version because those were prized collector's items. That model was based on the original semiautomatic G17 from 1987. It could fire in either semi-auto or full-auto mode. Only a few thousand were produced.

Ours were almost identical to the original but with modern improvements.

The magazine was a standard 19-round magazine with one round in the chamber. We always keep one round in the chamber. However, 17, 24, 31, and 33-round magazines were also available. We maintained a 19-round magazine in the gun for concealability, and I had a belt of 33-round magazines that I would cinch tightly around my belly—six of those. In total, I had 218 rounds, which should get me through a firefight or two …

I also had my two Karambit knives on both sides of my waistband, so I could easily reach either. The G had made some upgrades; these were made of a super-strong acid-resistant carbon steel alloy. Much stronger than regular steel, and hopefully—if I went berserk again like I did when they killed James—the knives would survive my stabbing and slashing attacks. We also all wore a T-shirt designed to stop pistol rounds and knife attacks. It would still hurt, but hopefully not penetrate.

Now, I was ready for bed.

I came out and nodded at Bob, who then showered and got ready. When he finished and went to bed, I slept on the couch in the main room. I quickly drifted off …

Beep, beep, beep.

I had been asleep for four hours—plenty.

When I got up, I heard Bob's alarm as well. A couple of minutes later, he joined me in the main room, and then we waited. A few minutes after that, we received a text from Anthony; he had brought us all to-go food. Bob went down to switch places, and Anthony joined me in the room. We wolfed our food down, and then he took his turn cleaning up and sleeping.

While he was sleeping, I heard back from Dave, who had texted me to call him.

"Tanaka," he answered.

"Hey, Dave, SITREP?" I asked.

"One lives alone and off-campus in her parents' detached home. Her name is Dorothy Scranton; she is the sorority president. White female, 5'7", 130, twenty-one years old. Long blonde, brown eyes, and no visible markings—no tattoos, birthmarks, or other identifiable features. A face picture is on your phone. Her parents are out of town, a cat is the only pet, and *21 Jump Street* has the house under surveillance now. How do you want to play it?" Dave asked me.

"Meet there after 21 Jump says she is home; we'll park a couple of houses down and proceed on foot—you and Alpha from the rear, Delta from the front. I need someone from Alpha to cut the landline, so the alarm doesn't go off. I'll pick the lock, and then Bob will let you in; we'll be on her before she can scream—standard stealth grab and gag. We shut the doors and let Christos do his thing and go from there, depending on what happens. Alternate, she goes all vampy before I can get her secured, and we go lethal and take her out, then EVAC and try again later on another," I said deadpan.

"Damn, you're scary."

"So I have been told."

"OK then, that is the plan. Let's meet near West Greentree Drive and South Beck Avenue once she is home. That should be about the right spot. I'll call when 21 Jump says she is in for the night."

"Copy, out," I said.

Dave hung up.

I sat at my computer while Anthony slept, learning all I could about vampires and the undead.

———

An hour later, Dave sent another text: "Change of plans. We're meeting you in your room. Be there at 2100."

I replied with a thumbs-up emoji.

Interesting.

At 2100, Dave came into the room. He was carrying a case of ammo. Although it was a plain box, I recognized its shape and weight.

"Merry Christmas," Dave said.

He plopped it down on the table with a thump.

"These are wood-core 9mm rounds for the Glocks," he continued.

"Never been tested—"

We opened the case; twenty boxes were inside, with fifty rounds each. A thousand rounds.

"Yeah, I asked for rounds for us, and he had them make a case of them! I owe Alan a drink!" Dave said, smiling.

"You and I both …" I mumbled as I inspected one of the rounds. It looked like a normal FMJ (full metal jacket) round, but the tip was serrated so that they couldn't be confused with standard rounds.

"He said they used rosewood with a thin ceramic coating instead of lead. The metal jacketing is normal but serrated to break apart on impact. So, you'll get normal bullet mushrooming, and the wood will go in as a solid bullet, then break into six pieces," he said.

"Even if it does nothing special, it'll still work as a lethal round, just like our Hydra-Shok bullets. I would love to see the coroner's face when he finds these bullets, though …" Dave finished.

We all nodded our approval. Then we started stripping and loading magazines—not all of them, but a few each, including the ones in the guns. I hoped they worked; we would know soon enough …

———

The Scranton Residence—Tempe

Dorothy was not a poor young woman.

The expensive three-story mansion she lived in may belong to her parents, but she never had to worry about money. We had taken a deep dive into her financials. At only twenty-one years old, she was worth six figures and had an 805 credit score. Her father paid all her bills on time. She drove a two-year-old Porsche 911 Turbo S, which was currently mostly in the driveway.

She had gotten home at 2150 and walked inside. The car was parked partially on the grass, and the surveillance team stated she appeared intoxicated as she went inside. They gave us the go-ahead to proceed. We got there in ten minutes and parked two houses down as planned. So far, so good.

"Delta Team, the front, Alpha, the rear. Delta secures the target after letting us in. The current time is … 2208. Entry positions and go on when Delta has the front door open. Questions?" Dave asked.

A short pause.

"OK, let's move."

We were already near the residence, so we were at the house in only a minute or two. Bob watched for anyone coming while I picked the lock. Just one more skill I can thank the SEALs for. As soon as I had the door unlocked, I quickly had a stun gun in one hand and flex cuffs in the other, with a roll of duct tape in my jacket pocket. I double-clicked my mic, and we went in. Bob scanned for threats as he went to the back door to get the other team. After letting them in, they all cleared the ground floor. While they were doing this, I waited by the grand staircase that led to the bedrooms upstairs, where Dorothy's light was on. *21 Jump Street* was still giving us operational details as they were still on the scene. I sensed something near me …

Turning, I saw something black with a bristled tail straight in the air; it was their cat. It hissed at me and ran like hell.

Sigh. Does any animal like me? … At least Frank does.

We crept up the stairs; I went first, then Bob. The others stayed below.

As we reached the top, we could hear soft music coming from her room. I slowly approached her open door. Bob got on the other side. He mouthed, "Three, two, one …"

We rushed in.

"AHH!" she screamed.

I forget how terrifying I am at full speed—or just in general.

Sprinting forward, I hit her with the stun gun and then dropped it. As she stiffened up, I pulled her wrists behind her and flex-cuffed them, then I spun the tape around her head with astonishing speed, bagged it so she couldn't see, and tossed her into a chair.

It was as if an angry six-foot-one spider had hit her.

Now that she was secure, I taped her to the chair. She was too terrified to resist. Then, I added two sets of metal cuffs to her wrists. Hopefully, unlike our last OP with flex cuffs, the metal ones could keep her secure if she changed …

Speaking of, something is wrong. Why didn't she go all vampy on us?

"Alpha, target is secure; come on up," I said into the radio.

A few moments later, everyone was upstairs. Bob stayed by the stairs to look down, and Steve stayed with him. Christos, Sammy, Harold, and Dave joined me in the room. I didn't have to tell Sammy and Harold to stay back; they already were.

Harold was filming, though.

Whatever.

"Christos, do your thing," Dave said.

He had some weird items with him, and he poured white powder in a circle around her. Dave and I backed up at an "L" and covered Dorothy. We had both seen what these things could do, starting with snapping flex cuffs.

Christos took the bag off her head.

A beautiful but scared-out-of-her-mind twenty-one-year-old woman looked at us, her eyes wide in fear. She had been crying and appeared intoxicated, but did not smell of booze.

Hmmm.

Christos came forward and moved another chair in front of her.

"I'm going to take off this gag so we can talk. Can you promise not to scream so my friends don't have to stun you again?" he asked.

She nodded yes.

He glanced in my direction. I stepped forward, took the medical shears from my pouch, and gently cut the tape. She cried out again as I removed the tape.

"Sorry, Dorothy. We had to protect ourselves," I said.

She nodded again as Father Leighe took over, tears streaming down her face.

"Dorothy, let me start by describing what we know and then ask you questions. Is that OK?"

"Y-yes," she stammered.

She was visibly terrified.

"Dorothy, the reason you're secured to a chair now is not because we came to kill you; I hope that is obvious—"

She relaxed a little.

"But, we need to stop this monster that has you in its thrall. Out of curiosity, am I still talking to Dorothy?"

She looked confused at first and then realized what he meant.

"Ye… (Burp)"—BLAHH!

She turned her head and vomited all over the floor; I noticed it didn't even faze any of us, as we were used to so much worse. Christos produced a handkerchief and said to her, "May I?"

"Yes," she replied.

He wiped her face.

"Thank you," she said.

"How are you not possessed right now?" Christos asked.

"I found out how to keep it at bay," she said.

None of us could hide our astonishment.

What miracle had she found?

"That is wonderful news, child! How?" Christos asked.

"Well, this feels like a living nightmare. That made me think of a fellow sorority sister whose boyfriend suffers from severe PTSD after serving in Afghanistan. He manages his nightmares by taking Prazosin. So, I got a bottle from him and started taking it. The monster did not like that and was trying to get control, so I took more. I told my parents that something bad had happened during our sorority initiation, and I was having nightmares. They assumed I had been raped …"

She shuddered at some horrible memory, then continued.

"I saw a doctor and got a higher dosage prescribed. Since then, I have been in a daze, but the monster is at bay. It doesn't bother me anymore, but I can feel it is still inside me."

She looked miserable. Father Leighe looked at us, and we nodded.

"Would you be willing to come with us? We don't want to hurt you; we want to stop this thing and get it out of you."

"Yes! Anything to get rid of this monster!" she said quickly.

We took off the cuffs and tape, and she stood up unsteadily.

"How much are you taking?" Christos asked.

"Three milligrams, about three times the norm," she said.

"Well, that is not too bad—" Christos started to say.

"Six times a day," she added.

"Is that what is recommended?"

"It is supposed to be once a day, at night, but I keep having to up the dose to keep it away," she said.

Oh wow. No wonder she seemed drunk.

"We are going to cuff you at the front this time. Do you understand why?" I asked her.

"I do."

She put her hands in front as I ran a metal KryptoFlex bicycle lock cable around her waist. Then, I put the two sets of metal cuffs on her wrists through the cable. Now, if she did go all vampy on us, we would have time to react.

Alpha Team did an intel sweep of the house while Christos asked her more questions, and we also took her laptop and phone.

After securing the house with her key, we left it as if we had never been there. The MCC had done their investigations and determined that her parents were in Amsterdam. Their tickets and accommodations showed they weren't scheduled to fly back for six more days, so we had time before she became a missing person.

We drove straight to St. Mary's Basilica, where Christos could set up everything he needed without outside interference.

After midnight, I finally texted a full report to ASAC Chayton at DENFO.

We finally had a "live" captured enemy.

———

US Capitol—Washington, DC
Senate Floor—Opening Debate
Congressman Halston

Although I did not hold a voting position in the Senate, I was invited to speak during the debates, and I gladly accepted the invitation. After all the usual formalities were observed, I approached the podium.

The Senate chamber is expansive, measuring 114 feet long and 80 feet wide, which makes it an impressive space. A balcony on the second floor overlooks the chamber below. The thirty-six-foot ceilings evoke the legislative halls of the nineteenth century.

I tapped the mic on the podium.

TAP, TAP.

PA is working.

I cleared my throat and began my speech.

"Do we trust the executive branch to do the right thing without oversight?" I asked.

"How about 9/11? Several FBI agents alerted their agency that foreign agents were learning to fly commercial aircraft ..."

I don't know if this is actually true, but it's not like that matters, anyway.

"They didn't have any interest in takeoffs or landings, however. Even without 20/20 hindsight, any idiot could see what they were learning it for. But the FBI, overall as an agency, was dumber than an idiot. Yes, I said it ... Now, the executive branch says there is an existential alien threat, sorry, correction *threats—plural,* that could not only devastate our country but destroy all of humanity?"

I paused.

"So, what was their answer? To come to Congress with evidence, like they did after the towers came down on 9/11? No, they did not. When that happened, we came together, all of us in the legislative branch, and created a gigantic new entity—the Department of Homeland Security ... We have mitigated that threat with hundreds of billions of dollars and millions of people. So, if there really are aliens here to destroy humanity, shouldn't the whole government be involved? Just like we were then when it was 'only' terrorists attacking?"

I let that sink in.

"I say this to you now, Democrat or Republican, we must have a complete and *unimpeded* bipartisan investigation into what the FBI and its OST division claim has occurred and what they know. According to them, it is also happening ... right ... now ... So, do we run in the dark with a tiny unsupervised group, or do we bring the truth into the light and create a whole department to combat it? If it is as dangerous as they say, we need Congress involved to address it with proper funding. Funding that ends with a big 'B' for billions of dollars. I don't know about you, but it sounds sketchy to me. I think there is a much higher chance they are up to something more sinister, like Iran-Contra, than that actual *aliens* exist. Either way, though, we must find out!"

I took a breath.

"This law will allow for the full investigation of OST and their activities and stop the FBI from having its own 'off-the-books' Gestapo! Vote yes … For your country and the protection of our citizens, for the involvement of the legislature, as a check on executive power, and for my daughter, Laura."

With that, I stepped away from the podium to great applause.

CHAPTER 11
OST DENFO

OST—Denver Field Office (DENFO)
Agent James

I HAD JUST FINISHED the Multiple Weapons Training Program at FLETC and arrived back in Denver. As usual, a blacked-out Suburban met me. This time, NMC Agent Harold Palmer picked me up.

We had all heard of Agent Lev's and OST's exploits with our newest OI. Reading up on the latest events, I realized what we were up against—a monster that could possess people.

People, plural.

That is terrifying.

Add in the damage to Lev, and I felt sick.

When she called to say she was OK early this morning, she did not tell me the extent of her injuries, not really. Now, her team had gone to Phoenix to join up with Second Squad in the OI investigation there.

That made me feel even more useless as we arrived at OST DENFO.

We entered the garage sally port, and, as usual, when the two doors were shut, two NMCs and a K-9 emerged.

The K-9 was Frank, though!

He had reached the point where he and Sampson, the original K-9, could take turns on duty. Sampson had finally gotten over his fear of Frank, Lev, and me; he was still visibly cautious, but now he could work with us without fear. During the OI, though, they wanted Frank there full-time instead of Sampson.

We parked, and after a pat on Frank's head, I headed straight to Chayton's office. His door was open, as usual. I knocked and entered when he looked up.

"Hey, boss," I said.

"Good morning, James," ASAC Chayton Blackwell said.

"You do know what I'm going to say," I said simply.

"Yup, and the answer is no. You're currently on training reserve and assigned to OST headquarters. Plus, we have *four* teams on the ground there now. We need you here to assist our QRF Squad—Third Squad—until you rotate back into Fifth Squad," Chayton said.

He saw my displeased look.

"Hey, I know the agreement, but Lev can handle herself, and I need you here. Honestly, James, I do. We don't know how many people this thing has gotten to or where. So, we need bodies in reserve in a bad way. Stay ready, James. We'll be in the fray soon enough, I'm sure. Besides, the SAC will return from DC this evening and wants to brief everyone tomorrow morning."

I was dismissed. I knew the look.

"You got it, boss. I'm with the government, I'm here to help."

We both chuckled, and I walked out.

Although I was still annoyed, Chayton was right. Twelve OST agents, including Lev and the NMCs, did not need little ole' James to help them—I think they can manage without me. But it still sucks not to be in the field with her. So, instead, I went to read up on what they had found. Maybe I could learn more about this new monster …

"Hey, James," Agent Michelle Newman said, looking up from her chair.

I had just come into the MWR room to work on my laptop. It was a relaxing room, but most of us used it primarily to catch up on our research and learning.

"Hi, Michelle," I replied.

She smiled and returned to work, her nose down to the computer. We both worked in silence. Michelle was in Third Squad, which had just arrived this morning to replace Fourth Squad on QRF. At least they had enjoyed a few days away from the office before coming in. During any OI, everyone is on duty. Fourth Squad was now on standby but not in the office, while Fifth Squad was away at various training courses. There were not enough dorm rooms to accommodate all agents here 24/7, but no leave or days off were granted during an OI. All agents had to abstain from alcohol and be ready at a moment's notice. That was the policy. However, it did result in a lot of overtime pay.

The nice thing about "regular" training courses at FLETC is the weekends off. Unless something unusual happens, most agents get at least one or two days off a week. So, I had been enjoying working "only" fifty hours a week.

I got up to stretch just as Frank wandered in.

Frank came over and let me pet him, then he bumped my leg and barked.

"Crap," I said.

Michelle laughed.

"Exactly!" she said.

I sighed and tapped my leg; Frank followed with his tail wagging. We were off to the mega-poop Olympics—

And Frank always took the Gold!

———

After a long afternoon and evening of reading and research, it was getting late. I had read up on everything that had transpired with the OI until now, but now I was reading "for fun". I yawned and stretched, and my copy of "Beast with a Thousand Young" fell to the floor. It was based on an esoteric Greek legend and did not look like it would have a happy ending …

Michelle looked up.

"Time to call it?" she asked.

"Yeah, I just reread the same page; I'm all done," I said.

She smiled.

I liked Michelle. In addition to being a great agent, she was pleasant to talk to. It was nice having time to get to know my fellow agents on QRF status. She shut her book as well.

"Yeah, me too," she said, yawning.

We walked back to QUARTERS together.

"See you tomorrow, Michelle," I said.

She gave me a mock salute and continued to her room as I went into my 150-square-foot dorm and shut the door. It was time to crash.

I took a shower before bed. We all did that; there was no cleaning service except at the end of the week before the next squad came in, so you wanted to keep your sheets clean. Then I brushed my teeth and climbed into bed. My pillow felt incredible as I dozed off …

Knock, Knock.

I slammed awake, and looking at the LED clock, I saw it was one a.m. Throwing on my pants and a shirt, I said, "Hold on a sec!"

Goddammit, this better be good …

I opened the door, and it was Michelle; I could see she had been crying.

"Michelle, are you OK?" I asked.

She nodded no and motioned to come in, so I stepped aside and let her in.

"What is going on?"

"My husband just said he is filing for divorce," she was almost sobbing.

As she moved to hug me, I let her. I knew it wasn't a sexual thing, as everyone knew about Lev and me. Plus, you would have to be insane to piss her off …

Michelle was crying as she put her head on my shoulder. Then she grabbed hold tight.

Too tight.

"Michelle—" I started to say.

Feeling her hug become overwhelmingly strong, I pushed her away from me firmly.

Something was happening!

I was only able to push her back a couple of feet, and she was just … staring at me. I don't know if I'm as strong as Lev, but I'm stronger than any ordinary human. If I weren't—

"I'm so (sniff) sorry," she said, with a look of complete remorse.

She looked genuinely sorry. Then her expression changed instantly, and I saw her eyes glinting in hunger. Her mouth spread open inhumanly wide, and hundreds of sharp teeth were exposed—

Oh … crap.

I don't sleep with my gun on me in the dorm room; none of us did. They were placed in the biometric safes in our closets. Besides, NMC provided office security, and they never went anywhere in the office without their MP5s

Michelle knew this. So, too, must the thing that possessed her.

I lunged for the closet.

Even with my ultrafast reflexes, she tackled me on the way there. We tumbled onto the floor, hitting the closet door and breaking it. She sank her sharp talons into my torso as I spun to face her; blood shot out of me. Luckily, I was already in combat mode, so I wouldn't feel it until after the fight.

If I lived.

She lunged forward to bite my groin, but I spun and felt a massive bite to my leg instead. The pain was incredible, but then it started feeling good, and I didn't want it to stop. Suddenly, I thought about Lev and knew what she would want me to do—

She would want me to kill this thing.

I rocked my torso forward, almost to the floor, and then spun back with a punishing elbow to her head. Black liquid "blood" sprayed from her mouth as she was knocked off me. I pushed myself up as she lunged at me again.

This time, I used judo—specifically, the tomoe-nage "sacrifice" throw.

I grabbed her sweatshirt as she came straight at me. Dropping to the floor backward, I put my foot in her stomach with my knee bent. Her razor-sharp teeth were coming straight for my face. I don't know if she was smiling because she thought I had fallen backward by accident or if that was just how a foot-long mouth with a hundred teeth looks. Either way, she thought I was done for. As she came in toward me and I fell onto the ground, I pistoned my leg outward as I went back.

She flipped over me and crashed into the already destroyed closet.

Shooting to my feet, I spun to face her as she got up. My flying knee to her face smashed her *into* the drywall at the back of the closet, knocking out several more of those deadly teeth of hers.

"MOVE!" I heard a man yell.

I jumped sideways toward the safe.

BANG, BANG, BANG!

Michelle took six shots to the torso from Chayton's pistol. As she was being hit, I put my hand into the biometrics of the safe. It popped open, and I grabbed my Glock.

Michelle, or what *was* Michelle, was recovering. She had black goo all over her from my strikes and Chayton's bullets. As she lunged at me, I brought my gun close to my body. We had all trained to use guns in Close Quarters Battle (CQB), so even as she was trying to grab me, I was putting rounds into her.

BANG! BANG!

She tackled me again.

Dropping my weapon, I grabbed her arm and spun. Unless this monster had studied MMA, I knew I was a better ground fighter than Michelle.

Let's just hope that is all the monster has available to it, I thought, as I spun over her and onto her side. I was on my back with Michelle in an armbar. My left foot clamped on her torso, my right on her head, and both legs squeezed. I knew if my right leg didn't stay tight, she could turn her head and bite it off.

Seeing motion, I saw Chayton put the barrel of his gun a few inches from her head and empty the rest of his magazine into it. She went limp in my grasp.

Michelle was dead.

In combat, you don't just get "tunnel vision," you also get "auditory exclusion." Just like you miss things peripherally when having tunnel vision, sound becomes distorted and different. You barely hear loud things and may not even notice them, but now I do.

The building's intrusion alarms were going off.

Chayton reloaded and yelled out, "ARMOURY!"

Grabbing my extra mags from the safe, I caught up to Chayton as we got to ARMOURY. There was a monster that used to be Joshua Butler standing between us and the door to go in. It had that inhuman smile—a smile that held chunks of human flesh, and his whole front side was covered in blood. It had several GSWs visible on its body.

As it charged us, Chayton and I both took a knee. We started firing precise shots into its head.

BANG, BANG … BANG, BANG … BANG, BANG!

It finally dropped—the destruction of the brain area seems to work once again.

The same as with the SIM creatures from our first OI.

We ran forward, and I covered Chayton as he started all the security checks to get in. The door swung open, and we ran inside, shutting it behind us.

———

Regrettably, we had no way of knowing who in the office remained human, so it was only Chayton and I for the time being. As we donned the ExoM suits and began to collect weapons, no words needed to be exchanged. Still, I was simply relieved to be wearing boots instead of being barefoot.

I glanced at the heavy weapons section and saw what I would use. The Navy SEALs had perfected a specific weapon for this situation.

Well, maybe not *this* situation, but a similar one.

The M32A1 40mm MSGL (multi-shot grenade launcher). It held six either medium-velocity (MV) or low-velocity (LV) grenades.

The SEALs found that more and more of their enemies wore body armor. As high-explosive rounds could not be used at close ranges or near friendlies, they were of limited use inside buildings or when friendlies were near the target. Their solution was something that could only come from the twisted mind of a Navy SEAL.

Low-velocity, low-explosive rounds (LVLE).

The standard high-explosive dual-purpose (HEDP) rounds, such as the ones in Lev's Mark 19 GMG, were high-velocity and did not arm until they spun the firing pin into position, anywhere between fifteen to twenty meters.

These bad boys, however, are armed right after leaving the barrel, in only one to two meters.

Combat experience has shown that at point-blank distances (under ten meters), the low-velocity rounds (traveling only 250 fps) would still penetrate the sternum, spin, and stop against the spine or, missing that, exit just out the back. It is lethal for the person hit, even when it doesn't explode. Working off that, they redesigned the standard grenade rounds to have a tiny amount of explosive at the core surrounded by dozens of .32 Cal buckshot. When it hit, the grenade penetrated and exploded, firing the buckshot 360 degrees around it like a mini-grenade.

The grenade and shrapnel would usually stay *inside* the target, perfect one-shot kills while limiting the damage around it.

In fact, even on a miss, the buckshot pellets were low enough velocity that standard body armor could stop them—unless the grenade stuck into the armor and exploded, in which case it had enough force to send frag through soft body armor.

We also grabbed our FN SCAR rifles, loaded the grenade launchers with the LVLE rounds, and then loaded the MSGLs with the same rounds. Lastly, we each grabbed a bandolier of LVLE grenades for our launchers.

We could hear the monsters outside trying to get in.

Although we would be safe here until reinforcements arrived, that is not how things work. We would kill as many monsters as possible and try to save any remaining agents. Considering the sporadic gunfire, some of them were still alive and fighting.

I lined up the MSGL at the door, and Chayton put up three fingers as he reached for the door release.

3 … 2 … 1 … Click

The door swung open to a nightmare.

Three monsters, who used to be agents Jim DeSantos, Elizabeth Sato, and William Durst, were waiting. All three started to rush in.

BURP!

I shot DeSantos first, hitting him high in the chest, and swung my aim to Sato. As I fired into Sato, the grenade inside DeSantos exploded.

BOOM!

His chest burst like a balloon, spraying black gunk everywhere.

CRACK … THUMP!

His head had launched into the ceiling and then fallen to the floor. That is normal for suicide bombers with explosive vests. I had seen that in CCTV videos of suicide bomber attacks, but this is the first time that I have seen it in real life. And to a friend, one that I shot.

BOOM!

Sato went down like a baby "alien" had blown out of her chest.

BURP!

I was switching to the last target, Durst, when Chayton's rifle/GL combo fired a grenade into him; I fired again anyway.

BURP!

BOOM! … BOOM!

When Durst exploded, he violently twisted to one side and then the other as the two grenades went off. Limbs went flying in a spray of black gore, and he fell to join the ruptured bodies of Sato and DeSantos. In the sudden silence, black specs were floating down, along with smoke hanging in the air. Body parts and burst-open bodies lay at our feet. Their insides were black and looked desiccated, and it looked like the organs had been dead for a long time.

"Undead, you think?" Chayton asked.

"Yeah, I think so," I replied.

I covered Chayton as he reloaded, and then I did as well. We exited ARMOURY and shut the door behind us. Then, we moved as a team through the office. Chayton also switched to having the MSGL in his hands.

BBBBBBBBANG!

The front entry vestibule machine guns were firing.

Chayton and I picked up our pace and headed for the front of the office. At least one NMC agent was alive and operating the guns.

BRRRRRRAP! BRRRRRRAP!

We came around the corner and saw NMC agent Jason Harris firing into one of the undead. Behind him, Harold Palmer was at the Oscar station, lighting up whatever was in the pedestrian sally port.

Chayton and I fired into the monster in unison.

BURP! BURP!

Jason dove to the ground and covered his head, believing we had lost our minds. He did not realize we were using LVLE rounds.

BOOM! BOOM!

Chunks of what was once NMC agent Tom Hussain now decorated the entry vestibule.

"CS has no effect! Switching to FAE!" Palmer yelled.

FAE stands for Fuel Air Explosive. We heard a loud hiss and then a snap—that was the igniter.

KA-BOOM!

The vestibule door from the sally port flew off its hinges, smashed into the opposite wall, and penetrated the drywall; a fireball followed it.

Luckily, we were not near it as it went up.

A horrible stench filled the air from the incinerated undead bodies within as the fire alarm and sprinklers started.

"Reloading," Chayton said. He finished and then palmed a grenade from his ExoM suit. It was a high-explosive concussion grenade.

"Ready with a grenade!" he yelled to us.

The machine guns in the port had been destroyed in the explosion, so Jason and Harold joined us to aim through the now wide-open sally port into the darkness of the night. Staying to the edges for cover, we could hear more of them moving outside. A lot more of them …

OST DENFO—Mission Control Center (MCC)
Agent Alan Loftus

It was 0100, and all was quiet.

I had been brevetted to the acting supervisor role for the MCC: same pay, extra responsibility.

Lucky me.

At least Frank had joined us. He was sleeping soundly near my workstation in the MCC. Everyone in the office had placed comfy beds in our various work areas. We had all made a game of seeing where Frank chose to hang out or where he decided to sleep. For weeks, an elaborate contest of who could provide the best affection and the comfiest bed—to lure in Frank—had been underway.

I held the upper hand, however.

Frank's favorite chew toy was a simple piece of rebar. I found it outside while taking a walk, where a white curb had been damaged. The foot-long chunk of metal was just lying there. I picked it up more as a joke, but Frank loved sharpening his teeth on it. He would contentedly chew on it for hours; it also served as his "fetch" stick. That dog was scary.

We all liked teaching him new tricks; Frank was brilliant. He had already mastered opening doors, finding any dropped food, and being around whoever gave him the most affection and treats.

He also played "patty-cake" with Elizabeth Sato (don't ask), "jump over the parked car" with Ed Baker, and "over the hedge" leaping fetch with Ruby Clarke, who was working with me tonight in the MCC. So far, he had cleared over forty feet on a running jump.

He was currently crashed out on his comfy bed here in the MCC; I looked at him with unbridled jealousy.

Ruby and I had gotten the coveted graveyard shift; lucky us.

Even though most supervisors worked Monday to Friday on day shifts, enjoying holidays, weekends, and snow days off, the regular agents worked around the clock, come hell or high water. As a temp supervisor, I didn't place myself above my troops in that way. Therefore, I took my turn handling the undesirable shifts and duties.

(Sigh.)

Beep, beep, beep …

I heard a timer go off on Ruby's watch.

"Dentist's appointment? Do you need me to cover for you?" I asked, smiling.

She turned to me and smiled.

"Funny but also ironic," she said.

"How so?"

She got up and walked over to me; I saw Frank snap awake and jump to his feet. He was growling in that scary SIM way.

"Speaking of teeth—" she said.

I watched in horror as her features changed.

Her eyes glinted inhumanly, and her smile stretched and stretched, revealing hundreds of sharp teeth; her nails grew into three-inch-long claws, and she lunged at me inhumanly fast. I barely had time to put up my hands, and then—

She was gone.

Frank had hit her full force and speed, knocking Ruby to the ground. He bit down hard on her skull.

CRUNCH!

Black goo sprayed out as she struggled, driving her talons into Frank's body. He made an even angrier and louder SIM growl and shook his head violently.

CRUNCH, CRACK, CRACK—POP!

Frank came over to me with his tail wagging! He had a new toy …

Ruby's head.

I realized, in terror, what I was witnessing—a colleague possessed by the new OI. I didn't need to be a math wizard (even though I was) to figure it out. I sprinted toward the door controls. Next to the ARMOURY, the MCC boasted the highest security and the most formidable doors.

I flipped the door switch to lock it, and a red light appeared over the door.

Only seconds later, someone (or some*thing*) violently tried to open the door. I heard muffled gunshots outside the door, somewhere in the building, as I hit the office intrusion alarm.

———

OST DENFO—Garage Entrance
Agent Edward "Ed" Baker

I'm one of the original NMC agents who fought in Bolsa Chica Beach, but right now, my job is fighting the Z-monster and boredom. I know someone has to take the graveyard shifts, and it was my turn.

I yawned loudly.

Sophie West had just returned from taking her "lunch," and I had to pee. Backing up my chair, I stood up, and she took my place. Wandering to the bathroom, I stepped up to the urinal. The relief was bliss.

"Ah, that's better," I said to myself.

As I pulled up my zipper, I heard the intrusion alarm going off. If I had been new, I might have thought, *false alarm.* But knowing we were in the midst of another OI, I realized it was likely for real. Besides, the intrusion alarm produced a specific noise, indicating that enemies were *inside* the building. Before it could be activated, a plastic cover in the MCC had to be flipped up. No "accidents" could trigger that, especially at one in the morning.

I brought up my MP5 before even leaving the bathroom, and it was a good thing I did. Sophie was coming into the bathroom, only it wasn't Sophie. She looked like some kind of demented vampire with more teeth than I could count.

She started to say something—

BRRRRRRRRRRRRRRAP-Click

She dropped to the ground dead, as I had put thirty rounds from her sternum to her skull.

"Wrong bathroom," I said to her corpse as I went by.

Reloading as I went, I came out of the bathroom. I could see the inner garage door was wide open, and I glanced at the camera's screen. Even at this distance, it looked like about a dozen of her pals were already through the sally port and heading into the GARAGE BAY.

I could never get there in time.

Luckily, I had another idea. As it was much closer to me than them, I sprinted for the MX and opened the driver's door just as the horde of vamps made it inside. They saw me.

I jumped in, hit the brake, and the driver's door shut automatically. The vehicle was now on. Flipping open the cover and pressing the fire control button, I felt cool air start blasting from the HVAC as "bio-defense mode" activated—along with the machine guns.

The rear tailgate and Falcon-wing doors opened as the Gatling guns emerged on their mounts. Gun two was the .50 Cal. It faced the rear, so it was useless unless I wanted to fire into the wall behind me. The right-side machine gun, an M134 Gatling gun, had an unobstructed angle of fire, however.

The first ones were almost to me.

BZZZZZZ! BZZZZZZ!

Whatever they were, they were no longer a threat.

I hit the ones closest to the gun first, then the ones about to get into the LOBBY, and last were the poor suckers in the middle. Some headed for the EXIT again, some the LOBBY, and the rest charged me.

All met the same fate.

The sound of links and shell casings clinking on concrete could have been heard if I weren't almost deaf from firing hundreds of rounds from the machine guns while inside a garage. Luckily, the BD Mode had come on when the weapons were activated, as the GARAGE BAY was now filled with smoke and black entrails from the undead things. One had gotten to cover and was hiding behind one of the Suburbans. The Suburban was between me and it, and the undead must still know our training. It must be behind one of the wheels, because I couldn't see its feet.

I floored it, and the tires fought for traction on the concrete floor— SQUEEEL!

The monster looked startled as my MX passed by; its cover only worked if I stayed still. As it began to run, I released the steering yoke and grabbed the aiming joystick.

BZZZZZZ!

A bunch of rounds missed, peppering the concrete wall behind it. The rest blew it into chunks.

Were there any monsters I missed? I didn't see any.

F— it, let's bring the fight to them.

Accelerating again, I caught the new ones coming into the bay flat-footed. As I nosed into the bay, I grabbed the joystick again. There was a loud racket as my "windshield" was starred from bullets hitting it. Thank God for good armor, but the sustained fire would eventually get through.

Both Gatling guns, Guns One and Three, are automatically synchronized according to the target's location. Anyone standing in front of the MX is bound to have a bad day.

And they are directly to the front.

The two M134s put out a combined four to twelve *thousand* rounds per minute.

BZZZZZZ! BZZZZZZ!

In less than a second, the sally port was clear.

Although I wanted to take the fight to them, my priority was securing this entrance, so I backed up slightly and got the perfect angle on the door. It could be shut now, and the monsters couldn't get by me before I shot them. Effectively, the MX was the new sally port defense.

I could get out and hit the switch to shut the doors, assuming the MCC hadn't disabled them, but I wasn't going to leave the MX to do it. These things were too fast.

Patiently, I waited, knowing they would eventually hope I was gone or going for the controls and venture in again.

I was not disappointed.

———

OST DENFO—Pedestrian Entrance
SSA Daniel (Undead)

Damn it!

We had not secured the sally ports, and now defenders were guarding both entrances. It sounds like they had Gatling guns defending the garage, which meant the MX. We were not getting by that.

Our only chance was the pedestrian entrance. If the MCC had been taken, all the doors would have been open, and the guns would have been offline.

How, in the hell, did they react that fast at one in the morning?

I sent everyone to flood the pedestrian entrance, except for a few at the back to ensure the MX stayed in place. The last thing we needed was that thing in the open shooting at us. Once everyone knew the plan, I did what terrible leaders do best—I ran away to save myself. Not because I was a coward, but because I had intel that Hellious still needed.

Besides, no matter how it all turned out, we won this battle.

We had turned their office into a war zone, and I had sent an email to every news agency I could think of at precisely 0100 hours. The email also mentioned that an unknown number of assailants would be attacking OST DENFO with heavy weaponry to "exact revenge for Laura and other Americans killed at the hands of OST."

I thought that was a nice touch.

So, their base was now public knowledge; they undoubtedly had lost agents in the battle, and I still could guide Hellious. Congressman Halston was going to have a field day with this!

Smiling, I put my Corvette into drive and pulled away, not in a cloud of tire smoke, but gently and at the speed limit …

OST DENFO—Pedestrian Entrance
ASAC Chayton

I got on my police radio.

"All responding units, be advised: Dozens of undead that can look human are attacking DENFO with small arms; they also have flash-bang grenades. Do not try to arrest them; they are deadly with their claws. We are all inside. Any person outside is considered a probable hostile. We'll shoot anyone, including you, who attempts to enter the building. Please respond."

One by one, units called in, saying, "Copy."

The MX in the back and our team at the front picked off a few more in the next few minutes. Jason went down from a bullet to the chest and one to the arm. The armor took it, but his arm was still pretty messed up. Otherwise, we didn't lose any more agents.

The next hour was a blur.

There weren't enough chewable antacids in the world for when SAC Cho found out.

We also kept our promise not to let anyone in. One intrepid (and stupid) reporter tried to enter through the pedestrian sally port, but we fired some rounds into the ground near him, which took care of that.

Once Fourth Squad arrived (they had been called with the "STAT" on their phones), we used a simple system to test them. We stuck them with a syringe and drew out a few cc's of blood—they all passed. Besides, whatever this OI was, it was clever. It would not be sending more undead at this point.

Now that we were back up to strength, we closed the GARAGE BAY sally port, and the MX came to the front to guard the pedestrian entrance. SAC Cho was on the way also.

This was bad.

All of Third Squad were undead and had been killed. SSA Daniel Foster, Third Squad's leader, was the only one on Third Squad still "alive," and he had escaped. NMC agents West, Miller, and Hussain and OST Agent Clarke were killed as well. So we had nine dead, and one enemy agent was at large. Still, it could have been worse—a lot worse.

If it weren't for Frank …

Never in my wildest dreams did I imagine a dog would save the day, but he did. We would have lost everything if Frank, by sheer luck, hadn't been in the MCC. If they had controlled that, the party would have been over. All the sally port machine guns would have been inoperable, and the sally ports would have been opened remotely. Additionally, the ARMOURY would have been sealed shut.

In short, we probably all would have died.

"I hope you all got to bed early. I think it's going to be a long day," I said to my fellow OST agents.

CHAPTER 12
OFFENSE

OST DENFO—Pedestrian entrance

Agent James

THE MORNING SUN battled with the emergency vehicles to create a kaleidoscope of lights. The rising sun's orange, pink, and purple clashed with the vehicles' flashing red and blue lights as its rays ascended the eastern horizon. Yellow police tape encircled a wide perimeter outside of our office building.

A sea of reporters stood in every direction, just beyond the tape. They had been there since last night, right after the attack. Their response was immediate, and we learned that someone had sent every major news network (and most of the smaller ones, too) our address and details of the attack that was about to commence. The emails were sent out at exactly 0100 hours. We had to take the phone offline as our number and address had been shared with the world. They had sent flow charts of our organizational structure, team members' names, and installation descriptions, including weapons and layout. Plus, an FN SCAR assault rifle was missing—

SSA Daniel Foster had royally screwed us.

None of us had slept well, and our nerves were frayed.

I stood at the front entrance, surveying the damage. What used to be the front entrance was now a burnt, jagged hole in the building. At least the garage entrance remained intact. The MX was no longer trying to be subtle; it had nosed into the front entrance, displaying all its machine guns. NMC agents Harold Palmer and Joshua Mills were inside. The MX was now manned 24/7 until we could repair the front entrance.

The exterior was peppered with little numbered yellow cones. Bullet casings, shriveled bodies (the vamps curled up—like dead human spiders), and police and forensic units were everywhere. We had already been contacted by so many three-letter government organizations that every letter of the alphabet had probably been used at least twice. Everyone wanted a full report right away! They didn't seem to care that we had just been in a significant battle and had wounded and dead to tend to, or that we had a publicly known, previously secret building to secure.

Sigh.

Chayton was right; it was going to be a long day.

I shrugged and called Lev. Earlier, I had texted her and let her know we had KIAs but that I was physically OK. I would not be mentally alright until we killed that OI.

"Oh my God, James—" Lev answered my call.

"Yeah, it is terrible. DENFO is wholly compromised, as are all agents. Everyone has been recalled to full duty, and we are on war footing. We lost all of Third Squad except for Daniel; we think he is the one who leaked everything about us to the world. He is undoubtedly undead as well. We also lost West, Hussain, Miller, and Clarke—all KIA. Harris took a bullet to the shoulder; he is at the hospital now, under guard."

"And the good news?" she asked.

"You and I, and the others, are alive to get our revenge," I said frostily.

"F— 'n A right!" she replied.

"How are things in sunny Tempe?" I asked.

"Good. We have a new CI; her name is Dorothy."

"Holy shit, *the* Dorothy? How?"

"I'll tell you later. Chayton just texted everyone; get your ass moving, Love."

"Copy, stay frosty." I hung up.

Sure enough, Chayton texted me while Lev and I were talking: "All DENFO not on guard duty, report to BRIEFING—Now."

Any sense of humor anyone had was gone; I hustled to BRIEFING.

Both Robert Cho and Chayton Blackwell were standing in the room to give the briefing. Chayton, usually inscrutable, showed signs of anger and stress. He must be *really* pissed off!

"Alright, everyone, let's cut to the chase. DENFO is compromised, all agents have had their identities compromised, and the media has taken video of everything. So, since we no longer have a goal to hide, let's go beat the crap out of them, too," Chayton said.

Everyone was deathly quiet but nodded enthusiastically; we had never heard him talk like that.

"Cho and I are making battle plans," he said, turning to the chalkboard. On it, we could see the roster of squads and teams, with blocks next to them showing where teams were.

"First Squad, Alpha and Charlie—in Virginia, monster hunting. Second Squad—in Tempe, monster hunting. Bravo Team from First Squad is with them now. They have found a coven, nest, or whatever the hell it's called, of these undead. They have one captured, believe it or not—"

There were a few who clapped at that.

"Yes, that is excellent news. We can use some of that right now ..."

He paused a moment.

"Third Squad, as you know, was compromised by the enemy and attacked us last night. Their SL, Daniel Foster, is the only 'survivor' and is at large and presumed to be undead and working with the OI. Fourth Squad, you're QRF and will protect this building—what remains of it anyway. Fifth Squad is on its way back and will report to DENFO for further orders. All off-site training is canceled until further notice. "

He paused again.

"James—you, Hamm, and Clay will take POV One to Centennial; you will be joining Second Squad in Tempe."

I nodded and said, "Yes, sir."

Walter "Walt" Hamm and I recently trained together at FLETC during our tactical surveillance course. He is an exceptional OST agent, and NMC agent Marcus Clay already has considerable battle experience. So, I have a strong team.

"OK, we all need to watch each other; this ever-expanding, toothy OI is the worst we have faced yet. Make sure you always keep an eye on each other; no solo trips against the enemy. We can't let them infiltrate us again ..." Chayton said.

Stony faces nodded back at him.

"That's it, get to work. Dismissed."

I looked at the two guys assigned to me, and without a word spoken, we followed Chayton to ARMOURY.

It was weird to see the QRF members all wearing ExoM armor and carrying heavy weapons in the office. We stowed ours in the car, as we planned on having to go "civilian" when we landed. We also brought some extra weaponry that the Second Squad had requested. Our car was so full that the NMC agent had some FN 303s on his lap.

We were in POV One and drove through the sally port. Except for a ton of bullet scars and black crap all over the floors and walls, you would never know there had been a firefight here just a few hours ago. The hundreds of shell casings and shriveled vamp bodies had been cleaned up.

On the way to Centennial Airport, a convoy of news vehicles, including a helicopter, followed us. We pulled into the secure area, and all the news crews could not go any farther. The aircraft also stopped. I'm sure they radioed for permission to enter the airspace and were told where they could put their request ...

As we pulled into the OST Hangar, our usual C-130 awaited us. The airman secured our car and gave us the preflight safety brief. Waiting and listening to that felt weird, but they had their orders, too.

The C-130 pulled out of the hangar, and in a few minutes, we were airborne and on our way to Phoenix. I was excited to see Lev.

———

Luke Air Force Base—NW of Phoenix
Naval Operational Support Center—US Navy

The C-130 touched down at Luke AFB.

When the car was untethered and the cargo door opened, we pulled the Tesla out and headed for the gate. We knew we were looking for at least eight vampires, probably more, once we found the coven. The decision was made to use that term since everything we had read about vampires "living" in a group said they were called that. Besides, since their leader was probably going to be a woman, it sounds better to say, "We killed the coven leader" than "We killed the den leader."

That makes it sound like we killed a group of Girl Scouts; creepy.

At a local diner, Phoenix City Grill, we met with Second Squad, Alpha Team, and their "new" Delta Team—Lev, Bob, and Anthony. As soon as I saw Lev, my face lit up, but I had to fight to hide my concern.

Her face was still a mass of scar tissue on the right side, but now the left had a bunch of scars on it also, and I could see a bullet wound in her cheek. Her arms were visible, still sexy and muscular, but now covered in dozens of scars from frag and more than one bullet wound. She had taken damage that would have put an ordinary person in the ICU for months ... Or a grave.

People were still staring; some had even stopped eating and left because of her. Lev looked like death incarnate and the human embodiment of war. Rambo's scars couldn't hold a candle next to hers.

She smelled nice, though!

Her perfume was strong; otherwise, she had a very faint smell of dead fish—the same odor I had now. It wasn't as bad as the full SIMS; they were gnarly, but it was still noticeable if the wind was just right. I wore cologne for the same reason. We were a match made in heaven ... Or somewhere else.

"Hi, Sexy!" Lev said.

She got up and gave me a big hug, and then we sat down.

"So, what's the OP?" I asked.

"It's a rescue mission; you'll love it. There are a bunch of juicy sorority sisters we have to rescue from their virginity," Bob said with a big smile.

"That sounds a lot like a movie quote," Lev said.

"Yup, glad you caught it," Bob replied.

Lev just shook her head.

"The actual OP is—we're going to take out the coven. Dorothy has found a way to keep the OI from controlling her, but it is temporary at best. She needs to keep upping the frequency and dose to keep it away, so she won't last forever. Plus, we tested her—no blood," Lev said.

"My God. A vampire that its master does not control. Bet there is a pissed-off OI monster out there somewhere," I said.

I liked thinking about that. I wish this OI luck—all bad.

"Right now, an FBI Tactical Surveillance Team—code name *21 Jump Street*—is working the sorority angle. We know they are in class at ASU and live on campus in one of the large dorm apartments. This damn monster is clever. It could have those women hidden in some obscure graveyard or house deep in the woods. Instead, they are living with a couple of hundred other students. It wants to maximize collateral damage to screw us," Lev continued.

She looked annoyed by her statement, but she was right. We would have to be very clever in how we approached this. The OI surely knew it had lost control of Dorothy and would react accordingly. Hopefully, it couldn't see through her eyes. It would be a bad day for us if it could.

"Right now, 21 Jump is watching them and getting us full schematics of the building—exits, stairs, elevators, room numbers of the sorority sisters, everything. Once they settle in for the night, that is when we go. Considering how late some stay up, we are thinking the wee hours of the morning again … We'll have to go in with non-lethals and take out the staff and students we come across first, then make our way to the sorority rooms. We'll field test the new wood-core rounds and report on first-contact effectiveness. I was thinking of the FN 303s with the NL stun rounds, and Glocks with silencers for lethal. What are your thoughts?" Lev asked.

We all waited a moment as the waitress brought out our food, which spilled over onto two plates per person—hearty diner food that would fill us up.

As we ate, we thought. We all knew Lev had the most training and experience, even though Dave was the squad leader. Any tactical decisions would defer to her.

I thought about our new ammunition. Alan, in the MCC, had taught me about the effectiveness of the new "stun" rounds. Those little babies seemed to work for only a few short minutes. The college students and staff would not be our friends anymore, but they would live. The wood-cores were unknown, but they should still work as regular bullets, regardless.

It would be a mess, and some sorority women would surely make it past us. However, they would encounter Delta Team's fire on the way out. It was a solid plan. The only hiccup was that it took several shots to the head to bring one of the vamps down; everywhere else just annoyed them. Additionally, regular explosives were off the table. We didn't want to harm innocent people if we could avoid it. *21 Jump Street* would handle any vampires that escaped through a window. Only those who behaved like normal people and didn't just "jump out" of the windows might get away. We hope most wouldn't think of that, as they were unaware of our tactics.

"It is a good plan, Lev. Weapons sound good to go. Park right out front and bum-rush in the ExoM suits? Or civvies and then open up in the lobby? That's all I've got," I said.

She nodded and then looked at Bob.

"That works, same questions. Plus, exfil in Teslas and alternate exfil is …?" Bob asked.

She nodded again. We all were thinking, and there was no ego in this. The plan would be the difference between success, failure, and loss of life—ours and innocent people.

Finally, she spoke.

"Weapons are a go, all silenced. ExoM suits. The plan is a go for the attack. Exfil primary is Teslas. Alternate is the TAC Team's cars, and we need their locations. The contingency is that the police have the building surrounded, and we shelter in place, have 360 security, and coordinate with them or the FBI. I don't have an emergency plan. Ideas?"

Bob got it first: "The emergency is that more monsters show up, maybe even *the* OI, and we have to engage. Our weapons may not be enough. What then?"

We all thought long and hard.

"I told James not to bring *the gun* because then I couldn't carry an FN 303 to help …" Lev said. She looked a little sad; she *really* liked that weapon.

"Lev, I did bring one of the MSGLs. They have both the HEDP rounds and those new LVLE rounds. You could carry one AND a 303? Plus, I know firsthand that it is a one-shot kill against them," I said.

The MSGL was a great weapon. Plus, we all knew it worked well against these monsters. And we knew Lev could easily carry and use both, one in each hand.

"OK. That makes sense. Let's do that. I'll carry the HEDP for emergency contingencies, but load LVLE for the OP. It sounds like we have a plan. *21 Jump Street* should have a detailed map with the sorority sisters' rooms marked soon. We all know the odds of them all being in their rooms are zero, but at least we'll get most, and hopefully, Delta will take out the rest in the lobby," Lev said.

We all nodded. It was a crap situation and far from a "perfect" plan. We didn't see a lot of other options, though.

"OK, Lev has the most experience, and we all think it is a good plan. Let's get prepped and rest up; it'll be a long night," Dave said.

Lev booked us more rooms at the Westin Hotel so we could all clean up and rest before tonight's OP. After the food was gone and we paid the tab, it was time to head to the hotel, plan the OP in detail, and get some rest.

Dave was right; it would be another long night. At least Lev and I were reunited.

———

US Capitol—Washington, DC
Senate Chambers
Congressman Halston
Continuing debate

"Although the loss of life saddens us, we can understand the anger of the American people. They are tired of secret agencies running around killing people for the 'greater good.' As you're all aware, the location of OST DENFO was somehow leaked to the public. Instead of just protesting, several of our constituents decided they had had enough …"

"Enough of the midnight attacks and murders of innocent civilians."

"Enough of attack after attack with no real explanation of what this 'OST' is doing."

"Enough of government malfeasance."

"We need to end this charade. I ask for your help in voting 'yes' on both the full committee bill and the Laura Act. My beautiful, brilliant daughter was a straight-A student at ASU. Now, she is a burnt corpse with a crossbow bolt and a bullet in her! And for what? Because some hack Catholic priest thought she might be a demon? What a load of bullshit!"

I paused—I was genuinely angry, not merely pretending. Cursing was a breach of decorum, but I knew it would enhance my speech, and it just slipped out. Naturally, I was the source of the leak. It took extensive digging, but I eventually located an FBI agent who had taken a position at OST. With my assistance, it was straightforward for Hellious to discover where she lived. She wasn't home, so Hellious ended up killing her husband instead. Once she returned, it was easy to make him "turn" her as well. After that, the rest of their squad fell one by one.

"Now, OST has been given, through the DA's office, a full-immunity deal with this 'exorcist' in exchange for his help against this newest 'monster' they supposedly face."

I deliberately paused with an angry look on my face.

"This 'monster' that they can never describe. This 'monster' that they can share no details or physical proof of. Amazingly, we never get evidence of these monsters that they supposedly keep fighting. Why do I say supposedly? Because there is no evidence of aliens or monsters! But do you know what there is evidence of? Obstructing Congress by refusing to supply any meaningful evidence about the dead. Not just my daughter, but an entire Secret Service detail and VPOTUS. But you already knew that—"

I paused for effect.

"Now, they have dozens of dead citizens, mowed down by machine guns! They have even more dead agents, and even some local police were killed by 7.62mm rounds, the same bullets that OST uses. Coincidence? Let's hear this clip from the early morning attack, recorded by 911 dispatch. This is ASAC Chayton Blackwell from OST, talking to Aurora Police dispatch. Listen carefully to his threat to their own brothers in blue—"

A recording started, and the sound of gunfire and explosions could be heard in the background:

"All responding units, be advised: Dozens of undead that can look human are attacking DENFO with small arms; they also have flash-bang grenades. Do not try to arrest them; they are deadly with their claws. We are all inside. Any person outside is considered a probable hostile. We'll shoot anyone, including you, who attempts to enter the building—"

I let the quiet linger after turning the recording off.

"Undead. *Really*? And where were these undead when the police got there? Who knows, but they did find a lot of dead *people*. Why? Because OST said, 'Do not try to arrest—only kill.' Since when do cops say that? And speaking of cops, the responding police officers were shot with 7.62mm rounds—rounds that came from inside the building, hitting officers outside. I wonder where those rounds came from …"

I hit my remote for the audio again.

"Any person outside is considered a probable hostile. We'll shoot anyone, including you, who attempts to enter the building—" Chayton's recorded voice filled the room again and then stopped.

"They said this to police dispatch. Minutes later, a shooting came from inside, a shooting that hit and killed two Aurora Police Officers and wounded four others," I said.

I was, of course, not telling the whole truth. The rounds *did* come from inside, but from the undead deliberately shooting at the responding police.

"I'm sick of this! Please vote yes and disband this threat to America once and for all! You can do it for my daughter, Laura. Or you can do it for the dozens of other dead, including the police they killed."

I walked away from the microphone. Again, applause from most and a standing ovation from the possessed and the dim-witted.

(Hellious laughed.) I love how gullible and foolish humans are. It makes this almost too easy...

You are not wrong, Hellious, I thought.

CHAPTER 13
BETA ZETA SIGMA

ASU

Greek Leadership Village—Beta Zeta Sigma Sorority

0300 hours

Agent James

WE HEADED into Tempe as a convoy of five Teslas.

The traffic was light, but a few people were still out and about. The desert sky was clear, and the nighttime temperature was much more comfortable than the daytime dry heat. We went south on South Mill Avenue until it turned east and became East Apache Boulevard. I'm glad it was a short six-minute drive, as the Teslas are not inconspicuous, especially when five are lined up in a row. We had decided to conduct the OP at three a.m. There would still be college students up and moving around, but significantly fewer than at any other time. We knew that, in hindsight, there would be no hiding that an OP had occurred.

Our only objective was to infiltrate, eliminate the sorority coven, and safely exit the scene. All of Second Squad, along with Lev's team (Delta) and my team (Echo), were set to participate in the assault. We had a total of ten agents entering the building. Additionally, one NMC was stationed in each of our Teslas, prepared to drive us away at a moment's notice.

Lastly, the FBI's *21 Jump Street* tactical surveillance unit had already surrounded the building. We had given each of them some wood-core bullets for their Glocks, but had no extra weapons to provide them with. As soon as they saw our Teslas, they were going to block all emergency exits with the bumpers of their cars. Emergency exit doors in most countries—including America—open outward. They do this so that thousands of pounds of people don't crush into a door that opens inward. It was a safety thing, and it worked great—unless a multi-ton car parked against the door.

To enter the building, Alpha Team would use Dorothy's student ID.

Any students trying to escape had to leave through the main entrance, where the Delta team would be waiting. Each team member also had a door ram. Lev and I did not carry the rams; a shoulder ram could easily open most doors. The plan was for each team to take one floor, one agent on each end, and then work to the middle. Then, as a team, they would descend the stairs back to the first floor to regroup and deal with the students trying to leave out the front door.

This plan was far from perfect, but it was the best we could do. If we didn't execute all floors and wings at the same time, we would give the sorority vamps time to mount a defense. I wish the SEALs could have joined us, but we had to work with what we had.

The CIs were left behind on this one. This was a "search and destroy" mission, so they would only be a liability and needlessly in harm's way. Fortunately, we didn't garner any undue attention (that we know of) on the way here.

As we pulled off East Apache Boulevard, we turned left and headed for the entry gates to the target building; we were all in our ExoM suits and ready for battle. Each team member carried the FN 303 less-lethal rifles with stun rounds and Glock 18 sidearms with wood-core rounds and silencers. Lev also brought the 40mm MSGL with LVLE rounds loaded.

The first Tesla through the gates was Alpha Team; we were the fourth team (Echo), and Lev was with the last team (Delta). The first team used Dorothy's student ID, and the vehicle entry gates swung open. As soon as they opened, the Tesla followed the left gate and parked against it so it could not close. The second Tesla did the same, blocking the right gate from closing. The rest of us zoomed through, and we made our way to our target building.

The sorority building's Beta Zeta Sigma's Greek symbols were visible above the fourth-floor windows of the Greek Leadership Village, Building B. The main entrance closed at ten p.m., so no one was "on duty" to greet us on our way in.

"*21 Jump Street*, SITREP," Dave said.

"You are a GO to deploy; the perimeter is secure, and all eight targets are inside the building," said Special Agent Harry Kennedy, the leader of the FBI TAC Surveillance Team.

"Copy, starting OP now," Dave responded.

Team Alpha (the ones with Dorothy's ID) went first in our group. When Dave gave the "GO," we all exited our cars simultaneously and rushed to the front door. We hustled across the lawn to the main door; no one was visible outside or in the lobby. Steve swiped Dorothy's ID on the proxy card reader, and the door clicked open. Dave held the door open while we all rushed into the lobby. As we ran past him, the door made a little alarm sound. I'm assuming that's from being held open too long.

Each team had been assigned a floor; our battle plan was nothing weird or complicated. Like this one, one of the principles of a "fast and loose" OP was the KISS principle (Keep It Simple Stupid).

As I entered the lobby, I saw two students sitting on a couch, working on their laptops. Both looked up as we stormed in. Their mouths hung open, and one said, "Dude!"

Moments later, they fell, jerking, to the ground—along with their laptops. It was not good for them or their laptops, but they would survive. It seems that the stun rounds from our FN 303s work …

As planned, Alpha occupied the first floor, Bravo the second, Charlie the third, and Echo took the fourth. Delta remained in the lobby on the first floor to prevent anyone from escaping. We each used the stairs at either end, and all teams emerged on their assigned floors.

I thought we had been very fortunate, as no shots or screaming could be heard.

Yet.

Walt and I each took a hallway wing as planned. Usually, an "Army of One" was not long for this world, but we had to make do. We had to separate to get as many vamps by surprise as possible. After the initial assault, we would then link up in the center to work our way down to the lobby together.

I hit door B-401 at the end so we could hopefully chase any vampires we missed toward the middle, where the main stairs and elevators were located. The other two staircases were at each end. The plan was sound; now, we had to see what happened next.

As I easily kicked the door open, I quickly scanned the dorm room. A young woman, whose face matched Christina Richards, was staring at me wide-eyed, but the man in bed with her I didn't know. I fired stun rounds into both as they awoke from sleep.

Nothing happened.

Except for their faces splitting into an all-too-familiar grin.

The two of them lunged out of the bed with frightening and inhuman speed. Even with how fast an air marshal can draw a handgun, it would be close on who got who first. Luckily, being part SIM, I was even faster than that.

I drew my Glock 18, already in full-auto mode, and fired a burst into each.

Ch-ch-chuff … Ch-ch-chuff

The suppressed rounds were hardly louder than a cough, plus the click-click sounds of the slide going back and forth. They stopped dead in their tracks.

Literally.

My first burst hit Christina from sternum to face, and she fell like an average person would—DRT (Dead Right There). The second burst hit her lover in the stomach and chest. The same result, except he dropped and started screaming.

AAIIIYA!

The scream was unlike any a human would make. His cries ended quickly, and I saw smoke coming out of the bullet wounds.

Wow! I needed to share this intel right now!

"All teams, wood-core is lethal to them, just like normal bullets on regular people," I said into my radio.

A series of beeps and radio clicks responded. Pressing the transmit button without speaking produces a "click" sound. When we can't talk, we do that instead—to indicate we heard what was said.

Hopefully, they all heard my transmission.

I heard horrible screaming from down the hall—a loud man's scream and then nothing.

Rushing into the hallway, I saw a group of men and women in various states of dress coming out of their dorm rooms. Some turned and saw me and screamed, "He's got a gun!"

All of them ran.

Half ran away toward the elevator in the center, while the other half came toward me. That half turned into vampires and sprinted in my direction.

Ch-ch-chuff … Ch-ch-chuff

I fired burst after burst, and the bodies piled up before me. I was thankful for my reflexes; they got close before the last one dropped. Smoke was wafting out of the barrel of my Glock and out of their gunshot wounds as I dropped the almost empty magazine and reloaded. I didn't see any more targets and quickly headed to where I last saw Walt.

––––––

Agent Walt

I quietly opened the door to Chloe Russell's room at the other end of the hall from James. Before smashing it in with the ram, I checked to see if it was unlocked—and it was.

She was in bed sleeping when I came in.

Lifting my FN 303, I put three rounds into the lump of a body in the bed. I couldn't see who it was, so I didn't want to kill an innocent college kid if it wasn't her—it turns out it was her, though.

She snapped awake, and the teeth came out.

As she leaped from the bed, the sheets went flying; then she lunged for me. I drew my Glock when she "turned," but her speed was incredible.

Ch-ch-chuff …

I fired my Glock as her open maw snapped down on my face.

"AHHH!"

I screamed in unearthly agony as she bit my face clean off. Luckily, I had tucked the Glock tight into my waist—CQB style—as she came into me. I fired round after round on full auto, blind, into her.

Ch-ch-chuff …

I just kept screaming as she bit me again, this time into my neck. I held the trigger down—

AAIIIYA!

She screamed as her head came off my neck, and I could feel my blood spurting out.

At least I wasn't going out alone …

———

Agent James

I stared in horror.

Walt was lying in an immortal embrace with Chloe Russell. His face was gone as though a giant ice cream scoop had gotten it, and a colossal bite was taken from his neck. Blood had sprayed all over him and her, the walls, and even the ceiling. Chloe lay dead on top of him; I could see where several rounds had hit her, and they were still smoking. Several rounds had also hit the walls and ceiling. It had been a terrible point-blank battle, one they both lost.

I lined up my sights and fired a round from my Glock into Walt's head, right into where his eyes would be. This was the "safety slug" we were taught about as FAMs, but never would use—until now. I couldn't take a chance he would turn, and he was clearly no longer alive, anyway.

"Two confirmed enemy kills, Chloe and Christina. Also, one confirmed KIA on our side; it's Walt," I radioed.

Boom, boom, boom …

I heard Lev's MSGL going off far below.

White strobe lights and fire alarms began sounding throughout the building.

No more surprise attacks for us.

As I exited the room, I saw the hallway was clear. No one was left on this floor unless they hid in their rooms. We had gotten the two sorority sisters on this floor, but now there were an unknown number of others. I had just reached up to key my radio when it came to life.

"All units, an unknown number of students are also vamps!" I think it was Dave. As he said it, I could hear the loud hiss of vampires and the chugging of a silenced pistol.

Things were going FUBAR fast!

I holstered my Glock and readied my FN 303. I ran to the central stairwell to descend to the first floor. Just as I reached the open door to the stairs, a vampire charged out to grab me.

Dropping low, I sprawled and rammed my head and shoulders into her stomach—

SNAP!

Her deadly teeth bit down where my head was only a moment ago.

Driving hard with my legs, I charged us onto the stairwell landing and then stopped suddenly.

She did not.

HHIIISSSsss … Thump!

She hit the next floor landing.

I drew my Glock and patiently waited; I didn't have to wait long.

As she sprinted up the stairs, the first thing I saw was her head—

Ch-ch-chuff

In a spray of black goo and smoke, her head snapped back, and she tumbled down the stairs.

Dead … once again.

I did not recognize her face; she was not one of the sorority targets. I re-holstered and readied my FN 303 again to run down the stairs. As I ran past her body, already curling up like a dead insect, I made my way to the ground floor. I took a few steps on each landing and jumped to the next, and quickly I was on the ground floor.

"Echo, coming out, floor one," I said on the radio.

"Come out," I heard Lev's voice. It was the flat-sounding, all-business voice I loved to hear.

As I came out, it was bedlam.

Students were screaming and running for the exit. Vampires were hissing and killing them, or charging Lev and Bob. The living and dead were everywhere, dozens of them. Some were jerking around from stun rounds, and others lay still with smoking holes in them.

Bob was hitting every person with stun rounds from his FN 303 rifle. Lev was doing the same, but she also had a Glock in her right hand, shooting vamps. I saw the MSGL lying on the ground, smoking. It only had six shots before reloading, so I'm sure she had already emptied it. Besides, the furniture, walls, and ceiling didn't decorate themselves in black, foul-smelling gunk. She had a bandolier of grenades for the launcher around her torso, but there was no time to reload it. A vamp was heading toward Bob as he was engaging another from a different direction. These things were *fast*.

I dropped my FN 303 on its sling and fast-drew my Glock.

Ch-ch-ch-ch-ch-chuff

"HHIISS!" It fell on its face and slid, six smoking holes in its back.

Hearing a motion behind me, I sidestepped and spun.

A young man darted past me as I leveled my Glock at him. My FN 303 was hanging on its sling, so I let him pass by unharmed. He dropped from Lev's FN 303 rounds a second or two later. I ran forward to the front doors where Lev and Bob were.

They saw I had the right flank now, so Bob switched to the left flank while Lev stayed in the center.

"Alpha, SITREP," Lev said into her radio.

Nothing.

"Bravo, SITREP."

…

"Charlie, SITREP."

…

"Coming out!" We heard Dave yell.

Dave came sprinting out the door to his wing on the first floor. Behind him was a small army of the undead. There were at least a dozen of them.

Ch-ch-chuff … Ch-ch-chuff

HHIISSSS, HHIISSSS

AAIIYA! AAIIYA!

My slide locked back, so I performed a tactical reload and kept firing. I was already on my third mag. Luckily, we were using those wood-core rounds.

One vamp ran for a window; it made it.

Ch-ch-chuff

Crash-Tinkle!

It went out the window with three bullets in the back. I saw flashes outside, and it caught a couple of rounds in the front as well. It fell and did not get back up.

We could hear the sirens outside now and knew time was almost up. There would be no escaping in the Teslas; we were not going to cause a dangerous chase, and it's not like our cars aren't easily identified.

"Responding Police, this is the FBI OST squad leader, Dave Tanaka. We are killing undead and stunning college students. FBI TAC Team will meet you. Cordon off all egress routes," he said into his police TAC radio.

"This is Sergeant Brisbing; come out and surrender with your hands up!" We heard through the blaring echo of a bullhorn, seemingly pointed in our direction.

Meanwhile, we were firing and reloading as fast as we could.

"No can do. Come in and join the party, or stay the f— back!" Dave yelled on the police channel.

He switched back to our channel.

"Contingency plan, I say again, contingency plan at ASU—" Dave broke the connection.

A vamp was right on him.

Ch-ch-chuff

He sidestepped as the vamp went to grab him; his shots killed it, and it fell to the ground.

The flood was turning into a low tide. Now, we could manage the numbers coming at us … unless we ran out of wood-core bullets.

———

ASU Campus Police
Sergeant Carl Brisbing

I had been a police officer for over ten years and had never witnessed something like this. Cars were backed up against all the emergency exits, and their plainclothes agents wore blue raid jackets that said, "Federal Bureau of Investigation, Federal Agent."

I was just giving the demand to surrender when I saw what would change my life forever.

A man came crashing out of a window, and I saw three exit wounds. At that exact moment, I saw him get hit twice more in the chest. But—instead of blood—black goo shot out, and smoke poured from the wounds. And then it fell lifeless to the ground.

It.

I saw the mouth that split its head almost in half, like a hippo. Row upon row of sharp teeth were visible even from this distance. Plus, it was *hissing*! It slowly curled into a tight ball, still smoking.

Just in case I thought I was hallucinating, we all saw what was happening in the lobby. It was dark outside, but the lobby was well lit, so we could see everything happening inside. We watched college kids going down and jerking like a Taser had hit them. And the ones that were shot with Glocks? They had long talons and those flip-open maws of teeth. Even their eyes were demonical—they shimmered in the night light, much like a dog's or a cat's would.

"All units, standby to assist the FBI Teams. Keep the perimeter. Do not engage, be advised … some of the students appear to be—" I knew I would regret what I said next "—they appear to be inhuman hostiles."

F—! I will never live this down.

I watched as the FBI agents took down anyone who got out. Eventually, the gunfire died down to a trickle and then stopped.

"Maintain perimeter; OST is clearing the building now," came over the police radio.

"I copy you, OST; we have the perimeter," I told this "Tanaka" fellow.

The SWAT unit and a bunch of Tempe PD cars were showing up. I had no idea what to tell them, as there was no rational way to explain it. As they deployed out the back of the SWAT van, I saw a bunch do that—ever so slight—head tilt. We did that subconsciously when our brains heard something that didn't make sense; I heard it on my radio as well.

"All units, this is Commander Baines, Victor One; you're not to engage or impede the FBI or OST, and will assist them in every way they need. Shift and Patrol leaders confirm orders on channel three. Victor One, out."

Holy crap! That must have been an order from pretty damn high to make Victor One "snap to" like that.

I'm so glad! I did not want to have to explain what I saw to them or anyone else … ever.

———

Agent Lev

I was so relieved to see James was still alive!

Especially knowing Dave and Steve had gone out on the ground floor in separate directions, with only Dave coming back. The last of the students were on the ground, convulsing. It was time to re-clear the building and retrieve our fallen after we cleared it of vampires. Agent Kennedy reported that several had tried to break out of windows and jump down, only to be eliminated by the FBI TAC Team on the perimeter. At least now we know they can't turn into bats, mist, or simply fly away.

"Any of our targets?" I asked.

"Yes, Cunningham, Brown, and Jones—all vamps, all KIA," he responded.

I thought about where we were at with our operation …

Our operation was happening in the middle of a college campus, so we knew it would be live-streamed by now.

Swell.

Wait a minute … that could be an advantage, though.

I signaled to Bob to cover me and pulled out my G-phone; I called Cho directly.

"SAC Cho," he picked up on the first ring.

"Operation has police assistance now; the executive order is working—"

"For now," he said.

"Yes, we know it won't last. Police are coming in now to secure students and get them out. OP is a partial success; we have confirmed enemy KIAs on Brown, Russell, Richards, Cunningham, and Jones. Amanda Collins, Jessica Lane, and Amelia Ali are still at large. We lost friendlies; Agent Hamm is KIA. MIA and assumed KIA are Robinson, Doyle, Wilson, Dixon, and Barker. Charlie Mike (Continue Mission) to recover or confirm KIA on friendlies and threats," I said.

"Copy SITREP," he responded.

"It will be live-streamed by now, so I want to use the TAC Team to show the vamp bodies to the students. That way, it will be all over the internet, which will be good for us …" I said.

There was a long moment of silence.

Don't take too long, boss, I have a job to do!

"Understood, proceed."

The line went dead, and I put the phone in my pocket. I got on the FBI TAC channel—

"TAC Teams, secure at least one vamp body and show it to the students who are filming. In fact, let them take a couple of the bodies."

"Copy," said the TAC Team leader, Agent Kennedy.

"OK, let's clear from the top and force them down to the TAC Team," Dave said.

"We need to break in every door and clear every room. Bring our KIAs to the central area of each floor and send them down the elevator if possible; if we have live agents, we'll take them to medical, or have their blood tested, and have them join us. Lev and James are on the entry team, and I'll provide security (hall guard duty). Bob, stay here and help *21 Jump Street* with anything funneled your way. Questions?" Dave asked.

"Good to go," said James.

"Ready," I said.

"Let's do it," said Bob.

We took the stairs to the top floor, covering the stairway above while the rest of the team moved. With only three of us, the tactics were easy.

The top-floor door was still open from where James had come through. We passed the curled body of the vampire he killed on the landing, went up the last set of stairs, and entered the hallway. The fire alarm suddenly stopped—the TAC Team must have gotten security to turn it off. That is good; the noise was only helping our enemy, not us.

"Starting top-down sweep," I said on the TAC Team channel.

"Copy that," said Agent Kennedy.

I switched back to our TAC channel and motioned to move out. Dave was still the OP leader, but I had the most combat experience and training, so I commanded the tactics. We moved to the end of the hall without any contact. The first door was open, and Christina and her undead boyfriend were still lying dead in the room. I snapped photos for positive IDs. We kicked in the doors and worked our way to the other end. We zapped a couple of hiding college students and moved on. At the last door, we grabbed the bodies of Chloe Russell and Walter Hamm and dragged them to the center with us. We put them on the elevator and hit the ground floor button; then, we descended the stairs to the third floor.

———

Agent James

We had reached the third floor and were starting on one end. Lev kicked the first door open as I covered whatever was inside.

I saw one of the vamps waiting for us in the darkened room. We could see her, though, thanks to our "SIM" capabilities. She was hiding in the dark with the lights off, perfectly positioned for whoever reached for the light switch or entered the door. I did not hesitate—

Ch-ch-chuff

HISS …

Thump.

She was down.

Suddenly, there was light; Lev had hit the light switch. Lev and I had no trouble seeing in the dark, and we also did not have any light-transition issues. Sudden bright lights did not affect us. We noticed them, but they did not affect our vision. This SIM thing is freaky …

We had found Amelia Ali.

When I took the picture, she was still smoking, including the rounds in her head. Her teeth and inhuman maw are visible in the photo. We moved on.

We kicked in door after door, mainly finding empty rooms. A few rooms had hidden college students or vampires. We shot them all—with different weapons, of course; we are not the monsters. As we prepared to go through the last set of doors, we heard Dave firing his Glock.

Dave's gun clattered to the ground as a round hit his hand.

"Son-of-a-bit—" he started to say.

Suddenly, his head snapped back from a round to his helmet. He fell flat to the floor, unmoving.

Another Glock was firing from down the hall!

Lev and I were about to enter a room when we both spun around incredibly quickly. Taking cover behind a door jamb, we could see our new enemy shooting from the far stairwell.

It was William Barker from Charlie Team. Or, what used to be him.

Ch-ch-chuff … Ch-ch-chuff

As he ducked behind the wall, Lev and I obliterated the door jamb he was hiding behind and everything around it. Lev kept firing as I charged. If the 9mm subsonic rounds managed to hit him, the armor may have taken them. So, he may very well be alive. If he weren't wearing ExoM armor, he would surely be dead.

I came around the door opening wide (we call it "slicing the pie") so I could see him first and not be right on him where he could grab my gun.

Thank you to every instructor who trained me in tactics.

I saw his gun and hands before he saw me, so I shot them.

Ch-ch-chuff

AAIIIYA!

The gun went flying as the hands drew back, smoking. It pulled back further behind the wall and into the corner of the landing, so I charged.

The vampire that was William was in agony and looked up from a crouch as I lunged through the door to shoot it. Slashing quickly with its talons, it hit my gun hand. My armor kept me from losing my hand, but it knocked my gun across the landing.

SMACK-Crack!

I threw a hook punch into its temple, and its head snapped to the left and separated. Now, it was dangling off to the left in a clearly lethal way.

But William wasn't dead—he was *undead.*

The wobbly-headed monster charged me and grabbed hold of my neck with both of its hands. I used Aikido to take his momentum—and add to it. Both of my hands shot up between his. Then, pulling down hard with my left hand on his right biceps, I forced his left elbow into the sky. Dropping to a knee, I windmilled his arms as I spun. The "heaven and earth" throw was challenging to pull off in combat—unless you're inhumanly strong.

He cartwheeled into the hall.

Burp!

I heard Lev fire from down the hall and saw a flash as his armor took the MSGL round. In that split second, from when I heard the MSGL go off to now, I turned away to dive for cover. The 40mm LVLE round would not penetrate his armor, so I knew it would detonate outside his armor and not inside him. I realized I was too close—

BOOM!

It knocked me down, almost off the stairwell's landing, but I scrambled back up. Grabbing my Glock off the floor, I aimed back into the hall. The thing that was William was unsteadily getting to its feet.

Its armor was shredded, and black goo was everywhere. One arm was gone, and the head was now completely disconnected from the spine.

It reminded me of Scott, the flight attendant from our first OI, so long ago ...

I aimed carefully.

Chuff

I hit him in the eye right where the visor had broken off. It was weird, as it was hanging almost upside down from normal. It didn't even scream; it just dropped straight down.

"Barker is confirmed KIA. All units, be advised that we have three MIA OST agents, assumed to be undead now. But check your fire; there is still a chance they might be human." Lev said into the radio.

As the other units responded to Lev's message, we saw Dave rejoining us. He had his bell rung, but the armor took the round. I saw blood dripping off his arm, now hanging useless at his side. Covering each other, we reloaded again. I also grabbed Barker's ammo and Glock, but his FN 303 was not with him.

Glunk ... clink, clink ... Glunk, Click!

Lev had reloaded the MSGL, so we moved out down the hall.

We found Dixon's body in one of the rooms; he was too destroyed to have been "reincarnated." It must have been a hell of a fight; he had killed a vamp, a male college student. I grabbed Dixon's body and pulled it to the center of the building. After putting our two dead agents and one sorority vamp on the elevator, we sent it down.

I hope they appreciate our care packages, I thought. *Grim, I know.*

We hit the stairs as the elevator door closed.

Two more to go …

———

We headed to one end of the second floor and then worked our way to the other. Dave still covered our rear as we moved down the hall. He was using his left hand now because his right arm was still hanging, useless. He had activated the CAT (tourniquet) for his arm to keep from bleeding out; his right hand was crippled from that GSW. He and Lev owned the hall as I engaged each room. I held my FN 303 in my left hand and the Glock in my right.

Another door flew in when I kicked it open, and I stepped inside—

This one was fast!

It was on me before I could fire; its deadly maw was heading for my face. I sidestepped and hit it in the temple with my Glock—

Crack!

Its head snapped to the side as it went by me and into the hall.

Burp—BOOM!

Chunks of black splattered into the room and all over my back and side. I felt some fragments bounce off my armor.

"Shit!" I heard Dave say.

I finished clearing the room and came out to see Dave with black gunk all over him. It was all over Lev, too, but she had stopped caring long ago.

"Man, these things are gross!" Dave said.

"Yuup," Lev and I said in unison.

Lev came up and snapped a picture of the dead vampire's face. It was Jessica Lane, another sorority member down; only Amanda Collins remained. She was the one who Dorothy said was the original "sacrifice" and talked like the OI. We didn't know if that made her any different or not, so we proceeded with caution. In one of the rooms, we found Doyle; he had been bitten apart. Disturbingly, his armor and weaponry were gone, and he had been stripped naked and mutilated.

I just hoped he wasn't still alive when that happened.

Wilson and Robinson were still MIA.

There was no basement, so the last floor—the ground floor—was next. We descended …

We nodded to the FBI agents in the lobby and went down the second-to-last wing, the one Robinson had not returned from.

As we entered the hall, all was still—no sounds or movement. Each door that went down continued revealing the horror of what had happened. When we started our assault, probably as soon as the fire alarm went off, any person still alive was attacked by these horrors. Blood splattered the walls, floors, and ceilings. Some beds were soaked in blood, and sometimes the bodies were still on them, or parts of bodies.

Apparently, becoming a vamp is an imperfect art, not a science. Why some turned while others just died is a mystery to me.

And I hope it stays a mystery to me.

The last door awaited us; Lev kicked it in as I covered the door.

HISSsss …

It was waiting, but the door flying inward had knocked it down.

Ch-ch-chuff

It's not very sporting, but then again, hunting isn't really a sport. Animals that only run away and can't fight back aren't "sport"—they are just targets.

So, maybe hunting vampires is a sport, after all!

The dead vamp wasn't Amanda. But we all saw, lying on the bed and clearly mutilated for our benefit, the tortured and dismembered body of Steve Robinson.

"Damn them!" Dave said through a clenched jaw.

"We'll kill them all, Dave," Lev said.

Dave nodded grimly and said, "Let's go."

We headed back into the lobby.

"OK, everyone!" I yelled.

"There is one MIA and assumed vamp, OST agent—Al Wilson, unaccounted for. He was on the second-floor team originally. Also, one target vamp is left—Amanda Collins. Both are extremely dangerous and probably armed with OST weaponry. Stay alert!"

I hoped they understood what we were up against. This last wing would be hell …

————

We passed through the open door to the final wing of the ground floor. Somewhere in here were Amanda and Al. Well, and God knows how many other monsters there were too …

This time, we took Bob.

He took the front guard, Dave took the rear, and Lev and I were the room entry team. A vampire hissed from the bathroom inside the first door we kicked open. We entered, and Lev waited while I got ready to kick the door—

The bathroom door flew open, and a vampire stepped out as it charged.

BURP! BURP! BURP!

The vampire flew right back into the bathroom.

Boom, Boom, Boom!

Black crap flew out of the bathroom. Lev turned and headed for the hall, and I followed. We came out of the room, just as several vampires emerged from doorways down the hall.

BURP! BURP! BURP! Ch-ch-chuff

BOOM! BOOM! BOOM!

From where Lev's grenades had exploded down the hall, parts of several vampires and black goo were on the walls.

Glunk … clink, clink … Glunk, Click!

Lev had reloaded the MSGL again.

We stared down the hall and waited. After a little while, we realized the ones remaining must be waiting in ambush. Oh well, off we go.

Lev and I got ready at the next door.

We kicked it open … and nothing was inside. We cleared the bathroom and then came out.

Finally, just two rooms were left.

Lev kicked in the next-to-last door and caught a couple of 9mm rounds in her chest. They lodged in her armor. Instead of entering the room as planned, I stepped aside, staying in the hall.

BURP! BURP!

Boom, Boom!

Lev didn't even have time to move as debris and black goo splattered her all over. She looked like some kind of demented Picasso painting.

"OST Agent Wilson is now KIA," Lev calmly said into the radio.

She spun to cover the last door, and a good thing, too. It opened suddenly, and Amanda rushed out like lightning—she was *much* faster than the others. Hitting Dave full force, she slashed her claws into his armor.

AHHH!—Crunch!

Dave screamed as he was flung into the wall.

Ch-ch-chuff

I hit her on full auto, and several of my rounds must have hit, but Amanda was wearing stolen OST armor, so they didn't kill her.

She went straight for Lev next.

Amazingly, she was even faster than Lev and me. As Lev went to fire her MSGL, Amanda sidestepped and hit the weapon with a clawed hand, knocking it down the hall. Then she whipped her talons toward Lev's head.

OMG, No!

I could see that Lev would not get out of the way in time.

So, instead, she rushed in. Amanda's forearm hit Lev's head instead, as Lev lunged in and hit Amanda with her whole body. They were propelled back into the room we had just cleared. I could hear the vampire hissing and Lev's SIM growl as they fought in close combat.

AAIIIYA!

The vampire screamed in pain as I came around the corner, but I couldn't help.

As they collided with the walls, a fierce battle ensued. Lev's dark-red blood sprayed alongside the vampire's black goo. Her armor had been torn open in several spots as the glinting blackened metal of Karambit blades and three-inch talons flashed.

I saw one of Amanda's hands go flying off. Then, more black goo from each flash of Lev's karambits. Lev was moving extraordinarily fast.

Hmm ... She did look like a blender.

Amanda's blackened entrails were coming out of her as Lev chopped off an arm and then, without slowing down, slashed both knives into Amanda's neck.

Amanda's decapitated head fell to the ground.

Lev looked at me, smiled, and gave me a thumbs-up—then fell unconscious to the floor in a pool of blood, hers and Amanda's.

CHAPTER 14
AFTERMATH

Honor Health Tempe Medical Center

Agent James

I WAS WORRIED.

Lev had not fully recovered from her ordeal with VPOTUS, and now this. Even though Lev was beyond human, there were limits—even for a SIM.

As I carried her to the waiting ambulance out front, I could see where the claws had gone clean through her armor. My God, that OI-possessed vampire was strong! No mist came out of it after Lev killed it, however. If that was just an OI-*possessed* vampire, I shuddered to think what the *actual* OI one was like. Was it stronger than Lev and me?

Now, I watched the woman I loved slowly breathing as the ambulance headed down the highway to Tempe Medical Center. We had some armed FBI agents following us, and the NMCs were driving our Teslas.

Dave and Bob were in separate ambulances en route to the same hospital; Dave had been hurt badly by the same super-vamp Lev fought. He would make it, but most likely be out of action for a long time, maybe permanently. That claw had gone through his armor and chucked him into a wall with incredible force. The armor undoubtedly saved his life, but I didn't have high hopes for what remained of his hand …

Bob was OK to continue, as he appeared to be the only one of us uninjured.

I had just given a full verbal AAR report to SAC Cho, as Dave was in the second ambulance and unconscious.

Technically, our mission was a success.

All eight sorority vamps were KIA, and we had successfully shown actual vampires to the world. Typically, in the past, that would have been an epic fail. But now that Congress was gunning for us, it was a plus for a bunch of college kids to plaster video of our OP and our vampire friends to the world.

Thanks to the lights and sirens of our ambulances, and because we were only a mile away, we made it to the hospital quickly. After the ambulance finished backing up to the loading dock, the paramedics hustled Lev's gurney inside.

The looks on people's faces would have been funny if they weren't so frightened.

Bob, Dave, Lev, and I were all covered in black stuff and red blood, and our armor looked like we had been in one hell of a battle. I walked to the ER triage nurse while Lev went straight to surgery.

"How can I help you?" she asked.

Her name tag read, "RN Angela Tate." As she looked up from her paperwork, she registered surprise.

"Well, well … I thought I had seen it all, guess not. I don't even know what to say—are you alright? Do you need to be seen?"

"No, Nurse Tate. Thank you," I replied.

"You should remove the armor and let the doctors look you over," she said. Her professionally trained eye had already seen many of my injuries.

"I'll be OK, just a sliced hand and some frag, nothing that won't heal."

She blanched. I keep forgetting that is not normal—our SIM healing.

"I'm not normal. Things like that will heal … but you're right. The removal of foreign bodies will help my recovery. Can you do me a favor and let me know how Tanaka and Levingston are doing?"

She shook her head like a disapproving mom and sighed.

"Yes, I can. Now, go to room seven and lose the armor," Nurse Tate said.

"Yes, ma'am," I replied.

I went to room seven, removed my armor, and sat quietly. We had left all our weapons in the Teslas, with the NMC agents guarding them. Even police must disarm to be seen as patients. That's why so many other FBI agents and police are in the building now—they *are* armed. This would be an excellent opportunity for the enemy.

When Bob got to my room, I handed him the gear. Miraculously, he was the only one who didn't get injured.

"Damn, Bob. I guess we should have gotten ranger training. Not a scratch on you," I said.

He chuckled.

"Too late now. Besides, they were too busy with you and Lev to notice me," he said, smiling.

"Anyway, I'll take this to the car. Get some rest, big guy," he said as he turned and left with my armor.

I lay my head on the pillow and rested; I was exhausted …

I woke up as Nurse Tate pulled the privacy curtain back. I looked at her expectantly.

"Your friend, Levingston, is in Room 4 in the ICU. She is stable and recovering. Multiple bullets were taken out of her from the GSWs, and a lot of pieces of fragmentation—both military grenade shrapnel and pieces of bone and building debris …"

She paused, and took my pulse, and I could see something was bothering her.

"She shouldn't be alive; what are you?"

I liked Nurse Tate; she was a pro and got straight to the point.

"For humans, from humans, but not human," I told her.

She looked a little ill and more than a little annoyed with my snarky response.

"I have seen a lot, but her vitals were not human; her body was filled with—"

"Tentacles. Yes, we know. So is mine," I said.

She nodded with tight lips and a little head bob.

"Maybe now I *have* seen it all," she said.

"You have not, and I hope you never do," I told her.

She looked at me critically and then spoke.

"Well, whatever you are, thank you. Everyone has seen the ASU videos, and I doubt anyone will sleep tonight."

With that, she got up and left, turning back to me as she went—

"It's time for you to wear that fancy gown. I'll return in a few minutes to help prep you for surgery."

"Thank you, Nurse Tate."

With a curt nod, she left. After she shut the curtain again, I made a call to SAC Cho.

"Hey, boss, some medical records at Honor Health Tempe Medical Center need to be 'lost' …"

CHAPTER 15
BILLIONAIRE

Seattle, Washington
Henry Rothensburger

"MR. ROTHENSBURGER, YOUR APPOINTMENT IS
HERE," the nondescript voice over my intercom said. Sitting at my
desk, I hit the intercom button and responded.

"Send them in," I said.

I was happy to be a billionaire.

There was only one thing I loved more than money—the power
that comes with it. This woman who contacted me said she could give
me more power than I could imagine.

Pfft, I doubt that.

The double doors to my ornate and spacious study opened, and a
team of security personnel entered the room.

I couldn't help but smile.

They moved and operated like my ship-shape team, many of whom
were also in the room. A moment later, the woman entered. She had
not even told me her name yet.

When she came in, my jaw dropped.

My God! That is the most beautiful woman I have ever seen!

She wore Gucci head to toe, and gold jewelry dripped off every limb and finger. Her entourage of toughs rivaled my security team—she immediately impressed me.

"Good afternoon, Henry. I am Hellious, and I am here to bargain for your soul," she said with a mischievous grin.

I chuckled.

If she were the Devil, she did not try to hide it with that name.

"I am not of this world, and I can make you energetic and immortal. If you join with me, that is …" she smiled as she said it.

"*Great!*" I said sarcastically. "But, uh, how exactly are you able to do that?"

She turned into a blur of movement and, faster than I could track, tore one of her security team's heads off with her bare hands. Black goo shot out of his neck where his head once was. The now headless body fell to the floor and curled into a tight ball. The rest of her team did not so much as flinch, which was damn impressive. My security team all drew their weapons, however.

"*Incredible …*" was all I could say.

She stood smiling at me, the man's head held in one hand, still dripping black goo on my deep, white carpet. I noticed her smile, even with her lips shut, now stretched inhumanly from ear to ear, and her fingernails were now three-inch-long talons. She continued smiling, saying nothing more. She opened her mouth slightly to reveal hundreds of sharp teeth.

I smiled as well because we both knew I would agree to her proposal. She offered to merge with me and give me unlimited power and immortality.

"Of course! You knew what my answer would be. Yes, assuredly yes," I gushed.

"It will be a violent change; we must be in private, so the others do not react … poorly," she said.

My security team still had their guns pointed at her, so I motioned to them to holster their weapons. As they were re-holstering, I spoke.

"Please, let's adjourn to my private quarters."

THUMP

The head landed on the thick white carpet where she dropped it.

She nodded and followed me through the door to my private en suite bedroom. I turned to face her. As soon as the door shut, she disrobed. Her naked body was beautiful on a level that was hard to comprehend.

How can a person possibly look so good?

She stepped up to me and hugged me with both arms. It was magical. I had never been with a person so uncontrollably sexy in my life. I could feel her hot breath tickling my neck.

CHOMP!

The pain took my breath away, but now …

This feels so good!

Smiling, I felt the walls close in as my eyes shut on this life …

———

I awoke on my bed.

Looking down, I was covered in blood—my own, I would assume. Standing at the foot of the bed, with that same impossible smile, was Hellious.

"You should shower and get new clothes," she said simply. I noticed she had already cleaned up and redressed. Now, her disrobing made sense to me.

"I would agree," I said.

As I stood from the bed, I felt like a twenty-year-old; I felt amazing!

Now, I was a vibrant, healthy eighty-four-year-old. My skin was starting to glow orange with vibrancy. The prospect of youthful energy and eternal life was too enticing to refuse. There was no doubt, for either of us, that I would eagerly and willingly follow Hellious anywhere and do anything.

"So, Henry, I have done my homework on you. The whole world knows of your deeds and exploits on your rise to power. You made your early fortune in the real estate industry, following in your father's footsteps. I know you have used illegal and immoral means to do so.

Your infamy of screwing over those in your employ is legion. You have even used the services of the mafia to quell competitors and critics, to intimidate or 'disappear' anyone who is in your way ... I salute you for accomplishing so much as a human," she said with a mock salute.

All I could do was chuckle. She was right; she had done her homework.

"And now we are going to make you even more powerful. My army of undead will release a creature even more powerful than I. It will know of your aid to me and will reward you handsomely."

She smiled, and her lips no longer moved, but I could hear her clearly in my head—

Now, we no longer have to speak aloud, Henry. I can communicate directly into your mind and hear you as well. I understand your desires. First, we will control America, and then the world. You will become the wealthiest man on Earth, with undead slaves to fulfill your every will and desire. Do you approve of our merger?

Oh, I do, I do. This is a great arrangement. We'll go far together! I responded quickly.

I'm glad you approve, Henry. As it turns out, there is a gift you need to buy me ...

What would that be? I eagerly want to know.

Nothing too much, just an island ...

A short while later, we found ourselves back in my study. I had showered and dressed, feeling better than I had in over half a century. Hellious explained her entire plan for Gunkanjima Island, stating that it would be perfect for our purposes—far from America's jurisdiction and prying eyes. One of her assistants plugged a flash drive into my computer, and we reviewed every detail of the plan on the big-screen TV on my wall.

There, on the island, she would create the giant altar that Hellious insisted was necessary for her power to be absolute. She informed me about the cult in Japan, the "Everlasting Sun," and its leader, Victor Hamatsu. They would assist her in the "grand summoning," whatever that involved. After our meeting, she would travel to Japan to perform this summoning and then wait for me to arrive with the first group of miners and workers. Additionally, once they started coming, there would be a nearly endless supply of bodies for protection. At least, there will be once we convince Japan of our purported plans …

———

With a few phone calls … I bought it—Gunkanjima Island was now ours!

Japan was eager to sell me the useless and abandoned island. Since tourism is its only revenue source now, my offer was much better. Although it chafed me to spend what we did, I did negotiate a lower price than the initial offer.

I would have paid ten times as much if I had to.

When the purchase was final, I started advertising for construction crews and mine workers. We told Japan we were reopening the mine because we believed rare earth metals were still below. Many cars and electronics use those metals now, but they are still scarce and valuable. Japan was excited to share the wealth and agreed to our enterprise, which would bring in tax dollars from both workers and exports from the island.

Too bad we had no intention of mining for metals …

As I prepared for my journey there, they were already hiring the first wave of miners. Things were happening fast!

Hellious had told me about her ambitious plan to thwart this OST group and to eventually control the United States government. Once that was done, there would be no one to stop us. The reach and power of the United States would allow us, as a corporation, to annex the island effectively. Additionally, Japan would be making so much money from the false exports that it wouldn't care. We would ship in raw metals to "find" in the mine and send them back out on the same ship. Indeed, we would lose money that way. Still, our other endeavors would eventually make hundreds of billions, especially once America started "special appropriations" with the Ways and Means Committee for these rare earth metals that we "found" in the mine.

They would authorize billions to get them, and I would become the world's first trillionaire. This monster was brilliant!

———

I still can't believe Gunkanjima Island is finally ours! Strange to be saying "us." I was accustomed to the word "me".

The mining and construction crews, their families, and their pets were now ready to come to the island.

That night, I took my private jet, a Gulfstream G700. With its 2,600 cubic feet of cabin, it could comfortably fit nineteen passengers. It had five spacious living areas and could travel up to 8,000 nautical miles at up to Mach 0.935. Mine, of course, was designed around the most important VIP in the world—me.

During the long hours of my flights, I caught up on my research on Gunkanjima.

As I enjoy talking (among other things) with one of my beautiful companions, I had Gemma sit and listen to me. She had permission to join the conversation, but mostly just sat there and listened, as usual.

"Did you know that Gunkanjima is also known as 'battleship island'?" I asked rhetorically.

"It is also known as 'Midori nashi Shima' or 'the island without green.' Developed by the Mitsubishi Corporation, the sixteen-acre island was established to operate the mine in 1887, as they believed it sat atop a vast deposit of coal, which turned out to be correct. Each year, over 400,000 tons of coal had been extracted from this mine. Throughout Japan's industrialization and during World War II, it continuously produced coal. By the 1950s, the island was home to nearly six thousand people, making it the most densely populated place in the world. However, by 1974, the coal reserves were exhausted, leading to the island's abandonment and its transformation into a ghost town. Over the next forty years, nature reclaimed the land. The streets and even the tops of buildings became enveloped in greenery. As nature invaded every nook and cranny, the buildings fell into disrepair, turning the place into a relic of its industrial past."

I paused to take a sip of Cognac and continued.

"In 2015, Korea and Japan reached an agreement to designate the island as a UNESCO World Heritage Site. South Korea and Japan agreed to identify Hashima Island, another name for this location, as a historical site on the condition that Japan acknowledge the history of Korean forced labor in its tours. To this day, Japan has yet to uphold its part of the bargain."

I shut my laptop and looked up. Her expression never changed; she just sat with a vapid smile and nodded yes a lot.

"They were horrible to those Koreans," Gemma said, finally showing real emotion.

I chuckled. I actually had a lot *more* respect for Japan after finding that out.

As part of the deal, I had to agree that it would reopen for tourism within a year and that any building renovations would comply with UNESCO World Heritage Site restrictions. I also had to allow regulators to review the site before mining operations could begin. Typically, that would require a multimillion- or even billion-dollar commitment. Therefore, the Nagasaki Prefecture was thrilled that I had agreed. By the time mining operations were ready to commence in earnest, our plan would have already come to fruition.

Our workers were paid, of course. They all received a substantial signing bonus, but none would ever see a real paycheck. I had arranged for all paychecks to go to the on-site bank. From there, the workers would set up automatic payments to be sent several days after they were paid. The beauty of the setup is this: I provided them with a generous sign-on bonus to keep them satisfied, and since it would take considerable time to get all the systems up and running properly, they understood it would take a month or more before their first paycheck. That paycheck would cover all back pay owed to them once it was online. I intentionally provided them with a three-month signing bonus to compensate.

I effectively "bought" each slave for three months of pay—a damn fine investment for an undead slave to work for all of eternity.

Sipping my Louis XIII Cognac, I gazed down at the clouds below. I savored my drink, reflecting on this exquisite elixir that required nearly seventy years to age as I swirled the amber liquid in my glass. This does not even account for the 200 years it took for the oak trees to grow—the very trees used to make the exceptional casks it needed. At around five thousand dollars per bottle, it represented perhaps a few seconds of the profit I made on my global investments.

DING

I heard the chime from the cockpit and knew it meant we were at one thousand feet.

There was no landing strip on the island, so we would land at Nagasaki Airport instead. The airport had one runway exclusively for private jets, and the other runways were for the loathsome commoners.

"Flight attendants, prepare for landing," came over the PA.

The two flight attendants, both exquisitely beautiful young women, made sure I was buckled in for the landing.

"There you go, Henry," the flight attendant said.

I playfully slapped her ass as she turned to walk away.

"Oh, Henry—" she chided with a smile.

I liked doing that. If a commoner did that, they would go to jail. But, for me, people were just "things" to be played with. Or even discarded.

I could feel, along with my immortality, my youthful vigor—and libido—had returned.

The plane landed on the runway as though sliding on glass; I had the best pilot money could buy. Unbuckling my belt, I rose to go down the opening jetway. My *help* would bring my luggage.

Several Japanese officials were there to greet me on the tarmac.

"Welcome, esteemed Henry-*san,*" one of them said, while they all bowed deeply.

I walked by them with a curt nod; I never liked business formalities.

"Yes, it is good to be here," I said as I walked to my waiting limo.

The limo took us to our freight ship.

Initially, I planned to take a helicopter there, but my security team advised me that the helipad had not been repaired and certified yet, so they did not want to risk an accident. That meant I would have to go on the same freight ship with the mine workers.

How revolting!

The ship was loaded with hundreds of workers and countless tons of supplies. But the real treasure was hidden in those supplies—

Weapons. Lots and lots of weapons.

The smugglers (not me, of course) would go to prison for the rest of their lives if those weapons were discovered. It was only a potential problem for others, though, so I paid no more attention to it and made my way to the captain's quarters. I knew that some of those weapons were for Hellious, and some were for my security team. They even brought explosives, which I will store in my penthouse until she tells me what they are for.

So, as I walked into the captain's quarters, I frowned.

What a dump!

At least it was a short ferry to the island. Even now on the island, they were sprucing up and supplying my master's quarters: an entire penthouse, the top two floors in one of the ten-story buildings.

Hopefully, it's much better than that captain's quarters.

After the ship reached the dock, we disembarked. My security team, which went everywhere I did, ensured all was safe from the ship to my penthouse.

The gangway led from the dock up and over the seawall, which was massive; it stood well over fifty feet. That and the lack of greenery gave the island a foreboding feeling. It must have been even more depressing back in the day. Now, at least, shrubs and trees were growing—along with grass and weeds—everywhere the eye looked. My trained eye, however, could only see the immense cost of refurbishing all the crumbling buildings and removing the invading plants— it was astronomical. I can see why the Japanese were so happy that I bought the island. It would take *billions* to renovate this island properly. I could see all this as soon as I got to the other side of the wall. Luckily, I would renege on doing any of that. Our renovation did involve getting the mine going again, but we were after a far more valuable resource ...

I could see where there were well-marked paths for the tourists, and they even went into some of the buildings, but most of the island was in disrepair. The "streets" were mostly just wide corridors that were too overgrown for cars; that is why a large ATV sat waiting for me. Frowning in displeasure, I got in. Although I'm used to the finest things in life, I have had to get my hands dirty occasionally. The ATV driver did his best to keep the ride smooth, but it was still rough. I looked around and saw decrepitude everywhere. The high walls, tall buildings, and relatively narrow streets made the interior depressing. Even midmorning, the sun struggled to reach the dark and dingy streets. Shadows played tricks and created a weird, haunted feeling, especially as the wind blew ancient newspapers and trash in little wind swirls. I could smell the sea breeze as it made strange and unsettling sounds—it whispered or howled through the streets.

I shivered. It was perfect for the lowlifes who would be toiling here.

My thoughts came to an end as we pulled up to my building. Typically, I would be ill from all the jostling as we reached the island's far end. Instead, I felt fine.

This new monster in me was something, for sure.

The northernmost end of the island had several buildings built into it. Being on a natural hill, the buildings on this end of the island were higher than the others. Unlike the ones below, many upper floors had a panoramic ocean view. The buildings formed a V-shape, with the large central mining facility in the center of the V.

The roads here were not designed for the main coal deliveries. Right now, they are not even serviceable for anything other than an ATV. Luckily, the workers mainly walked and used services underground and at the mine. A full monsoon could occur, and business could still be done. I had to admire the engineering.

The mine brought up over a thousand tons of coal *daily* during its heyday. Hellious told me we would mine for a much more profound treasure below. Ironically, those precious, rare metals we told Japan about (ignored at the time) *were* in the mine, but their extraction would also require more and more workers—

They were the actual prize.

————

My security detail and I entered the building.

It was still in disrepair, but the elevator was in excellent condition, and it whisked us up to the penthouse.

Finally.

The penthouse was ornate. Many of the buildings on the island were ten stories, as was this one. I picked the one on the highest part of the island, which gave me panoramic sea views. Since the Mitsubishi GM came here to oversee operations, the penthouse was already built for maximum luxury. So, it was not hard to return it to its former glory. The roof above had ample entertaining space, perfect for any parties (when necessary) or for relaxing and enjoying the ocean view and breezes. I heard movement from the doorway—

A beautiful twenty-year-old came in.

"Good morning, Henry," she said, kissing me.

She was one of my beautiful "girlfriends" who also brought me my Cognac and meals. I smiled and nodded my thanks. I didn't remember her name and, frankly, didn't care. Even though she was over sixty years my junior, she was always eager and ecstatic to please me.

As were all my "girlfriends".

I had watched, with amusement, as some of my dumber billionaires got caught in scandal after scandal. This never made any sense to me. A beautiful woman you paid for sex was a hooker, and you were "guilty" of soliciting a prostitute. But if they came willingly to be a "girlfriend," to include sex whenever you wanted, you were free and clear. So, they all signed contracts showing their willingness to "hang out" with the rich guy on his yacht. The ones who didn't please me? Back on land at the end of the voyage, with my thanks. They were not "required" to do anything.

Word of mouth was all that was needed. They arrived with their own pens.

Out of a hundred, only a dozen or so stayed. They were the smart ones, and they did all that I asked unquestioningly. For that, they were showered with money and other "gifts". And how many men help their girlfriends financially? Many do. So, there is no crime there.

I chuckled and admired the view again, both of her and the ocean beyond.

The freighter ship was unloading now. With the distance and excellent soundproofing, I could barely hear the bangs and movements on the other side of the island. The GM had picked his humble abode wisely.

I looked down from my window at the little specks of people far below. They dreamed of a better life for themselves and their families.

Hah! What a bunch of suckers and losers …

———

Gregory Yashido

I looked up at the sky far above. The wind blew, bringing a chill from the ocean breeze. The holiday season was fast approaching, and my son and daughter were excited. A large group of people walked alongside me.

"Hi, I'm Susan," a woman said to me.

I looked over at her; my mind had been drifting as I walked.

"Oh! Sorry, I was lost in thought. I'm Greg," I said, shaking her hand.

"Are you one of the new miners?"

"I am, are you?" I asked. I didn't really think she was, but I did not want to appear sexist if she said yes. Most miners, however, are male.

"Oh, no, I'm a teacher. I'll be teaching at the school."

"Wonderful! Classes start on January 5th, right?"

"That is correct. You must have children then, Mr. Greg."

"Yes. They are excited to start; their names are Levi and Jules. He is ten, and she is eight. Yoko is my lovely wife," I said.

"Well, I look forward to meeting them all," she answered with a warm smile, waving as she turned to head to the school. I continued walking to meet Yoko and the kids at our new apartment.

I smiled at my good fortune.

It was indeed an honor to have been chosen. Having been involved in mining my whole life, I competed with many others to be selected to come to this island. With a Bachelor of Science in Construction Engineering Technology, I was chosen to help restore the mine and oversee the other workers. My wage was easily double what I could get on the mainland of Japan.

If I could find work at all.

The Japanese labor market had been in a depression for some time, so construction work was hard to come by at any wage. So, I thanked the powers that be for my luck!

When I arrived at the assigned apartment building, I took the stairs to the third floor and went down the hall to unit 313. As I opened the door, they all came to greet me.

"Daddy!" shrieked Jules as she ran into my arms for a hug.

"Hi, Dad," Levi waved.

Yoko came over and gave me a short, sweet kiss.

"I have the honor of taking the first chalk into the mine. I may be back late, so just save me some leftovers?" I asked Yoko.

"Of course, my love. Congratulations on your new job! I'm glad you're going with the first group. What an honor!" she beamed.

I kissed Yoko and my kids goodbye and then headed for the mine. While they settled into our new apartment, I would join the first group going down into the mine.

This was a historic moment! My family was so excited that we would work and live in the place we had only visited as tourists. Unlike in the nineteenth and twentieth centuries, everyone here was a valued and "at-will" employee. We could leave the island anytime on one of the ships returning to the mainland, not that I ever would.

The three-month stipend I got was more than I made last year!

Whistling happily as I walked over to the other workers, I joined the other happy faces waiting to go down into the mine.

Growing up in Japan, my father, Shino, worked in the mines. So, I learned to be fascinated with them from an early age. Seeing how my father and the other men toiled long hours in these conditions, for meager pay, I was determined to be one of those other men with the survey maps, like the one I now hold. The ones called "engineers" who made more money and didn't toil like the other miners. I still wanted to be there and even to get my hands dirty, but I did not want to work like a slave for twelve hours a day.

"Welcome, everyone. I'm the superintendent of operations, Samuel Takishido. Thank you for your part in bringing Gunkanjima Island back to its former glory and beyond!"

We all clapped, and some shouted in celebration.

"Well, without further ado … Chalk One, to the mine!" Samuel yelled.

There was more clapping and pats on our backs as I joined the other nineteen miners of Chalk One. Once the twenty of us were on board the giant freight elevator, we shut the heavy metal grate and started the one-thousand-meter descent to the bottom.

We were honored to be the first men in modern history to begin the restoration. I could see my pride reflected in the other men's faces. I smiled, knowing I was honoring my ancestors, bringing honor to Japan, and providing for my beautiful family.

The light slowly faded as we went down, deeper and deeper into the mine.

CLANK, THUD!

We had reached the bottom. Two of the men lifted the grate, and we all got off.

"We are off!" the foreman, Haroto, I think his name was, yelled into the speaker. I heard someone say something back, and then the elevator clanked and rattled loudly as it rose back up the shaft. Everything was suddenly quiet.

That's weird.

Even though we were the first crew down, I expected at least *something* to be operating here. Typically, at least one machine would still be running on seawater or geothermal power.

"OK, men, looks like a cold start—nothing is on. Each of you pick a corridor and head down it. We need to figure out what we have, what we need, and what needs to be fixed. My team, let's get some lights up in this chamber. Let's go!" Haroto yelled.

I joined three others going down one of the four corridors. We all had survey maps and would need them, as this place was a maze, like most mines. Our flashlights were powerful but insufficient against the subterranean mine's lightless gloom.

"Hey, I'm Jim," said one man.

"I'm Tom, this is Hono—"

They turned to me.

"Gregory. Just Greg is good," I said.

"Cool. Let's go fix some stuff," Tom said, smiling.

We were all happy. Mine work can be dangerous, but this mine housed thousands of people and brought up hundreds of thousands of tons of coal in its day. It was not some flimsy mine, so I was not concerned.

It was probably safer than almost any other mine in the world …

―――――

We walked for a while—this place is enormous! I was fit for my ripe age of thirty-three, so I still had a spring in my step. As we walked, I marveled at how cool the mine was compared to the surface above. Millions of tons of water were high above our heads.

Patter, patter, patter …

"What was that?!" Jim asked.

We all shined our flashlights down the dark corridor—just a vast tunnel cut into the rock, maybe twenty feet high in the center.

"I don't know. It sounded like—" I said.

"A bunch of people running!" said Hono.

"How? Aren't we the first ones down?" asked Jim.

"Good question," Tom added.

"They must have messed up; that was definitely the sound of people running. Let's go check it out," I said.

I turned to continue and only heard my footsteps. Turning back around, I shined my flashlight toward them. They were standing there like frightened schoolkids.

"What is wrong with you all? Let's see who came down here before us; they can help! Obviously, they sent down some engineers ahead of us by mistake," I said, turning around again.

I heard them walking with me this time. To be honest, it *was* a little scary. But we are grown men who work in mines! We don't get scared every time there is a little noise or management screws up. So, we are the second crew and not the first, so what?

Patter, patter, patter …

"Hey! Who is there?" I yelled.

It was running feet; I heard it this time, without any doubt. There was no response.

"We can use your help; quit messing around!" I yelled.

Again, there was no response.

I would have a serious talk with the men acting this way.

Continuing, we came to a fork in the tunnel.

"OK, guys, how about Hono and I go left, Tom and Jim go right?"

They looked at each other and shrugged. Tom and Jim disappeared down the right corridor, as Hono and I started walking down the left one.

Our steps echoed, and it was hard to tell where the sound came from. There was a constant, slow drip of water on the damp floors. Having worked in many undersea mines, I knew they were all like this. There was no worry that the ocean would suddenly collapse through the roof on us, but water always seemed to find a way to seep inside.

I thought I heard more running in the tunnels, but now I realized my mind *was* playing tricks on me—

AAHHH!

"What was that?" Hono yelled.

I guessed it was one of the other two men.

"They could be hurt; let's head back to them," I said.

Unlike the other jittery men, my mind was not filled with boyhood fear. Sure, I was a little rattled by the unusual noises, but my primary concern was that one of the other two men, distracted by fear, had injured himself. He may need assistance.

Hono was frozen in place from fear.

"Let's go, Hono! They aren't paying us to stand here, and they need our help!" I yelled at him.

That worked, and we got moving at a quick walk. There was no running in a dark mine unless you wanted to get hurt like one of those other two idiots. We backtracked to where they were. Luckily, the survey map was accurate, and we didn't have far to go.

When we came around a bend, we saw the dark shapes of the two men ahead. As I suspected, one was on the ground, and the other was helping him. As we got closer, I recognized Tom's pants and boots. I shined my light on the two men. Tom was on the ground and—

What the ...?

A Korean man, young, maybe twenty years old, bent down over Tom. But something was wrong with his features; his whole body was black as night and covered in scaly warts. He was naked, and parts of his body were missing; whole chunks were gone, like animals had partially eaten him.

Crunch, crunch ... gulp. Crunch, crunch—

He snapped upright suddenly and turned to look at us. His eyes glowed amber, even as I turned my flashlight away to run! My last glimpse of him was of his nightmarish face—

It had a giant chunk *bitten* out of it.

Hono screamed at the top of his lungs and ran down a different tunnel. I saw the light from his flashlight dancing down the other tunnel and then fading from view.

I WAS terrified now!

The thing we saw chased after him. I knew because I recognized the sound now—

Patter, patter, patter ...

AAHHHhhhh ...

The sounds disappeared down the tunnel. Hono and whatever was *eating* Tom were gone. Carefully, I backtracked to the mine entrance and the elevator. I entered the large, well-lit chamber and, sighing in relief, called for the freight elevator to come down.

Nothing.

Angerly, I hit the call button again.

And again, nothing.

I grabbed the speaker and saw that it was unpowered now as well.

The power had been turned off. Maybe they were doing something to it above or just turned it off before the next crew came down.

OMG! The next crew!

No matter what happened to me, I couldn't let the next crew come down. I also desperately wanted to get out and back to my family. My thoughts were of Yoko, her beautiful long hair and smile, and my children, Levi and Jules. I had to get back to them!

There was an emergency ladder, but it had collapsed long ago. So, the only way up or down was that elevator.

Why hadn't I inspected that before all these men were down here?

AHH!—

Another man's scream—cut short this time.

It sounded very close.

My mind wanted to run, but there was nowhere to go. I looked out at the edge of the light, where it disappeared into long, dark tunnels in every direction.

Patter, patter, patter …

I shined my light down the tunnel.

Patter, patter, patter …

Another tunnel—

Please, God. Get me out of here!

Clink.

I heard something get bumped in a tunnel, so I shined my light down it.

Nothing. No, wait!—

Frantically swinging my light back into the tunnel, I could see several distant lights in the gloom. Could it be Hono or one of the other miners?

I could just make out several pairs of amber lights glinting far away in the diffused light of my flashlight. I suddenly remembered where I had seen those amber lights reflecting in the dark—

Oh, no. Those lights are sets of amber eyes looking back at me!

I dropped my flashlight and grasped the grate covering the elevator shaft. With both hands and a strength I didn't know I possessed, I pulled it open, stepped inside, and slammed it shut behind me, swiftly flipping the safety lock into place.

Turning around, I looked up. The unforgiving rock of the elevator shaft dimmed into the blackness above me. I walked forward and put my hands on the wet rock at the back of the mine shaft. There was no purchase, no way to climb. Even if I were a skilled rock climber, the rock's dampness would guarantee a deadly fall at some point during the thousand-meter climb.

Patter, patter, patter …

I froze.

Patter, patter, patter …

Closer now. So many of them.

I heard breathing. No yells, no screeches—just breathing in short, ragged breaths. I slowly turned around from the elevator shaft's rocky face to the metal grate I had shut.

There were dozens of them—

All were Koreans, all were pure black and in varying stages of decay, and all had been partially eaten—probably from each other when they died.

Just like Tom and the others.

They tried to reach in, and some were biting the metal with sharp teeth. Every maw had multiple rows of razor-sharp teeth. And their hands, blackened and dead, had long nails that scraped on the metal.

That was the sound I heard in the tunnel before.

I silently prayed that they were stupid, but I saw the looks in their eyes—they were already looking for ways to get in …

———

"Chalk Two, you're up!" yelled Samual Takishido.

There was more clapping and cheering as the elevator was powered back up, and another twenty men boarded it to descend into the mine.

CHAPTER 16
THE VESSEL

St. Mary's Basilica

Dorothy

FATHER CHRISTOS LEIGHE and I went to St. Mary's Basilica.

He took me into some back office, through a secret door in a bookcase, and down steps into a byzantine labyrinth of tunnels and rooms.

Well, I guess I got my ten thousand steps in, I thought with a chuckle.

The room was ornate and arcane. I observed strange, ancient tomes lining the walls, sconces and braziers lit with unusual flames, and recognizable and unrecognizable items in jars and other containers. Everywhere I looked, I felt the same impression—*a wizard's chamber? For a Catholic priest?*

I sat down in a very plush and ornate oversized chair. It was amazingly comfortable, and I started dozing …

"How was your nap?" Christos asked, waking me. He had a strangely amused look on his face.

I felt amazingly refreshed!

"Good! How long did I sleep?" I asked.

"About two hours," he replied.

Wow! It felt like seconds, but it was as though I had a solid night's sleep. Something I hadn't had since August when I was "turned."

"That chair is the Great Chair of Ware," he said.

"Where?" I asked. I wondered what on Earth he was rambling about …

"Ware, W-A-R-E. The chair you're sitting in was created in the early 1600s. The man who built it also made the Great Bed of Ware. It was a priceless and magnificent four-poster bed with a canopy that could sleep eight comfortably. During the Renaissance, a bed was a sign of wealth and passed down through the generations. Sometime around then, the first 'incursions' of demons and devils started showing up in our plane. Along with that came the advancement of science and things from the other plane, things we would call magic. The reason the stupid and gullible people of the world started crying out 'sorcery' and 'witch' was simple. Both science and this 'magic' were inexplicable to the commoner. So, in typical human fashion, they vilified and destroyed what they couldn't readily explain."

He paused. Probably to catch his breath, I thought; I felt like I was back in college.

"Anyway, he made that chair, somehow infused with something from this other plane. Anyone who sits in it falls into REM sleep almost instantly. That is why you feel so good," he said.

"Wow. No weirder than possessions and vampires, I suppose," I replied.

"Very true. Now that you're feeling better, let's get to work. I have a plan, but I'll only do it once you understand the risks and only if you choose to proceed—"

"That isn't scary at all," I said sarcastically.

He chuckled.

Even though he was a good fifteen years older than I was, I felt attracted to Christos. Perhaps it was because I couldn't have him. I always want things more the harder they are to get. Or maybe it was because his voice and charisma were simply beautiful.

"I'm going to put you in a trance and use exorcism to try to talk to the OI. Then, hopefully, you can sense where it is and even what it is doing."

"What then?"

"The goal will be to find where the actual monster is. Then OST can help us fight our way to it …"

Christos looked sickened, and I didn't like how he looked at me with deep sorrow.

"I love you as God loves you, Dorothy. All of humanity may depend on this next move," he said, then continued, "The only plan I have involves sacrifice—yours, to be direct."

He looked at me with compassion and empathy. Christos was a fantastic man. Even when the news was all bad, he genuinely cared for you.

I was terrified by his look, so I could only nod yes.

"Once we get to where this monster is, we must kill it. Only then will its 'mist' come out. I noticed it still needed to find cracks to get out. So, if we can seal it in, it cannot leave and will be trapped. Further study has shown me how to keep the mist from leaving an area, at least for a while. But the monster won't know that—it will just know it can't leave. Here is where you come in: It will be weakened and will then look for someone to jump into, someone it already possesses. As a mist, it is powerless without a summoned "dead" body to use. Someone who was either involved in the reading of the book or the summoning of the creature. Otherwise, it would have killed me during my exorcism of Laura Halston—

He looked sick as he continued.

"The only way to condemn it forever is inside of a host," he said.

And there it is. I was to hold this monster in me forever.

Christos put his hand on my shoulder; I was trying not to throw up. This was the most horrifying thing I could ever hear. To know I was already dead—and would surely die when the monster did—was bad enough. Now, I would be with it for all of time.

"When it goes in you, which it surely will—to have a body to use —you will be ready. Part of an exorcism is forcing a demon or devil to show itself. So, we can ready you to hold the monster inside you, against its will. Then, we have you climb into a hermetically sealed container and lock it shut. It will torture you to let it out, so you must be locked inside with no way to get out."

I looked into Christos's eyes. He seemed so empathic and compassionate, and I could tell that he felt the same horror I did.

"I don't want to stay with it. I want to check out," I said.

Christos nodded; he knew what I meant.

"I understand. We can put a bottle inside for you to pump in carbon dioxide and cyanide gas; you will fall asleep, and it will all be over. If there were another way, child, I would do it," he said.

My terror only grew because I knew he was right—I was technically already dead. I had no heartbeat, and from what I saw of the others, my insides were decayed and black. There was no "return to life" for me. That damn thing already killed me back in August during that moonlit initiation.

So, I was eager to return the favor.

The idea of *it* suffering forever made me smile. Before I went, I would give it one final "F— you". My nightmare would end, as its began.

Tears were streaming down my face as I weakly smiled at Christos.

"Thank you, Father, for allowing me to stop this thing and end my suffering. Let's get started ..."

The process was long and excruciating; I purged my mind of all emotion as I steeled it for my full possession to come. It had been nice to be free of it, but I needed to let it in for the plan to work. We can only hope I can just "let it in" whenever I choose to. That was one of many things that could go wrong. There were no other options, however. We either succeeded in this mission, or humanity's days were numbered. As I was feeling the probing of both Christos and *IT*, the epiphany happened—

Hello again, Dorothy. I am impressed. How did you keep me away?

You aren't that tough; it was easy. Look in my mind and see how—

Fascinating. You know I cannot. Still, you have returned to me. I am Hellious. Welcome home.

I could see it—thank God for my psych meds! It was on an island, and I could see all the decrepit buildings and a seawall. Far in the distance was the mainland. I tried to memorize every detail. And now I know its name! The same giant monstrosity of Hellious I saw on the mountain during the sorority ritual was before me now; only it was real and not just a red mist. It was still too terrifying to comprehend fully.

Impressive! Goodbye, my sweet!—

"OWW!" I screamed.

The pain was intense as Hellious broke the connection—

Finally, I was free!

I smiled. To be free of possession was like a wave of happiness. No longer in its thrall, I was free to be me again! This is the moment that Christos had prepared me for.

Hellious, of course, did not "free" me to live—it did it so I would "die" before I could get to it. We had prepared extensively for this moment, and I was able to keep the smallest thread of mental contact, unbeknownst to it. Christos placed an oxygen mask over my mouth and connected me to an IV. I would will myself to stay connected to it and alive until Hellious became *my* victim!

———

Tempe
Agent James

"Thank you for filling us in," I said to Christos.

Hanging up, I thought hard about what he told me. We also learned the name of our OI—Hellious.

I thought about what we had accomplished so far—OST had stopped the vice president and the sorority coven.

Whatever vampires we missed at ASU must have quickly left the campus. Luckily, our "mandatory" blood draw was explained and followed. After the videos came out, we decided on the best way to get compliance: just tell the students the truth. It sounds overrated, but when you tell *smart* people what is happening, they happily comply. If we forced them, they would scatter and get lawyers—as they should! Our compliance was at over ninety percent. The other ten? Let's just say they went from their school database to *our* database.

They were in a category that OST had created for known or suspected monsters.

Instead of KSTs (Known or Suspected Terrorists), we had KSMs. Not very original, but it works. Those missing college students were now on that list. The ASU students themselves insisted on having regular blood drives. Not only would it help those in need, but it would also be a good "monster checkup" and keep them from returning. This OI was intelligent; it would pick a softer target than the "new" ASU campus.

Furthermore, based on certain votes in Congress—specifically from those who would never have supported the bills presented by Congressman Halston—we had similar entries in our KSM database. Additionally, the Alpha and Charlie Teams from Lev's squad verified that many of these "KSMs" were politicians in both the House and the Senate.

Intel confirms we know it can create and control multiple undead.

This monster was a serious megalomaniac. It wanted us all and was well on its way to achieving that goal. Who else was undead or possessed?

We needed to stop Hellious, and soon. It would not be long before the Senate voted to end OST for good. Then, the OI would run unopposed.

I thought more about Christos's plan, then typed another number into my phone. After a short wait, Alan answered.

"MCC, Supervisor Loftus speaking."

"Is this *the* supervisory special agent in charge of the MCC?" I asked, smiling.

"It is! Is that you, James?"

I chuckled, "The one and only."

"Thank God for that."

We laughed.

"What do you need, James?"

"Well, I know you have been briefed on Christos's plan. I was thinking about adding something to our little present for Hellious."

"Shoot."

"It seems to me, if wood-core bullets work, maybe we should add a layer or two of that wood sandwiched into the tube's exterior. Keep the OI quiet and unable to contact others …"

I waited. I could almost smell the burning odor of intense thinking.

"Good idea. I'll ask them to add that to the lead layers I recommended."

"I should have guessed." I chuckled. "Alright, gotta run. Thanks for the chat."

"Anytime, brother, anytime."

The line went dead.

Our additions were worth a shot, at least. It's not like anyone can Google "how to trap a Hellious" on the internet.

Furthermore, we still didn't know precisely where Hellious was, even with Dorothy sharing every detail she could recall. Alan at the MCC collaborated with other brilliant individuals to locate the island Dorothy had seen, so we should have some options soon. What Dorothy revealed was already frightening: an island surrounded by a seawall in the ocean. The good news is that there can't be many "abandoned islands" worldwide. Most islands are worth a fortune to the right, extremely wealthy buyer.

While we waited, I called SAC Cho.

"Cho," he picked up on the third ring.

"Good evening, boss. I sent you our intel on Dorothy and our plan. Can we mobilize QRF-Oscar again? We need a bigger team this time. At least a platoon; I'd prefer a battalion, though—"

Cho laughed with me. We both knew it was pushing it just to get a platoon. It wasn't that we were unimportant, but—just like us—many of them were otherwise engaged in their current operations. It's not like Navy SEALs are just waiting around for us to call them.

"Hey, boss, any luck on the island?" I asked.

"No, although Alan is confident they will nail it down soon, what-ever that means," he said.

"OK. We're at an impasse here—my team can deploy to help find monsters in DC or Tempe, but I think the endgame will be on our mystery island …" I said.

Cho and I both thought for a while.

"Agreed. Return to DENFO, and we'll go from there."

"Hey, boss. Speaking of DENFO—"

"Yeah, work in progress. We have started repairs on the front door, and the rest is pretty cleaned up. We have a permanent camp of protesters, counter-protesters, and media outside our building, but it's going OK. All agents passed the 'blood test,' so we are good on that front at least."

"Alright, we'll take the C-130 again; see you soon, boss."

"See you soon," Cho said, hanging up.

I pondered our next steps. There was not much more to consider. We had one plan, and it wasn't just our best plan—it was our only plan.

———

OST DENFO

My flight landed without incident at Centennial, and we drove back to DENFO.

Pulling into the garage sally port at OST DENFO, the NMC guys and Frank came out. Frank was struggling. He was "on duty" and had a job to do, but when he saw me, his tail was going a mile a minute. Watching him be so professional made me smile. It was killing him— he wanted to come see me so badly!

After completing the procedure, we pulled in and backed into the GOV Two space. As we climbed out, I started walking out of the garage. I saw Agent Baker at the port controls.

"Hey, Ed. Sorry about what happened here; are repairs going OK?"

"Yeah, they are on it," he replied.

"Thanks for saving our asses—again."

"No prob, James," Ed said.

As I turned and walked away, I gazed around me. Everything was back in order. While the evidence of what had happened remained, it was functional once more. I entered the lobby and made my way to Chayton's office.

I knocked on the doorjamb, and he looked up.

"Hey, James. Good work, as always," he said.

"Thank you, sir. Good job with DENFO."

He nodded and motioned to the empty chair in the office. Understandably, everyone was very subdued. I sat and waited as he finished something on his computer.

"OK. I have all the AARs and updates. Alan and the MCC folks are working on the island angle. Where are we at besides that?" he asked me.

"Well, Lev and Dave are recovering in the Tempe hospital; Dorothy and Christos are ready for the OI capture; now we need to organize QRF-Oscar and get intel. Once we know where this island is, the real work begins. The pre-operational planning, the sandbox rehearsals, the five-paragraph OPORD, etc. Where do you want me?"

"I had been considering that. I'm sending you back to Joint Base Andrews to meet and train with QRF-Oscar. They also have *the gun* and said it is repaired now, so let Lev know when she wakes up."

He told me that matter-of-factly because he knew I had been checking in on her nonstop since she went to the hospital. Lev had been steadily improving, and they expected her to regain consciousness soon.

Chayton continued, "JSOC has given us SEAL Team 8 again. This time with a full platoon—sixteen SEALs."

"That is great!" I replied.

"Yes. Considering everything happening outside of OST, we were lucky to get that many," Chayton said.

"True," I replied.

"I realize you just got back, but let's load up a Suburban with all the gear needed for the OP and get you to Centennial. That was the main reason I wanted you back. The Tesla can't hold all the gear the assault team will need. Besides, you can rest on the C-130," he said, smirking.

"Yeah, thanks a lot," I said, but I was smiling too.

We got up, and I followed Chayton to ARMOURY. In addition to the ExoM suits, I grabbed weapons and equipment for the OP. Several agents helped me; it was *a lot* of stuff!

I was bummed we couldn't take the MX, but the SEALs had their DPVs if we needed vehicles. Besides, the MX, along with Frank, was a big part of us still having a field office at all. So, they would be staying.

Once we had everything loaded into the Suburban, Chayton shut the ARMOURY and went back to his office. NMC agent Marcus Clay joined me in the SUV and entered the driver's seat.

"Where to, boss?" he asked.

Smart ass, he knew where we were going.

"Disneyland. And make it snappy!" I said.

"Will do."

Marcus pulled the Suburban out of GOV Three, and we went into the sally port. I missed having the Tesla, but we were hard-pressed just to fit everything into the Suburban. I felt bad for its suspension. Once the outer door opened, we were on our way to Centennial Airport. Luckily, the media had found nothing to see or report besides our leaving and what car we were in, so they didn't bother to follow us. We got to our hangar, loaded up, secured the Suburban into the C-130, and were on our way.

It was becoming routine at this point.

I put my head back on the Suburban's headrest and drifted off as the C-130 took to the sky.

———

Joint Base Andrews—Virginia

The rear cargo door on the C-130 lowered as soon as the hangar door shut.

When the door was fully down, Marcus and I opened the back of the Suburban and unloaded gear into the hangar. A group of men, clearly Navy SEALs, came forward to help. As soon as we finished emptying the Suburban, one of them approached me.

"Agent Grey, I'm Lieutenant Taylor, commander of SEAL Team 8," he said, holding out his hand.

"An honor, sir. Thanks for keeping Lev out of trouble," I replied, shaking his hand.

"Hah—like anyone could control her," he replied.

"Yeah, you're not wrong—" I said.

LT Taylor shook out his hand, grimacing.

"Wow, you're as bad as Lev! We need to teach you to control that thing," he said.

"Oh yeah, sorry about that. I still have a lot to learn … speaking of … we all know I'm not a Navy SEAL, so fill me in on what role you want me to play in this OP."

Lieutenant Taylor looked at me and thought about it. Finally, he smiled and nodded.

"Of course. Let me introduce you to the platoon first. This is the Second Squad: Lieutenant JG (Junior Grade) Decker, and Petty Officers (POs) Preston, Myers, Phillips, Owens, Burch, Duffy, and Silva," he said.

They all nodded or waved.

"My Squad, First Squad, has some familiar faces and, unfortunately, some new ones."

The SEALs all nodded somberly; they had lost SEALs Cole and Price, who were killed in action, along with Brooks, who was wounded in action.

"I'm the Platoon and First Squad Leader; over there are Petty Officers Smith, Parks, and Acevedo," he said, pointing to the new SEALs.

"And Petty Officers Carr, Reynolds, Evans, and Lamm were on the VPOTUS mission with Lev," he concluded.

They all nodded my way.

"Don't worry, we all wear name tags and will simply be Squad One and Two, with teams Alpha through Delta on each squad," LT Taylor said.

I nodded.

"Nice to meet you all. I look forward to helping however I can. On that note…" I looked at LT Taylor.

"I have one role you could fill well on the ground," he said.

I cocked my head.

Damn, I probably look like Frank right now.

"We'll call you … Fire Support Zulu, or just Zulu for short."

A bunch of SEALs were smiling my way. They all had that look like they were sharing a funny joke only they knew. And I was the butt of that joke.

"Behold!—" LT Taylor said with a dramatic flourish of his hand.

PO Jason Evans stepped aside, and I saw something I hadn't seen since the 1980s.

The *Predator* Gatling gun.

The movie *Predator* came out in 1987. In it, Blaine uses an M134 modified to be fired by a single operator. They had found a massively muscular man for the role. His weapon fired blanks, but it was a working prototype of what lay before me now. The pressure from firing live rounds would have knocked him on his ass, or at least made it almost impossible to use accurately, but they probably figured that I could handle it.

"We won't have you go into combat without test firing it first—" LT Taylor said.

He motioned to PO Evans.

"Take him to Range Five; give him a few thousand rounds of familiarization fire," LT Taylor ordered.

"Yes, sir. Follow me, James, sorry, *Zulu—*"

Evans turned and walked to the waiting DPV.

I went over and picked up the M134. It was light, just a hundred pounds or so …

Hmm. This should work nicely!

I carried it over, placed it in the DPV, and climbed into the passenger seat. We rolled out of the hangar and headed for the firing range.

The Desert Patrol Vehicle wasn't much for comfort, but it was pretty cool. The engine made a fierce growling noise, like a motorcycle engine with a good muffler. Not too loud, but still mean-sounding. It could go full electric with the turn of a knob—helpful when you wanted to go quietly—but still used gas for most of its journeys.

We pulled up at the range and saw a gruff-looking man in a US Marine uniform.

"Morning, Gunney," Evans greeted.

"Good morning, Petty Officer … Is that James?" he asked, glancing in at me.

"It is. We are going to get him acquainted with the M134 and the .30 Cal. Heading to Five, do you want to fire a few?" Evans asked.

"I wish! I need to watch some FNG recruits so they don't blow their dicks off. Next time," the Gunnery Sergeant said.

We waved and drove off to Range Five. After parking the DPV, we climbed out.

"OK, let's get you suited up," Jason said.

He helped me into the rig and familiarized me with it, including how to wear it, fire it, clear malfunctions, and even take it off quickly. I leveled it at a car about 300 meters away.

BZZZZZZ!

My first salvo was terrible. Half my rounds missed against a stationary target—a car, no less.

PO Evans roared in laughter.

"OMG, you *really* suck at that!" he laughed.

"Thanks for the confidence boost," I replied, frowning.

"No worries, mate. You and Lev are the only ones who can even fire the damn thing. Let me teach you how to fire it like a soldier, not a blind ape …"

———

We rejoined the rest of the team that afternoon. I wouldn't win any gold medals with my shooting skills, but at least now I could use it accurately. Besides, with a cyclic rate of 1,800 rounds per minute, I could miss a few and still hit my target. However, the pack only held four hundred rounds, so I would have to be judicious with my trigger finger. I had also practiced with the .30 Cal machine gun on the DPV, so I could use that if necessary.

The SEALs had colluded with Alan at the MCC, and his mystery armorer had gotten us a ton of the wood-core rounds, so all rounds in the weapons were now wood-core. I had four hundred rounds in the ammo backpack for the M134, plus an additional six hundred (in separate, two-hundred-round satchels) for the other SEALs to take. No matter how strong Lev and I were, there were still limits on the *volume* of things we could carry.

The SEALs typically carried suppressed MP5SD SMGs, while the non-snipers also had M4s with M203 grenade launchers attached. The snipers on the two Delta Teams were equipped with RM338 LMMG machine guns instead of M4s. Combined with a spare barrel, tripod, and 500 rounds, these weapon systems weighed a total of one hundred pounds. The A-gunner carried the barrel and extra rounds (instead of the tripod) along with an M4, resulting in a much more mobile system.

As usual, we all carried first aid gear, water, and food bars.

Each of us would also carry one M18A1 Claymore explosive mine. Each mine had also been modified with a plank of serrated rosewood on the front. It was in the M7 bandolier, which had the clacker and wire to detonate it. The mine contains a layer of C-4 explosive behind about seven hundred 3.2 mm steel balls set into epoxy. The rosewood would also break into about the same number of pieces. It should destroy a lot of vamps in a 60-degree arc out to several hundred meters.

Also, we were all issued M111 offensive grenades. They can be used during combat while minimizing danger to friendly personnel. The grenade was designed for when lethal fragments are not desired— to reduce collateral damage.

I had used grenades before in the army but was out of practice. So,

I was lobbing a blue (inert) M111 training grenade around like a toy. Usually, this is a huge no-no, but I needed the practice. They had me throwing it into waste baskets, through windows and doors, and anything else the SEALs could think of, which was a lot. With my increased strength, I could easily throw the grenade well past 200 meters. Hitting was a different story altogether, though.

At least I could outshoot them with a pistol, but that was about it; they excelled in every other aspect of combat. As they should, given their training.

In my short time with the SEALs, I learned everything I could from them. They knew my training background and built from that. I practiced MOUT (Military Operations in Urban Terrain) with them until they were comfortable that I understood how they did small unit tactics. Nothing could match their years of training and experience, but at least it would keep me out of their way and, hopefully, not get anyone killed—

Like it was divine timing, right after a long day of training, my phone rang; it was Lev!

"Hi, baby! How are you feeling?" I answered.

"Like a spring chicken … hit by a tractor," she said.

I laughed.

"So, pretty much back to normal then?" I asked.

"Yes, that sums it up. I'm OK, Hon. Thank you. How about you?"

I noticed the other SEALs smiling and shaking their heads.

"I was just learning how not to kill your SEAL friends by accident," I added.

PO Carr gave me a thumbs-up on that comment.

"I appreciate that! Tell them I'm on my way. See you at about … 1830 hours."

"Awesome, I can't wait. By the way, *the gun* is fixed and here waiting for you," I said.

"Sweet! Keep her company, and I'll be there soon."

"Copy that. Out." I broke the connection.

The gun, her Mark 19 Mod X, sat waiting. Loaded with thirty-two highly effective LVLE rounds, her combat bag had another drum of

HEDP rounds. The SEALs had fully repaired it and improved it again. Now, it had heavy metal armor in front of both the front and rear grips. So, it could deflect more damage from the user's gun hand if she fired it again without cover. There were still scratches all over it from the battle. It reminded me of Lev—scratched and dented but still beautiful. It had worked well for her so far, and she would also carry the MP5SD with a hundred-round drum magazine, just like the other SEALs.

At 1830, we sat down to eat Chinese takeout. We had gotten Lev her favorite: two orders of sweet and sour chicken and white rice. A short while later, she walked in, and everyone turned—

Her face had many new scars on the left side, and a chunk of her left ear was gone but already growing back. Her arms and hands looked like she had survived a war … or two or three.

"Hi there, sexy fellas!" she said, beaming.

"Hey, it's our favorite frogwoman!" yelled PO Carr.

"I f—ing hope so! Since I'm your only frogwoman," she said.

They all laughed, and she walked over and joined us. She grabbed me and gave me a deep kiss.

"Oh, man! Really, Lev?" LT Taylor said.

"Yuup." She and I said (again in unison).

The other SEALs just shook their heads.

"OK, looks like my baby is ready—"

Lev turned and went over to her baby, the Mark 19.

She picked it up with one hand, gripping it like an eight-pound M-16. Nodding in appreciation, she moved it around, reacquainting herself with its weight and movement.

"It has the LVLE rounds, I can tell by the weight," she said.

"That is correct—" LT Taylor said, smiling, then added, "HEDP rounds in the combat pack, as usual."

"That'll work. Any news on the OP?" she asked.

LT Taylor shook his head no. Then he turned to the platoon—

"OK, everyone! Finish eating, then prep the DPVs and stow your weapons and equipment on the bird. I don't know if we can use the DPVs, but I want them ready. After that is done, grab a rack and some

ZZZs. This is probably our last chance before this OP starts," LT Taylor said.

"Aye, aye, sir," from the SEALs.

We gobbled down our dinners, prepped, and then racked out.

I woke from a deep sleep to see LT Taylor talking on a SATCOM phone. He was jotting down some things and then hung up.

Stretching, I glanced over at Lev. She was awake and watching; she hadn't even raised her head. LT Taylor saw us and motioned for us to join him, so Lev and I got up and went over.

"The OI is on Gunkanjima Island, in Nagasaki, Japan," he said.

"Damn," Lev said.

LT Taylor and I nodded in agreement; we all knew what that meant.

Japanese airspace meant we couldn't just deploy like normal. Without permission, we would have to do a HAHO (high-altitude, high-opening) jump without any vehicles (to avoid radar detection). Also, we would be enemy combatants in a foreign country. Even if we won, it would be challenging—maybe even impossible—to extract. POTUS would be unable to secure consent for the OP from a hostile Congress, and there would not be time for formal permission anyway. We were essentially invading Japan with a SEAL platoon.

Oh well, even if it caused a war, at least humanity would survive.

LT Taylor went over and turned on the bay lights. Nothing even had to be said. The SEALs all got up and went over to the briefing area.

"I hope everyone enjoyed their sleep. We are a go for our OP," he said, turning to the whiteboard and a large monitor. An overhead view of a vast island was displayed on the screen.

"This is Gunkanjima Island, located in Nagasaki, Japan. It is a former coal mining facility and will be the location of our target. The island was once the most densely populated place on Earth. It's less than one square kilometer in size, but a high seawall surrounds it. Japan established it in the late 1800s to mine undersea coal, and by the

1940s, it had produced hundreds of thousands of tons of coal, primarily from Korean enslaved laborers. The island is filled with ten-story buildings and underground facilities. It is a maze of restaurants, schools, courtyards, stairs, and other structures to accommodate the almost six thousand people who once lived and worked there. A labyrinth of underground corridors, staircases, and mineshafts interconnects it all. There is even a commissary somewhere down there."

He paused for a moment.

"It has recently been bought by a billionaire named Henry Rothensburger. Based on intelligence provided by OST, we now have one hundred percent confirmation on the island. Our OI is holed up somewhere on the island; it is our primary target. All we know is it isn't human and is *much* bigger than a person. I truly hope that makes it unique as a target ..."

The looks on the SEALs' faces matched his—the "what world are we in now" look.

"We are currently looking at a total of approximately 2,350 people on the island. A ship carrying 1,113 individuals, all civilians, made a trip to the island shortly after it was purchased. The manifest listed nothing else except them and a large "support structure". Regarding OPFOR (opposing forces): We know Rothensburger's security detail is comprised of former operators, and we expect them to be on the island, as his jet flew to Nagasaki Airport. We have also intercepted ship records indicating that another 1,230 individuals, along with standard supplies, have recently arrived at the island. They will primarily be mining crews—"

LT Taylor paused and looked a little sick.

"—and their families," he finished.

"Oh, man ... that sucks," said PO Evans. The other SEALs nodded in agreement.

"Yes. It does ... We must assume all civilians in the target area are compromised by the OI. It will still be a free-fire zone on the island," LT Taylor said.

We all sat quietly for a minute as the gravity of the horror sank in.

This monster was going to make us kill innocent civilians, including women and children.

"That son of a bitch!" PO Kevin Smith finally exclaimed.

"Yeah. No one is OK with this, but we have to do it," LT Taylor said.

"Check?" he asked.

We all said, in turn, "Check, sir."

"OK, let's pull up our topography and figure out our battle plans …"

We studied the reports on the mine's construction methods, as Alan at the MCC had contacted some mine construction engineers. If we didn't use the grenades in one of the mine tunnels, we *should* be OK.

The satchels were a different story.

Each SL carried a US M2 assault demolition, a.k.a. a "satchel" charge. It could be detonated by wire (with a "clacker") or using a timer.

The explosives were reduced from twenty pounds of C-4 to five pounds. That amount, used in a large open room in the mine, again *should* be OK and not bring the Pacific Ocean down on our heads, as long as it isn't too close to a wall or support structure.

Not exactly reassuring, I thought.

I hope we don't have to use explosives down there.

CHAPTER 17
HAHO

Gunkanjima Island—Nagasaki, Japan
Agent Lev

SEAL TEAM 8 and OST were preparing to leap from the C-130J at 30,000 feet using the high-altitude, high-opening jump—one of the most challenging maneuvers in parachuting. I looked over at the other SEALs, along with Dorothy and Christos, who had been inhaling pure oxygen to eliminate nitrogen from their systems and prevent decompression sickness, commonly known as "the bends". They also wore polypropylene undergarments to protect against frostbite in the minus 47-degree air.

James and I wore our full combat load without needing oxygen or cold-weather gear.

From my many previous jumps at the Yuma Proving Ground in southwest Arizona, I had learned that I simply didn't need it. The cold didn't affect me, and I could go without oxygen for several minutes or hours. Plus, I did not suffer from the bends.

The SIM part of me changed me so that I don't need to worry about time and depth while scuba diving or breathing during military free-fall. Although James was not a SEAL, he had shown a similar capability. However, I still insisted we had oxygen on him, just in case we were wrong.

Military free-fall is one of the most physically demanding and dangerous skills in special operations. It is typically done under the cover of darkness to hide our presence from OPFOR. The maneuver has its dangers, though. Protective goggles could crack, eyes could seal shut from the frigid cold, or the soldier could lose consciousness during the jump. There was a list of things that could go wrong with every operation.

Christos was strapped to PO Evans, and PO Carr had Dorothy strapped to him. The civilians looked scared out of their minds, understandably.

"Hey, Lev—will you try the HANO jump today?" Carr asked.

They all laughed. They had joked earlier that I should do a "High Altitude, No Opening" jump.

"Next time, guys," I said.

Christos looked at me in fear.

"Petty Officer Evans is a pro, don't worry," I told him.

I didn't mention that Jason Evans had never done a tandem jump with a passenger before. It was weird; he was wearing Christos like you would a papoose. Also left unmentioned was that Christos was both a liability and an asset. He was in average shape for a man his age, maybe even on the fitter side, but he was not in the insane condition of the Navy SEALs. However, Christos was the only one of us who had successfully exorcised demons before. And one of those "demons" he faced (and lived to talk about it) was the one we hunted now.

Dorothy was also critical in stopping this, and her days were numbered anyway. That sounds horrible—because it is.

We had to put her on *additional* psych meds just to keep her sane now.

I definitely can relate.

The name alone gave me night terrors. Hellious—it meant "inferno" in Latin, and we had yet to see it use fire.

On second thought, best not to dwell on that—

The cabin lights went red; we were almost in the drop zone.

"Two minutes," came over the PA.

We assembled for the jump.

The "casket" would land before me since I had tethered it for the jump. We had decided to name it that because saying "weird, torpedo-looking thing" took too long. It was heavy, so I would land like a ton of bricks, even after releasing it before touchdown. It had extensive padding—an excessive amount, really. If it broke, the mission would fail before it even began.

James was not certified for parachuting, so PO Parks carried his Gatling gun tethered like mine. James was jumping in tandem with PO Phillips.

PO Smith had *the gun.*

I could see that James was nervous. Sure, he had been in combat multiple times—and even died in battle—but jumping out of a plane at night into the clouds below was still scary.

"You good, James?" I asked.

He gave me a thumbs-up and a shaky smile.

The jump lights came on.

"GO," yelled LT Taylor.

We all dived into the freezing night …

As soon as we cleared the aircraft, we deployed our glider chutes.

The reason for the HAHO jump was simple: our aircraft had to follow a specific flight plan and avoid invading Japan's airspace. Thus, we jumped from thirty thousand feet and glided twenty-five miles to our target. As gliders and individuals, we would not create a significant radar signature and would be difficult to detect with the naked eye. This way, we could reach our target and catch them off guard. Let's just hope vampires can't see well at night—

Crud.

Far below, we exited the cloud cover. As we dropped to ten thousand feet, we could see Gunkanjima Island—an inky black island in an inky black ocean. We angled toward it; luckily, we were dead on target.

Our LZ (Landing Zone) was just now visible on the island's edge. Hopefully, the enemy would not detect us until well after we landed.

We had researched Gunkanjima Island, and, in short, it felt like a nightmare for us. There was only limited information available, along with the current satellite topography, which we had memorized. However, there were many unknowns: the enemy's types and numbers? Uncertain, but likely substantial. The underground terrain? Uncertain. The OI's capabilities and location? Unknown. Thus, this was likely the worst-case scenario for us, and the best-case scenario for our enemy.

This damn monster was brilliant.

It must have known we would be in a foreign country and heading to an island without backup. Plus, it was a complete maze. We now know the OI creature possesses multiple people and can create an army of undead to protect it, so that was a given in our planning. It was going to be an ugly battle, to be sure.

As the wind whipped by my face, I looked at the other SEALs. The island loomed before us. We could see lights on in some apartments and even some halogen lights run by generators. Those would need to be disabled if we went into that area.

Although we had the advantage of night vision, I feared they did too—innately.

I could see just fine without NVGs, as could James, so I'm betting the vampires could as well. We knew they didn't meet the strict definition of vampires, but since these were real and not just legends, it's fair to count them as the "real deal" even if aspects of them didn't match the fairy tales.

We angled for the high end of the island and our LZ. Our intel said the mine shaft was there, so we were hoping the mine was meaningful to the OI.

Otherwise, we were SOL.

Trying to control even that one part of the island would be difficult enough.

In addition to James, Christos, Dorothy, and me, there was a platoon of Navy SEALs: two officers and fourteen enlisted, forming two squads. So, we were eighteen combatants against over a thousand possible vampires, a billionaire and his security team, and some monstrous OI creature.

It's just another easy SEAL/OST mission.

We did not plan to "kill" every undead on the island. Our mission objective was to transport the casket to the OI, eliminate it, and then capture its mist form inside the casket. Only then would Dorothy end things for good. However, we still had to get the casket off the island afterward.

The Navy would do that.

SEAL Team 5, based out of Pearl Harbor, had SEAL Delivery Vehicles SDV-1 and SDV-2, which had already launched from the Dry Dock Shelter on the back of a submarine. The Mark 8 Mod 1 was their latest version and could send encrypted radio transmissions to the sub. They would transport us to a waiting Navy submarine just outside Japan's territorial waters.

There was also a Mark 9 Mod 1 SDV coming.

The Navy's newest SEAL Delivery Vehicle wasn't a delivery vehicle at all, unless you consider its two torpedoes a "delivery". It was designed to attack surface ships instead of deploying SEALs. Stealthy and designed to target and destroy ships, it was currently armed with only one torpedo. The other tube was empty and had been retrofitted to store the casket. The Mark 9 SDV would surface in the ocean, and the SEALs would load the casket into the torpedo tube. Then, the SDV would return to the nuclear-powered submarine in the Pacific, the USS Greeneville.

The only good news so far was that the US Navy was already conducting a joint exercise with Japan to prepare against China's ever-growing imperialism. Therefore, the US Navy's presence wouldn't spook Japan's Navy. Even now, the US Navy is performing a "drill" with its SDVs—just for us.

Our LZ was in a small courtyard not far from the mine, and it was quickly approaching. Releasing my line on the casket, it landed right in front of me. Then, my boots hit the ancient pavement hard. I landed with my feet together and fell to my side, rolling with the momentum until my feet spun over me and hit the ground. This was the parachute landing fall (PLF) technique that all airborne troops use; it absorbs the impact of landing, especially when landing hard, which I definitely experienced. I snapped to my feet after finishing my roll.

Everywhere I looked were tall buildings, crumbling streets, and random vegetation pushing out through every crack, nook, and cranny. The desolation was palpable. An eerie wind blew through the island. It's hard to believe thousands called this place home; it was creepy.

Of course, its purpose was clear—to provide coal for Japan. That's it.

I quickly disconnected from my glider chute and examined the casket. After removing the expansive padding around it, I looked it over. It seemed in perfect shape, and I breathed a sigh of relief. The entire mission would have failed if that casket had been broken or unusable.

The rest of the team and our CIs also landed safely and without injury.

Everyone except James and me was wearing NVGs. If there was any light, James and I resembled many of the world's other animals—superior to humans. I approached PO Smith and retrieved *the gun*. I noticed that PO Parks was assisting James with the M134. We quickly stashed our chutes, formed a hasty 360-degree fighting position, and quietly waited.

No one had spotted our landing, and no one was injured—one minor miracle down, countless more to go.

We moved out, putting our CIs in the middle of the squads. Team Charlie One pulled and carried the casket. It had a frame attached to wheels that pulled it, at least when the ground was smooth enough. The two men took it by its handles the rest of the time.

The SEALs had their MP5SDs out and had their M4/M203s slung on their backs. In contrast, the two snipers on the Delta Teams had their RM 338 machine guns instead of M4s. The sniper teams found strategic spots to overwatch us as we moved. Their machine guns could reach out and touch more than two miles, far beyond the island's length. So, they quickly saw what lay before us.

We all had earpieces, so we could talk on the same channel or split into separate squad channels. After no enemy contact at the LZ, we made our way toward our objective—the mine.

"We have multiple hostiles on route one," Delta One radioed us.

After double-checking our map, we took an alternate route, one that went around the sentries the sniper saw. Moving tactically, we bounded as we moved, first one team covering while the other moved, then flip-flopping. We made it to the mine access building without contact.

Miracle number two.

There were two doors in. One was a pedestrian door we found to be locked from the inside, and the other was a large one for moving machinery. The large metal loading door would make a racket when opened, but we saw no other way in, unless—

"LT, permission to go in quiet to the roof and find another way in for the platoon," I radioed.

"Granted," LT Taylor replied.

"Delta Two, join her on the roof and give us a roost up there," LT Taylor said.

"Wilco," responded Delta Two.

Levering myself onto the catwalk, I helped Delta Two up, and then we made our way to the top of the building. I had left my Mark 19 with the team below, as it was noisy to fire and awkward to carry up to the roof. For now, I had a silenced MP5 in my hands, but even it makes some noise when fired.

I looked around until I found a hatch for storing mining supplies. It was not designed for people and had a long drop to the floor. Unspooling my rope, I attached it to the hatch's frame. I could see the two SEALs setting up to cover the two streets leading to the mining building with the RM 338.

I silently wished them luck.

Then, carefully opening the hatch, I dropped in my rope and started my free-fall descent. I went quickly; the only sound was the zipping sound as I descended the line.

The sound was enough.

When I landed, I could see a half-dozen undead vamps stealthily heading my way across the open floor. There was almost no light in here, and if I had been human, I never would have seen them coming. I thumbed my MP5's selector to semi-auto.

Chuff … chuff … chuff …

Chuff … chuff … chuff …

They dropped silently. There were no screams of agony as I hit each with a precise round to the head.

So far, so good.

I pushed on the outer door for pedestrians, and it didn't budge—that's when I saw the heavy cable and padlock. Moving to the lock, I took out a couple of small bottles of acid. Squirting each into the lock, I heard it hiss and pop. I unfastened the lock and removed the chain. Turning quickly, I scanned for more threats.

Nothing.

I gently opened the door.

SCREECH.

Not too loud; we should be good.

"Door open," I radioed.

"We see you; we are en route," one of them responded.

After the SEALs entered the large room, we moved out past the undead bodies. No hands reached out to grab us; they were truly dead now. Our pre-operational planning indicated that this building would house the elevator that would descend to the mine. We could see a closed steel grate in front of a large freight elevator.

"Delta Two, we are in position, all clear," PO Silva radioed.

"Copy," LTJG Decker replied.

Delta Two was on the roof, protecting us from outside threats. The other teams in Squad Two and I would defend our EVAC from the mine. The reason for sending James down instead of me was simple: his Gatling gun could be used in the mine, whereas my weapon was more effective against troops in the open. Additionally, firing *the gun* in narrow mine tunnels would be terrible—even catastrophic—for everyone, including us. The same applies to our offensive hand grenades.

After securing and barring all the doors inside the room, we established our fallback positions for cover within the building. Alpha Two and Bravo Two then began setting up their fields of fire (FOF) and hardcover (to stop incoming rounds) inside the structure. Meanwhile, Charlie Two and I coordinated our exterior defenses. Charlie Two had a strong field of fire on the open space leading to their position, including the avenue of approach (AOA) from one street. I covered the other FOF/AOA on the adjacent street.

We knew we would start any large-scale engagement out here, so I joined Charlie Two to cover the streets outside. If we were being overrun, we would fall back to cover from inside the mineshaft room. Our fallback places were already set up with cover and additional fields of fire.

Plus, we even set some booby traps for our enemies, setting up Claymores on the likely "avenues of approach" on the two streets leading to the mine. We took all the Claymores from First Squad, as they would not need those in the mine. So, we had six mines "daisy-chained" to explode simultaneously for each approach. Once we fell back to the interior, the leftover six were set up the same way—to detonate into the clearing outside the door to the mine building.

Movies always make it look like special operators are just lucky and adept at "going with the flow". Although that is a trait we do have, it is what we do when our planning *doesn't* work out. But we always have plans and fallback plans. This OP is no different.

Well, except for the vampires and a giant creature from another plane.

We completed our exterior defenses and then went inside. The room we entered was massive; equipment and places for cover and concealment were scattered throughout. We assisted Alpha and Bravo in finishing the defenses, including our fallback positions. We relocated and eliminated what we could in our fields of fire, although many items remained unmoved. We noted reference points and ranges and established individual AORs for each shooter. Final protective fire was designated as the point at which we all would shoot if we were overrun en masse.

After our defenses were complete, I settled on top of a large piece of machinery outside. I have no idea what it does. It provided an unobstructed, wide-open field of fire on my avenue of approach. Charlie Two set up to cover my flanks and give me additional fire support, and they watched the other avenue of approach. We went to our positions, and each of us checked in. It was time to start the party.

"Squad Two, eyes open; we are getting a little loud with the elevator now," LT Turner said. Everyone copied on their radios.

When they opened the grate, it screeched, surprising no one. We could not do anything about it; the freight elevator would be even louder.

CLANK, CLANK, CLANK!

The elevator was loud as hell in the formerly quiet air. My nerves were on edge; if they were here, we were about to have company.

"I don't like it," I said.

"Me either, stay frosty," said LT Taylor.

Things had gone *too* well. We were all walking into a trap, for sure.

CLANK, THUD!

I knew James and First Squad would be getting into the elevator now. We had long considered what to do with the CIs and the casket during our pre-battle planning. Our best guess was that the OI would probably be down in the tunnels, so that is where the CIs and the casket needed to go. We could be wrong, but they had to go somewhere, and we couldn't just leave them topside until we figured it out. Dorothy, Christos, and the casket would have to work in unison when we turned the OI into "mist".

There was still no sign of the enemy. I had loaded the HEDP rounds into *the gun* and laid the LVLE drum mag next to me for quick reloading.

CLANK, CLANK, CLANK!

I listened to the elevator inside the building as it headed below. It was so loud you could hear it clearly, even from outside. If any more vampires were here, they would be coming soon.

Swinging my weapon, I referenced my aiming points again: the Mark 19's barrel facing one of the streets leading to the building. The clacker for the Claymores was next to me as well.

Now, we wait.

———

Gunkanjima Island—The Streets
Yoko Yashido

I no longer think of myself as a proud Japanese mother or even as a human. As the vampires started a deadly chain reaction on the island, people fought or hid.

It didn't matter which.

Everything happened so fast, and there was nowhere to run. Ultimately, I had locked us in a storage closet and hid my children. Unfortunately, one of *them* found us. I tried to fight it, but there was no hope. At least it didn't see my children, whom I had carefully hidden in some of the boxes—

But, once I was turned ... *I still knew where they were hidden.*

My beautiful white dress, a gift from my husband Gregory, was now stained red with my children's blood—Levi and Jules, who were lost somewhere in the mob of the undead now.

There was a moment when the agony of what I was doing was so great that it caused me to break through the fog of being a vampire. A distant part of me still feels the agony of biting down on Levi's neck. Any humanity I had left disappeared when I finished Jules as well— their terrified screams and pleading were all but a distant memory now.

Hundreds of us are now running down the street toward the mine. The loud clanking of the elevator inside the mine entrance captured our attention. My only desire now is to feed and make more of us. It is time to find the humans who dared tread on this unholy island.

CHAPTER 18
THE MINE

Gunkanjima Island—Under the Pacific Ocean
Agent James

CLANK, THUD!

The freight elevator stopped. The typical industrial grate opened from the top and bottom.

I aimed at the farthest tunnel as the SEALs pulled the grate open.

As we exited the elevator, we quickly moved to one of the tunnels. Standing in a large semi-lit room surrounded by dark tunnels was a deathtrap if they started shooting at us. Once in one of the tunnels, we made a hasty 360-degree fighting position and got ready.

"OK, four tunnels, one team each. Transponder check," LT Taylor said.

"James, Christos, Dorothy, with my team in this tunnel. Tie the casket to Zulu so he can pull it as he walks," LT Taylor said.

The floors here were uneven, but there was no major debris, so I hoped pulling it wouldn't slow me down much.

"Yes, sir," PO Reynolds said, tying the casket to me.

All of us had IFF (Identification—Friend or Foe) transponders. We used them not only to see each other's locations with GPS (which doesn't work down here) but also because they emitted a specific light when viewed on NVGs—so we knew not to shoot a "friendly" in the dark. It is bizarre not to wear or need NVGs, as Lev and I could still see their transponder light, even without the NVGs. We carried them anyway because, in absolute darkness (which is extremely rare), we could not see. Luckily, they just flipped down into place from the helmet.

We split up after we all looked at each other and verified that they were working. I know splitting up is a terrible idea. However, it was necessary because there were four tunnels, and there was no way of knowing which one, if any, led to our target. Time was of the essence, and our options were limited. Each team headed to one of the other three tunnels. We covered them until they got to their respective tunnels. They made it without incident.

LT Taylor, PO Smith, Christos, Dorothy, and I turned and moved through our tunnel. The tunnel was spacious enough for us to maintain our formation without proceeding one at a time, which was beneficial as we needed to keep Christos and Dorothy safely in the center.

The SEAL's tactics were close enough to ours that we seamlessly covered each other past intersections and Y-junctions or when it enlarged or shrank in size as we moved.

Patter, patter, patter …

"Contact, twelve o'clock," LT Taylor said.

We had gone to our team's channel, so we didn't talk over the other teams.

Clicks from Smith and me, in confirmation.

Patter, patter, patter …

This time, it was coming straight at us.

Something big was coming our way. As it got closer, we saw that "it" was actually dozens of vamps packed tight in the tunnel ahead.

Ch-ch-ch-ch-ch-chuff …

AAIIIYA! AAIIIYA!

Ch-ch-ch-ch-ch-chuff …

AAIIIYA!

There were way too many to kill in time. So, the SEALs hugged the walls as we had practiced.

"Zulu, you're up!" LT Taylor yelled.

BZZZZZZ! BZZZZZZ!

The light from the Gatling gun was blinding in the dark corridor. The flashes from the six barrels, rotating at 1,800 rpm, created a kaleidoscope of horror.

As the light strobed, I could see dozens of small, naked, blackened bodies charging us. They had the open maws and talons of vampires and screeched as they broke into a shambling run toward us. Unlike the vampires we had encountered so far, they were in varying states of disrepair; some limped because of the missing chunks in their legs or other decrepitude, while others moved faster. All looked as though they had lived here for decades or centuries, as many appeared highly decayed. They crawled and jumped over the ever-increasing bodies in front of them.

BZZZZZZZZZZZ! C-c-c-c-click

The last shell casings and links fell to the stone floor, and the smell of cordite gun smoke filled the air. I let off the trigger; the weapon was empty.

The sudden silence rang in my ears. Firing a Gatling gun inside a tunnel is surprisingly loud! The tunnel ahead was filled with a black soup of body parts, entrails, goo, and bodies—scores of them.

Chuff … chuff

The SEALs were giving "safety slugs" to the heads of any vamps that looked like they could still be "alive". We didn't need to have a SEAL crippled by a bite as we walked by and over them. I noticed that LT Taylor didn't even bother calling out contact to the other teams. You could probably hear my weapon from anywhere in the mine.

Oh, crap.

It was as if LT Taylor had read my mind—

"All teams, go loud; the jig is up," LT Taylor radioed on the platoon channel.

I marveled at the SEALs' discipline. They moved as though a single piece of machinery. Even now, they were perfectly arrayed to deal with any incoming threat. LT Taylor switched to his M4, as did the other SEALs. Each M4 had the M203 grenade launcher mounted under it. PO Smith came over with two more satchels of 7.62mm rounds, and we reloaded the Gatling gun. After reloading, we continued down the tunnel and entered a vast chamber.

"My God," PO Smith said.

I saw Christos crossing himself. Dorothy looked like a ghost; she was clearly in shock.

"Hey, you two, stay frosty!" I said to the CIs.

They just nodded their heads vacuously.

I didn't blame them. Three and a half years ago, before I joined OST, this would have put me into shock as well. Now, it was just another day at the office as I critically assessed what lay before us.

The chamber had been dug out for an astronomical amount of coal. It was huge! The ceiling was one hundred feet high, and the room was probably one hundred meters in diameter. All the mining equipment had been moved to the sides of the room, and a gigantic altar had been placed in the center. Many hundreds, maybe a thousand or more, bodies lay on the ground. Not the blackened undead we had killed; these were dead humans. All looked unharmed, like they had just gone to sleep and never awoken. We knew they were dead because of the horrible smell of decay and excrement that the recently departed gave off. These were not the miners; they all wore regular civilian clothes and looked like they came voluntarily. Men, women, and children.

Jesus, another damn cult? Really?

I took a good look at the altar. It looked like some kind of white stone and had runes, symbols, alien language, and atrocious creatures carved into it. There was no pedestal, so where were the summoned creatures if it worked like it did with the last OI? I looked around me. There was no sign of monsters, a pedestal, a book, or anything else.

Several tunnels branched off from this one in almost every direction.

I saw Christos systematically taking pictures of everything on the altar.

I hope it makes a lovely scrapbook for him.

"Alpha One—we are in a large chamber with an altar and hundreds of dead discovered. All teams converge on my location," LT Taylor radioed the squad.

We heard the other teams acknowledge the order.

"OK, James, this is your area of expertise. What now?" LT Taylor asked.

"Well, if it is like the other OI, we must destroy this altar. Last time, there was a pedestal and a book also. So, I don't know what this means," I said.

Within minutes, the other teams had joined us.

"OK, Smith, set demo on the altar," LT Taylor ordered, handing him the explosives he carried.

"Copy," Smith said, taking the satchel and moving to the altar.

The other SEALs and I watched our fields of fire as PO Smith set the demo charge.

Seeing a lake of dead bodies all around us was surreal. They had all been facing the altar when they died, so it was as if they were all worshipping us in death.

"Done," PO Smith said.

He had just finished when we heard a rumbling noise. It wasn't loud, but it was coming from every tunnel.

"Incoming, all directions," LT Taylor said.

They came. Hundreds of blackened bodies came out of every tunnel toward us.

"Squad One, heavy contact," LT Taylor said on the platoon frequency.

Burp, burp, burp

BOOM, BOOM, BOOM!

The SEALs' M203s blew dozens of them apart as they entered the main room.

AAIIIYA! AAIIIYA!

BZZZZZZ!

They fell like dominoes in front of me. I slowly shifted my aim horizontally as dozens dropped to my Gatling gun, but more came.

BZZZZZZ! BZZZZZZ! C-c-c-c-click

Out of ammo.

I pulled up my MP5SD.

They were having trouble getting to us now. They had to climb over the ever-growing piles of "dead" undead bodies.

Each team poured fire into the undead. The flood turned into a trickle and then stopped.

"OK, set up a perimeter, and let's—" LT Taylor started to say.

HHHAARRRGGGHHhhhh!

My insides went cold.

Something huge made a growling alien howl that reverberated through the mine. Strangely, it sounded close and far at the same time. I pulled out my knife and cut the line connecting me to the casket; I would need mobility against whatever made that sound.

I heard the SEALs reloading as LT Taylor sprinted over to me. He had the last two-hundred-round satchel. Without a word, I dropped to my knees, and he started putting rounds into my M134 pack as I reloaded the first rounds of the link into the weapon. I had fired all four hundred again.

"Squad Two, heavy contact!" Came over the platoon frequency.

All units above were now being engaged. The war had started in earnest.

———

Gunkanjima Island—Mine Rooftop
Team Delta Two
SEAL Petty Officer Silva

I watched the roads and scanned the hundreds of windows; it was a counter-sniper's dream and our nightmare. There were so many places we could be engaged from that we would need a battalion to cover every one of them at once. Oh well, we work with what we have. I was the A-gunner for PO Duffy, the sniper/main gunner. We usually had one-hundred-round drum mags, but we had set him up with a three-hundred-round link to start the party.

I heard a weird rumbling sound from the two streets below. Down below, a giant sea of people rushed into the courtyard.

We had found the miners' families.

"Squad Two, heavy contact!" I radioed the platoon.

BRRRRRRRRRRRRRRRRRAP!

The RM 338 was putting out nine rounds per second, and the mob of vampires slowed from one street as they had to step over bodies to continue.

Same with the other side.

KA-BOOM!

B-B-B-B-B-B-B-B-B-B-B-BOOM!

Giant groups of vampires on the other street flew into the air; pieces and whole-body parts flew as Lev's Claymore mines detonated. Then, her Mark 19 threw HEDP grenades into the remaining mass of moving undead. We must have killed a hundred or more in the first few seconds. The undead attackers wore regular clothes and mainly consisted of women and children. It was horrible—

POP!

I felt a warm sensation on the right side of my face. I could smell the coppery smell of blood and something else. Looking to my right, I saw Duffy lying motionless. The side and back of his skull were gone from where a rifle round had hit him. Instinctively, I rolled toward him.

PLINK!

A round hit where I just was. I continued rolling and grabbed Duffy's machine gun as I went behind a section of concrete wall. It looked like Rothensburger's counter-snipers had found us, so I stayed low and crawled to another area. From there, I would look for the shooter.

"We have snipers," I said on the Squad frequency.

A click came back.

———

Gunkanjima Island—Courtyard Outside the Mine
Agent Lev

As the mass of undead passed the string of Claymores, I hit the clacker.

KA-BOOM!

Hundreds of undead were destroyed in an instant. Pieces and parts of them went everywhere in a shower of black gunk, but hundreds more came from behind them.

Hitting a horde of vamps didn't require much skill. This is what the Mark 19 automatic grenade launcher was designed for—troops in the open. In this case, the vampires were exposed and closely packed together.

I can hear the staccato auto fire from the RM338 coming from the roof. They had an angle I didn't, so I knew the hordes from both streets would be visible soon.

I was not disappointed.

A giant mass of hundreds of them came from each street.

B-B-B-B-B-B-B-BOOM!

Dozens upon dozens of monsters blew apart and into the air. From the flash of the grenades, blackness shot in every direction—

KA-BOOM!

I also heard the explosions as the other SEALs detonated the Claymores on their street.

AAIIIYA!

A cacophony of their alien screams reached my ears. Between the gunfire, the explosions, and the vampires' screams, it was Dante's *Inferno*. My ears were ringing from all the noise.

"We have snipers," came over my earpiece.

That was PO Silva. I clicked my radio in confirmation.

Without hesitating, I switched to dealing with the snipers. Besides, I knew I would be their next target. Jumping from the top of the machine, I landed and rolled. I had no way of knowing if I was being targeted or even if I had been shot at already; there was just too much noise. Moving at top speed across the courtyard, I scanned the rooftop and open windows for the building the sniper must have fired from. I surmised they were probably in the VIP building on the top floors. I picked that building, and I hope I chose it correctly.

High above, from several blackened windows, I could see flashes from rifles coming from within, as a high-powered round whistled by my ear. These guys were pros. They would shoot and move, just like we do. Luckily, I could move much faster than humans, and I had one advantage that they didn't—grenades cover a wide area.

I unloaded every remaining HEDP grenade into the top two floors.

B-B-B-B-B-B-B-BOOM … Click

Flashes and detonations lit up the night.

KA-BOOM! BOOM!

Rothensburger's detail must have had some impressive explosives of their own, as secondary detonations devastated the top floors of the building. The building went dark after massive detonations inside shattered tons of glass, steel, and concrete, and it all came crashing down on the monsters below.

They shrieked as the falling debris filled the street with an ungodly noise, and a cloud of smoke billowed out from the street below. I could hear the other two SEALs on Charlie Team firing into the remaining streets of the undead.

"Fall back," I radioed to my squad as I ran to retrieve my other drum magazine of LVLE rounds. I loaded the magazine quickly and then sprinted toward the mine building.

The horde would be upon us soon, so we fell back to join the other SEALs inside. We had to prevent the undead from reaching the elevator. Now, we would need to confront them face-to-face from within the building.

Hellious

My plan was going perfectly.

I had deliberately given the OST assault team some resistance; I needed them to feel they were succeeding. Of course, they would know it was a trap, but I needed them to wonder where and what that would be.

Knowing they would eventually guess my location, I set my trap.

Sure, I could have left for somewhere else, but this group had earned my respect. Besides, the summoning was long ago completed, and *my* master was already heading this way from across the cosmos.

I had already won.

Knowing what I had done was the only thing that would spare me when it arrived, for it would destroy all.

Humanity was already doomed.

Even if I didn't rule them all by the time my master arrived, it would finish them.

So, I decided they had earned the privilege of being killed by me.

It was a shame that the thousand-plus cultists could not be used as undead, but the ritual had consumed the entirety of their life force and killed them instantly. I needed living people to possess or even to be created by my undead; we couldn't kill a corpse.

The blackened miners were an anomaly.

I had not expected *the rift* to raise them from the dead. The power of the altar, once the summoning was complete, must have been strong enough to bring them back. Strangely, they remained connected to me, and I controlled them just as I did the other undead. Without my telepathic control, all my undead would become inert and die forever. I could feel that the new undead were linked to me in the same way; my legion of undead was truly massive now.

Waiting patiently, I was no longer concerned about being seen in my proper form. I could hear them talking in the giant summoning chamber, and I would enjoy snuffing out their lives. This was not a group to play around with; I would kill them all quickly and efficiently. My ability to sense what was around me was alien to them. I could already see, hear, and smell them individually. They had also brought in some kind of weird tube.

Hahaha.

I wonder what on Earth these humans had in mind, considering the strange things they did. No matter: I entered my hive mind and let the undead know it was time to finish the attack.

———

Agent James

We heard the rumbling again and faced the tunnels.

LT Taylor had reloaded my Gatling gun, albeit with only 200 rounds, and we were ready for the next wave.

Right as they got near, they stopped. Not having targets yet, but with the defensive advantage, we waited for them to initiate the attack.

BOOM! Crash, Tinkle, Crash!

From only a hundred feet away, an industrial loader, along with giant mounds of dirt and debris, flew from the wall and into the air. It was concealing a tunnel we didn't even know was there. As some of the SEALs turned to face the new threat, hordes of undead flooded into the room from every tunnel.

HHHAARRRGGGHHhhhh!

The thing entering from the new tunnel was massive.

Standing over twelve feet high and probably just as wide, it resembled nothing from this Earth. Its body was a giant amalgamation of undead bodies, with dozens of arms and heads sprouting from a massive ball of organs and bones in the center. Under it all was a mass of undead legs that it was running on. Strange tubes were sticking out of its central body as well.

And I could see most of the arms were holding weapons.

Lots and lots of weapons.

At the same time, as dozens of those arms fired weapons, we also engaged.

BRRRRRRAP! BZZZZZZ! Bang, Bang, Brrrrrap!

The noise was deafening.

"OI contact!" yelled LT Taylor into the radio.

I saw one SEAL, PO Acevedo, fall from the gunfire, but we had shredded one whole side of the monster. All the vampire arms and heads on that side were "dead" and had dropped their weapons. The OI's central body of undead torsos was scarred but intact; not a single round had penetrated it.

BZZZZZZ!

I concentrated my fire on one spot in the creature's center.

HHHAARRRGGGHHhhhh!

Black goo finally shot out.

If it bleeds, we can kill it!

PFFFFFT!

The tubes sticking out all over it started pumping out a greenish gas.

"Gas, gas, gas!" I yelled.

I ducked down, grabbed my gas mask from its pouch, and snapped it into place, silently praying it would work. The SEALs put theirs on as well. One of them, who had gotten his on already, grabbed Christos and put his on.

Dorothy had no time and no one near to help her.

Oh my God, no!

She was enveloped in the gas, coughed a couple of times, and then started to look puzzled. I could see that it did not affect her.

The SEAL next to her was not as lucky. PO Reynolds was closest to the monster and still donning his mask when the gas hit him. Even though he held his breath, it got into him anyway.

AHKKKH!

He screamed a blood-curdling scream as he puked out blood and fell to the ground. He tightened into a fetal ball so hard we heard his bones cracking. Like a bug hit by bug spray, he was curled up super tight and was dead.

F— me!

The greenish gas filled the room now, making it hard to see.

PFFFFFT! PFFFFFT!

It was like we had hit a ten-ton stink bug—it just *kept* spraying gas.

It must have turned around to its other side because the gunfire started again.

BRRRRRRAP!

BZZZZZZ!

The SEALs and I were returning fire. I saw another SEAL go down as my head jerked to the side; I registered the pain. A round had hit my helmet and gone through; I could feel the blood running down my face.

Spinning back around, I sprayed the horde coming from behind us.

BZZZZZZ! BZZZZZZ!

I saw the giant OI run forward and crush PO Lamm beneath its feet.

BOOM!

A chunk of the monster dislodged from its body, and it ran around madly, trying to crush the SEAL who shot it with an M203 grenade. The giant chunk of its body hanging off reminded me of one of those cars you see on the highway, with its damaged bumper flapping dangerously in the air as it moves. Black goo was coming out from where it had been hit.

I took a deep breath and aimed.

BZZZ! BZZZ! BZZZ!

HHHAARRRGGGHHhhhh!

Black goo sprayed out again as my rounds sank into where its exterior did not protect it. Another SEAL fired a grenade round at its vulnerable spot, but it turned just as he did.

Plink! … BOOM!

The grenade bounced off and exploded harmlessly in the air. Well, harmless to it anyway.

I felt fresh blood gush from a deep frag wound in my arm.

Things were not going well. Dorothy and Christos were hiding on top of a piece of machinery, and we had at least three SEALs dead already. On top of that, the undead were almost to us as well, so I turned my weapon on them.

BZZZZZZ! C-c-c-c-click

The undead were no longer a problem, but I was out of ammo.

Again.

Releasing my harness, I dropped the Gatling gun and ran to one of the discarded M4/M203s. I grabbed the downed SEAL with one hand and the rifle with the other, taking them both with me. I recognized that PO Evans was dead, but I needed his grenades and ammo.

I stepped behind a piece of machinery to reload the rifle and the grenade launcher.

Leaning around my cover, I saw that LT Taylor was trapped between some heavy machinery and the altar. He ran toward the altar as it lifted the machine he was hiding behind and flung it into the air. I watched him grab the M2 satchel's clacker in his hands; that was what he had been running to get to.

"GET DOWN!" I yelled at Christos and Dorothy.

They heard me and flattened out on top of their cover.

LT Taylor yelled, "FIRE IN THE HOLE!" as he ran in front of the demolition charge on the altar, but the OI had caught up to him. As I ducked for cover, I saw several of its undead hands grabbing him, and he squeezed the clacker—

KA-BOOM!

I felt debris, loosened from the ceiling above, rattling down on me.

Leaning my head and weapon back out again, I saw the remaining parts of the OI. They were still smoking from the explosion that killed it. Black goo, chunks of black vampire body parts, tubing, and pieces of the monster's body core of horror decorated the chamber.

———

Dorothy

My mind was shattered.

What I saw was the same monster that was in the mist on that fateful moonlit night. But now, it was made of real things. It was like it had taken dozens of undead and blended them all into one monstrosity. I wailed an inhuman sound as I flattened out on top of … whatever the hell this machinery was. I heard the soldiers yelling, and then my ears were stinging from a giant explosion. Through my tears, I stood up.

It was finally dead—I could see the pieces of it on the ground. My horror grew, and my insides tightened as I saw the horrible red mist emerging from it again.

"NOW, CHRISTOS, NOW!" I heard James yell.

Christos got up next to me and started yelling out his exorcism in fluent Latin.

The mist moved toward a large fissure in the cave's stone but suddenly stopped in midair. Swirling erratically, it began to descend to the ground. Once there, it shifted toward Christos and me. Spinning and undulating wildly, I could sense the anger and surprise of the OI.

It was not going to escape as planned.

I looked down at the casket, and James was already running for it.

In a daze, I felt as though I was watching from above and not truly present. Numbly, I climbed down and ran over to the strange tube we had brought. Crying, I understood that my time was about to end.

James was already opening the cover. As he opened it, I climbed in and grabbed the canister of gas. Pulling it close, I got ready to commit suicide.

As James started to step away, I lunged out and grabbed his arm.

"Tell people what I did! Please!" I pleaded.

"Bet your ass I will!" he said.

I nodded and lay back, my hand on the trigger to release the deadly gas.

Hyperventilating, I took a final look around me.

My insides went cold. The horrible, evil things in the mist were creeping over the edge and into where I lay, frozen in place with fear. I could feel its intense rage. The telepathic screams were painful as the last part of Hellious slowly finished crawling over the edges and into the casket with me. Sobbing, I could feel the mist start violating my body.

SMACK! CLINK!

James had slammed the casket shut and locked it.

In a panic, without consciously thinking, I squeezed the trigger to release the gas. There was a loud hissing sound, and I smelled a weird smell as I breathed deeply. Then, I had one final thought as I felt myself shutting down and dying, and screamed with all my remaining energy at the creature that had ruined so many of my friends' lives.

———

James

As I slammed the casket shut with Hellious and Dorothy inside, I felt a wave of shock. Being this close to such indescribable horror must be what Lev had experienced.

From inside the sealed tube, I heard a muffled yell.

"I TOLD YOU I WOULD WATCH YOU DIE! … IF IT WAS THE LAST THING I DID! … DIE YOU BASTARD!"

Those were her last words.

Right after the casket was sealed, the last of the other vampires dropped like their strings had been cut.

AAIIIYA! AAIIIYA!

I watched in horror as the blackened undead, still coming in from the tunnels, spewed black goo from every orifice and fell into tight little balls like dead insects.

"OI is neutralized and captured; the casket is secure and ready for transport," LT Taylor said to the platoon.

"All undead are … dead," he added.

"Roger, same up here, all hostiles eliminated. Sending Bravo now with the elevator," Lev said. We heard it start its descent …

CLANK, THUD!

Our elevator had arrived.

Two SEALs got off the elevator and helped retrieve their fallen, as I put the casket on the elevator. Christos was next to it, giving Dorothy her last rites.

We headed for the surface.

Once we got out, we saw the surviving SEALs. The teams up top had engaged both security forces and the undead. By the time we killed the OI, the undead had reached them. The battle up top had claimed three more SEALs: POs Owens, Duffy, and Birch. At least this time, Lev was walking around and not about to fall unconscious. She saw the look on my face—

"Oh, James …" she said.

Nothing more needed to be said; she understood I had finally faced her full horror. No one can come that close to something so indescribable and come away wholly sane.

We traveled to the seawall for extraction. Lev and I carried the casket between us, and the other SEALs carried their fallen. As we reached the seawall's top, we could see the ocean churning below.

Roping down, the SEALs got our inflatable Zodiac ready. We lowered the casket to them, and they loaded it onto the Zodiac. We climbed down and joined them on the rocky outcropping.

As SEALs, putting on SCUBA gear was second nature to us. However, for Christos, it was a new experience. Observing this, PO Parks approached and assisted him in donning the equipment. After he finished helping Christos into his scuba gear, we entered the water and boarded the Zodiac. They started a small, quiet motor, and we pulled away from the island.

"Fish in the water," Lev said into her SATCOM.

We didn't travel far.

SPLOOSH!

The Mark 9 SDV surfaced a dozen meters away. In amazement, I watched the SEALs helping Lev and me load the casket into one of its torpedo bays. The torpedo tube slammed shut, and the submersible vanished silently into the ocean below.

"Fish in the barrel, Romeo Tango Bravo," came over the SATCOM.

EPILOGUE

US Capitol—Washington, DC
Senate Chambers
Congressman Halston

I WATCHED ANGRILY as the Senate came to order.

We had all seen the "vampires" that attacked ASU.

This time, OST not only didn't cover it up, but encouraged the ASU students to tell the world. So now, in addition to OST's voluntarily divulging information on the monsters, there were these damn snot-nosed college kids! They had added their thanks to OST and showed, in an annoyingly scientific way, precisely what had attacked them. They shared about the black insides, showed the teeth and claws, and shared about their school's new blood drive program.

This is a fascist's worst nightmare!

We were on the brink of total world domination, and they had to ruin it by exposing the truth (and reality) to those who had been deceived. I listened to others talking, and this time, I wasn't even invited to speak on the Senate floor!

In typical cutthroat politics, Congressman Liam DeMarcus (the

Speaker of the House) suddenly wouldn't return my calls. He acted as though we had never spoken, and he hardly knew me.

Finally, the time for the vote had come. I held my breath. There was still a chance that enough people were stupid enough to believe our lies, and we could prevail.

"Yea," "Nay," "Nay," "Nay, with prejudice!" "Yea." The drown of yeas and nays went on and on.

Until … we had lost resoundingly.

The final total was twenty-two yeas and seventy-eight nays.

No bill of mine had ever lost by a more considerable margin. Except for the possessed and the Freedom Party, every Senator had voted no. Even some of the Freedom Party voted no!

So, not only was the subcommittee not going to become a full committee, but the Laura Act died without ever being voted on.

I was furious!

Standing, I was ready to scream at the top of my lungs!

But I suddenly had trouble breathing, and something seemed caught in my throat.

There were screams, and I saw the Sergeant at Arms yelling something—but I couldn't hear anymore. The Capitol Police were swarming in, and the senators were being whisked from the room.

My insides felt like liquid fire, and I worried I was about to have diarrhea, vomit, or both. Suddenly, I felt the most excruciating pain I had ever felt! My whole body spasmed, and I screamed an inhuman scream—

AAIIIYA!

I vomited black goo, defecated, and curled into a ball. From my side on the ground, I could see the other possessed legislators curling into tight balls, covered in black goo that was pouring out of their every orifice.

It was so dark now … like I was in a mine.

———

USS Greeneville—Off the Coast of Japan
Agent James

The USS Greeneville reported a "mechanical problem" and had to leave the joint training exercise early. To safeguard it, the naval exercises were canceled, and the entire carrier group returned to Honolulu, Hawaii. The casket remained safely on board, and Christos stayed by its side during the whole sea journey.

We knew the mist was losing its mind as it frantically searched for a way out. It was trapped, with no host to possess and no way to telepathically communicate—either because of the wood and lead or just because it was sealed in.

Christos was studying all the pictures he had taken. The glyphs around the altar were particularly interesting, and when he returned, he would give a hell of a report to the Vatican! We were also going to analyze the glyphs and everything related to the operations.

Crime Scene News—Denver, Colorado
Samantha

I can't believe they fulfilled their promise!

Our story went viral immediately after it aired. As promised, the agents' and SEALs' names, along with other sensitive or *class-e-fied* details, were redacted.

Harold and I received bonuses and renewed lucrative contracts to stay with CSN, which was inundated with news and speaking requests. We were also offered contracts with other news agencies. Luckily, CSN was able to afford our new and huge salaries.

I also covered a new bill to establish the "Department of Supernatural Affairs," or DSA. It was expected to pass with flying colors, and soon, OST would have more support than they had dreamed of.

Japan was quite upset with the USA, not for stopping the OI but for invading its sovereignty without informing them; no surprises there. I also helped cover that topic.

Lastly, I wrote Dorothy's eulogy, expressing the debt of gratitude she was owed for sacrificing her life to kill the OI. One detail I had to leave out was that it was still "alive" but captured. Perhaps my journalistic integrity is waning, but I now understand why certain things are too dangerous for the public to know—and must be classified.

I sighed.

Goodbye, naive Samantha.

Cosmic Deity
The Edge of the Milky Way Galaxy
1.9 Million Light Years from the Galactic Center

It felt a sensation, one that an ancient being had called out to it.

The power to achieve this was immense. The energy needed to send the signal was minimal in comparison to it and the cosmos, yet significant for a non-celestial being. A pathway to new life had been revealed.

Now, it has a new place to conquer.

The summoning was much more than just a call to where its new victims were; it also allowed it the means to get there. The summoning created the nexus between its plane and theirs, whoever these "humans" were. Now, it had the physical path to get there.

Humans had just started to understand what they called "entanglement theory" and the existence of dark matter. What they did not know is that faster-than-light (FTL) travel was not only possible but was regularly used by Cosmic Deities.

The mass of the Cosmic Deity is measured alongside stars and planets.

Humanity's conceptualization of something massive collapsing into something tiny with immense density, such as a black hole, was within their comprehension. The idea of something with tremendous mass transforming into something with little or no mass, or even *negative* mass, was not. Nor did they have a proper understanding of how FTL travel worked. They were learning; it was too bad their time was coming to an end …

Heading their way, at speeds they could not comprehend—it would reach them soon.

ACKNOWLEDGMENTS

I'm deeply grateful to all the individuals and experiences that have influenced and shaped my books.

First, I want to express my continued gratitude for Mark Everett Stone's BSI series of books, which greatly influenced me. I highly recommend exploring his works.

Also, H. P. Lovecraft and his Cthulhu monsters, GURPS Horror©, physicists everywhere for the parallel universe concept, and the Internet for helping to bring about the end of humanity.

A big thanks to my beta readers and editors for all their help in creating a quality product.

Finally, I want to express my appreciation for my experiences with the federal government as an enlisted soldier and officer in the military, a uniformed and undercover law enforcement officer, and an instructor.

Thank you for reading my books. I hope you enjoy the ongoing adventure—and the new horrors the Occult Strike Team faces.

ABOUT THE AUTHOR

RK Jack is a retired government agent with over thirty years of experience in federal law enforcement and the military. He has served on SRT and VIPR Teams and held uniformed and undercover positions, including twenty years as a Federal Air Marshal (FAM).

He deployed for OP Desert Storm as an enlisted soldier and later became a lieutenant in the US Army National Guard.

Now that he is retired, he is busy writing books that depict the military and police not as stoic, unfeeling superheroes but as real individuals with genuine feelings and fears. These fallible men and women demonstrate their heroism by confronting their fears to protect others when duty calls, just as they do in real life.

His first book in the series, *The Devourer From Beyond,* introduced us to the Occult Strike Team as the world faced its first occult incident.

Now, years later, a second super-being from another plane has surfaced. He hopes you enjoyed this book, the second in the OST series, as much as—or even more than—the first.

Feel free to see more of his books or contact him at his website: rkjackauthor.com

Happy horror!

CONNECT WITH THE AUTHOR

I hope you are enjoying the OST series of action horror books!

As always, I would greatly appreciate it if you would leave an honest review for this book and/or the first book in the series, *The Devourer From Beyond*. Your opinion matters a lot!

This is the second book in the Occult Strike Team series, and it picks up where the first one left off. The adventure will continue with the third book in this exciting series ...

I currently live in Denver, Colorado, and can visit your book club or group upon request. You can reach me anytime through my website: rkjackauthor.com.

Thank you for your continued support!

GLOSSARY

AAR After Action Review

AFB Air Force Base

AOR Area of Responsibility

APC Armored Personnel Carrier

APD Aurora Police Department

ASAC Assistant to the Special Agent in Charge

BATFE Bureau of Alcohol, Tobacco, Firearms, and Explosives

BB Battle Buddy (military)

BFF Best Friend Forever

B&E Breaking & Entering

CAP Close Air Patrol

CAT Combat Application Tourniquet

CCTV Closed-Circuit Television

CO2 Carbon Dioxide gas

CS CS gas (military), also "Counter Sniper"

CSI Crime Scene Investigation

CQB Close Quarters Battle (military)

D&D Dungeons and Dragons (a role-playing game)

DENFO Denver Field Office

DEVGRU Development Group—SEAL Team 8

DL Driver's License

DM Defensive Measures (hand-to-hand fight training)

DOE Department of Energy

DPV SEAL Desert Patrol Vehicle

EDIP Explain, Demonstrate, Imitate, and Practice (instruction method)

EDP Emotionally Disturbed Person

EMS Emergency Medical Services

EMT Emergency Medical Technician

EOD Explosives Ordinance Disposal (military)

EVAC Evacuate

FAM(S) Federal Air Marshal (Service)

FFL Federal Firearms License

FLETC Federal Law Enforcement Training Center

FN FN Herstal (A company that makes firearms)

FOF Field of Fire

FPF Final Protective Fire (military)

FPO Federal Police Officer

FRAGO Fragmentary Order (military—comes before an OPORD)

FTL Faster-than-Light

FTX Field Training Exercise (military)

G Government

GOV Government-Owned Vehicle

GMG Grenade Machine Gun

GSW Gunshot Wound

GURPS Generic Universal Role-Playing System (a role-playing game)

HEDP High-Explosive Dual-Purpose grenade rounds

HIPAA Health Insurance Portability and Accountability Act

HIT High-Intensity Training gear (hand-to-hand protective suit)

HMMWV Heavy Multi-purpose Multi-wheeled Wheeled Vehicle (AKA a Humvee)

HUMINT HUMan INTelligence

HVAC Heating, Ventilation, and Air Conditioning

IFF Identification-Friend or Foe

IR Infrared

JTTF Joint Terrorism Task Force

JSOC Joint Special Operations Command (military)

K-9 A trained police dog

KIA Killed in Action

KSM Known or Suspected Monster

KST Known or Suspected Terrorist

LEO Law Enforcement Officer

LVLE Low-Velocity Low-Explosive grenade rounds

LZ Landing Zone (military)

MCC Mission Control Center

MMA Mixed Martial Arts

MO Method Operandi (AKA a standard method of operating)

MSGL Multi-Shot Grenade Launcher

MX Tesla Model X SUV (modified for heavy combat)

MWR Morale, Welfare, and Recreation (military)

NATO North Atlantic Treaty Organization

NER Church of the New Era Revivalists

NMC Nuclear Materials Couriers (Federal Agents with the DOE)

NSC National Security Council

NVG Night Vision Goggles

OCC Office of Chief Counsel

OI Occult Incident

OP Operation

OPFOR Opposing Forces (the "bad" guys)

OPORD Operations Order (military)

ORP Organized Rally Point (military)

OST Overwatch Surveillance Team (also Occult Strike Team)

PA Public Address (system)

PACE Primary, Alternate, Contingency, and Emergency (military)

PAX Passenger(s) (airline)

PLF Parachute Landing Fall

PMCS Preventative Maintenance, Checks, and Services (military)

POV Personally Owned Vehicle

PT Physical Training

PTSD Post-Traumatic Stress Disorder

REM Rapid Eye Movement

RON Remain Overnight (airline term)

QRF Quick Reaction Force

RDO Regular Day Off (airline)

RFID Radio-Frequency Identification

RO Registered Owner (of a vehicle)

ROI Return on Investment (amount of profit from an investment(s))

RTB Return to Base

SA Special Agent

SAC Special Agent in Charge

SATCOM Satellite Communications

SEAL Sea, Air, and Land (a specialized warfare unit in the US Navy)

SFB Space Force Base

SIM Simulant, or Simulant Infected Monster

SITREP Situation Report (military)

SL Squad Leader

SMG Submachine Gun

SOL Shit Out of Luck

SOP Standard Operating Procedure

SPEC OPS Special Operations

SSA Supervisory Special Agent

STU-III Secure Terminal Unit/Equipment (model 3)

SWAT Special Weapons and Tactics

TL Team Leader

TT Tentacle Thing

VIPR Visual Intermodal Protection and Response (uniformed SWAT for FAMS)

VPOTUS Vice President of the United States

WIA Wounded in Action

WOG Wrath of God